I0451448

The Gideon Files, Book Three

Gold Peony

Ande Li

 ROOM 808 PRESS

Publishing Imprint for Addison Maxima B. Arevas & Ande Li

Copyright 2019 Ande Li at Room 808 Press

ISBN-13: 978-1-951575-02-1
ISBN-13: 978-1-951575-05-2

Source: Digital copy

Cover image: popovartem.com, Stock photo ID:410565868, Apr 25, 2016. Photograph. Shutterstock. Web.

Acknowledgements

For those who pursue their dreams, wherever they lead, without promise of wealth, glory or reward.

Prologue

1865 Fujian Province, China

Jin Mudan stared through the mesh wire at the humans who had trapped her, watching their pacing from her cage on the withered grass. Her legs were shaky from her exhaustion and fear, and her paws were raw from pressing against the coarse, biting metal weave. In all the years that she had survived on her own in the wild, she had always been careful to avoid the humans' snares, but tiredness and unrelieved hunger had finally weakened her enough, that she was drawn into the cage by a piece of boiled chicken. For that momentary lapse in judgment, she could pay with her life.

Shortly after she was born, decades ago, her mother had named her "Gold Peony"—translated into the local human tongue as "Jin Mudan"—for the way her golden coat formed a rosette when she was curled into a ball. Now, recalling her idyllic youth as a kit, warm and full at her mother's teat, Jin Mudan coiled tightly into a compact round and whimpered mournfully at her desperate plight.

A small human child looked over at her and tugged at the adult's clothing, and Jin Mudan assessed the relationship of the pair quickly: father and son. Her body didn't allow her to speak with humans, but she understood their languages. Ever since the foreigners arrived on the land over twenty years prior, she had had to learn the English and French languages, in addition to

1

the local Chinese dialects, but it was a necessity for her survival; it was easier to evade hunters when she understood their intentions.

"I'll make a deal with you, *ba-ba*," the child proposed, following his father around the yard, as the man looked for a cudgel or blade. "I'll feed the chickens and clean out their pens every day for a week, if you don't kill the fox, and you let me have it as a pet."

"Son, foxes don't make good pets," the father cautioned, picking up a machete. "They're wild, can't be trained, and don't like being kept in captivity." The man looked sympathetically at her cowering in the corner of the wire trap and lowered his machete. "Baron would likely use it for his next foxhunt, which would mean an exhausting and horrible end for it, either being shot or ripped apart by the hounds."

"You think it would be more merciful to kill her inside a cage?" the boy cried.

"I don't want to kill it, either, but Baron pays us to watch his game and farm animals, so we need to protect the chickens more than we need another fox in these woods."

"She's probably very hungry," the boy said. "We've been getting more rats and snakes on the farm since Baron had the road built, so she probably can't hunt like she used to."

"There's nothing to be done about that," the man said, reaching for the crate. "Maybe I'll take it to the river and drown it inside the trap. It wouldn't suffer long."

Jin Mudan yelped her panic. To be drowned, trapped in a cage with no means of escape, was possibly one of the most terrifying ways to die. She shivered and whined, turning her eyes to the boy for mercy.

"Please, *ba-ba*! I'll take care of the chickens for *two* weeks—a *month*—if you set her free," the child tried, grabbing his father's hand. Before the adult could argue,

2

the boy said, "I'll even sleep outside the coop and chase her off, if she tries to get inside."

"Why do you care what happens to a mangy little fox?" the man asked. "Look at her coat—it should be shiny and red, not dull and sickly yellow like that."

The boy looked into the crate at her. "She's not mangy, just very skinny and scared. And I like her fur—I bet it would shine like gold, if it was clean and brushed."

"Don't even try giving it a bath," the father warned. "She'd probably bite, if you tried to touch her."

"I won't touch her," the boy said, crouching to be at eye level with her. "I just want her to be safe."

The man shook his head. "One month, and you watch the chickens at night. If we lose even one hen to her, we throw her in the river the next time we catch her. If Baron catches wind of this at all, I may lose my job."

"I understand," the boy nodded solemnly. "Can I feed her before we set her free?" At his father's incredulous stare, he said, "If she's not as hungry, maybe she won't be in a rush to come back."

"Or, she'll come back sooner because she thinks we'll have food for her."

"I thought you said they can't be trained," the boy reminded innocently.

The man laughed. "Okay, son. Let me see if your mother has some meat or fish trimmings to spare. We'll take it to the edge of the farm, so it can just go back into the woods."

As the man went back to the house, the boy sat on the ground and stared raptly at Jin Mudan, beaming at his victory. "You're safe now."

She looked back at him in wonder, too. She never thought she would ever owe her life to a human, much less a small boy. She untucked herself and sniffed at the plump little fingers that he held out, smelling fruit and sticky rice starch under his nails.

He giggled at the tickling touch of her whiskers against his fingertips, then sobered at the sound of approaching horses. "That's Baron. You have to be quiet now." He found a dirty grain sack and threw it hastily over the cage, but Jin Mudan had a sliver of visibility under the edge of the coarse fabric. "Remember, don't make any sound!"

Jin Mudan recognized the pungent odor of the foreigners: fatty meats, wine and spirits, and cloying perfumes and cosmetics to mask their natural smells and colors. In particular, she recognized the Baron, who held and used the land under orders from monarchs who never set foot on it, and never would. The Baron was a stout, pink-skinned man who reminded Jin Mudan of the pigs squealing in a nearby pen, with sharp green eyes that belied an indolent appearance.

"Bo, my dear game warden," the Baron greeted in the English tongue from atop his chestnut mount. "My men tell me that you caught a fox in one of your snares, an exceptional little creature with a yellow coat?"

The man bowed his head and replied in the language of his lord, albeit with an effort: "I'm sorry, I no longer have it, as it died in the trap. The description was too generous, anyway; what looked like yellow fur was yellow soil, caked onto a thin, ragged coat."

"Ah!" the Baron bemoaned dramatically. "My search continues, then. The bounty is still to be claimed, men!" he rallied, and his mounted entourage hollered enthusiastically, as the group rode off.

Warden Bo shook his head, as he returned to the house. His son stood outside, watching his father gather some pieces of gristle and tendon into a bowl, and Jin Mudan's mouth watered at the smell of the meager meat trimmings.

"You lied to Baron," the boy said. "I thought you said we should never lie."

4

"I said you should never lie to those who love you, and the Baron has no love for us," the game warden clarified. "More important is the obligation to honor one's word, once given."

He crouched and looked in his young son's eyes. "You and I had an agreement: you promised to watch the chickens, if I let this fox go. That agreement is still binding, and your integrity means more to me than any hollow promise from the Baron; even if I let him have her, I would get nothing more than a grunt of thanks, if that much."

"But Baron said there was a bounty. He wouldn't pay you, even if you find what he wants?" the boy frowned. "That's not fair!"

"No, it isn't, but it is the way of some of these foreigners," the game warden said tiredly. "They come with a pledge to enlighten us with their civilization and religion, but most of them just come to strip us of our treasures, and they will leave once they've taken what they want. At least if I agree to work for the Baron, I can try to limit the damage to our lands, otherwise, he and his kind would kill and use up everything that lives here, like a swarm of locusts. Don't ever think that the Baron cares about our home and its creatures."

Bo's son raised his chin. "I don't want to be like that. I will keep my promises."

"Good," the game warden smiled, ruffling his son's hair. "You are already a better man than that Baron will ever be."

The man lifted the cage with Jin Mudan inside it, and she braced herself, but he was more careful this time, knowing that his son was watching. Carrying the bowl of meat scraps carefully, the boy skipped ahead and reached the eucalyptus stand by the edge of the farmstead's clearing first. As he waited for his father to arrive with the cage, he made a small bed of clean grass to hold the

5

trimmings, instead of emptying the bowl directly into the dirt.

The man laughed at his son's meticulousness. "You know that it can't be your friend," he said gently, unlatching the cage door. "Animals don't think like people do, and a fox has no place on a farm, just as you would be lost and confused in her wilderness."

"I know," the boy said, standing back to let her come out on her own. "But you always said that we should help others whenever we can."

"You know I meant people, not animals," the man clarified.

Jin Mudan flashed the man a knowing glance, and the boy noticed the furtive gesture and laughed. "I think there's something special about her, more than just the color of her fur."

She darted from the crate and paused to sniff at the trimmings. She didn't trust the humans or the lack of cover in the clearing to eat anything there in the open, but she picked free a tough, sinewy chunk of meat trimmed from a beef shank, that would be enough to sustain her for a day or two. She started dragging it away with an effort and looked at the humans tentatively.

The boy crouched but kept his distance. "Go on," he said gently. "You can take it. As long as I'm around, no one's going to hurt you." He looked up willfully at his father. "I promise."

Chapter 1

Present Day

Everyone that Jonah Gideon knew in New York was aware that he had died. The angel Gabriel had warned Jonah that it was going to be jarring, confusing and disquieting for his friends, to see him alive again, and seemingly unchanged.

Once the shock wore off, Gabriel had advised, they would be overjoyed and relieved, but in the meantime, his friends wouldn't look at him as they used to.

Gabriel was right. As Jonah sat at the bar of the Red Lotus lounge, nursing his glass of ice water, he was aware of the unsubtle scrutiny that his friends were giving him. They didn't realize that he was almost as lost as they were about how he had arrived.

Not the mundane logistics of his actual arrival—he had caught a shuttle flight from Logan to Newark, taking much more time getting around on the ground than he had spent anywhere on the plane, then caught a cab into Manhattan—but not all of the conditions and circumstances that led to him being given a second chance at life had been revealed to him in the hours before he returned to the earthly realm.

"Is anyone as weirded out as I am, by how normal Jonah seems?" Morgan semi-mumbled, running his hand through his mop of red curls, as he often did when he was nervous.

Xani nodded, twirling a long red curl around her finger. "Considering what he's been through, he looks well and well-adjusted."

Jonah Gideon looked down the bar at the twins, and Cindy, who seemed more recovered from her shock than the others. Her wide brown eyes, only a shade lighter than her skin, were cool and analytical. "I'm right here, guys," Jonah said, "and I can hear you perfectly. You can just talk to me. Is anyone going to tell me where Mina and Adam are?"

"They're not here," Cindy said, moving down the bar to stand across the counter from him.

Jonah was confused. When he picked up his belongings from Aciré Hart, in Boston, she had told him that the Xing siblings had returned to New York. "Where are they, then?"

Cindy held out her open hand. "Let me see your hand."

Jonah gave her his right hand, without question, and watched her study both sides of it, as well as his fingertips and fingernails. "What are you looking for?"

"I need to make sure that you're you." She glanced at Micah, who was observing them from the door. "I trust Micah to verify your identity and determine whether or not you're a danger, but that doesn't mean you're entirely innocent, either." She released Jonah's hand and nodded her head towards the back rooms. "Come on back with me. Let's have a chat, just the two of us."

Jonah followed Cindy into the office, as Xani and Morgan returned their attention to serving new customers who had just passed Micah's inspection. He waited until Cindy shut the office door for privacy before he spoke.

"What's going on? Don't you believe me?"

"I believe that *you* believe who you claim to be, but one can't be too sure," Cindy said, perching on the edge of the desk. "You can either strip, or you can let me kiss you—it might be a little awkward if you do both, so let's just stick with whatever you find less invasive."

Jonah was taken aback by Cindy's mandate, but he deliberated on the options quickly. He trusted Cindy, and he needed her help, but while he was sure he didn't have anything that Cindy hadn't already seen or have herself, earlier in her life, he liked to maintain his privacy around his body. "Let's keep it simple, with a kiss."

"Okay, honey," she said, getting to her feet and holding out her hands. "Come here."

They both laughed uncomfortably, as they stood closer, given their shared platonic feelings. Cindy was beautiful, sexy and confident, but to Jonah, she was off-limits. She was with Morgan, just like he was with Mina—

Cindy kissed him without warning, setting her slender brown hands gently on his shoulders to keep him from pulling away, but once he felt her lips on his, Jonah was drowning in a wave of her fae light, blinding and hot like direct sunlight, but blissfully welcome, as though he had just emerged damp and chilled from winter hibernation. Her warmth became unpleasantly intense after a moment, but she moved her hands to hold onto his.

"Just a couple seconds more," she whispered against his lips, and held onto him, with a firm grasp.

One-Mississippi, two-Mississippi. With an enormous effort, focusing his thoughts on getting back to Mina, Jonah lifted his head and pulled his hands out of Cindy's grip. "Enough!"

Cindy settled back on the edge of her desk and folded her hands in front of her. "You pass," she smiled.

"What the fuck—"

"You remembered Mina, and your memory of her kept you grounded and protected you."

"What if I hadn't?"

"You would've likely been consumed by my light, and gone mad when I deprived you of it," she said.

"Shit. And you're just a *quarter*-fae?" Jonah marveled.

"You remembered that," Cindy beamed. "Yes, some traits skip a generation, but my illumination was passed down from my mother, and it's something I can turn on and off," she said casually. "I don't want to play too often like that, now that Morgan's in the picture. He has to tolerate enough from me, as it is."

Jonah took a seat on the couch. "Now that I've passed your test, will you tell me what happened?"

Cindy tilted her head inquisitively, a tight curl falling over her sparkling dark eyes. "To you, or to Mina and Adam?"

Jonah was surprised at being given a choice. "I'll take both, if that's an option."

"The easy one, first: Mina and Adam are on their way to San Francisco."

Jonah thought about what was there. "They're going to visit their parents."

Cindy nodded. "They can find the answers on how to help Adam more easily there, than here."

"Help him?" Jonah frowned. "He seemed fine when I last saw him."

"Physically, yes, he's fine, but straightening out his mind is like trying to unmix a drink," she said. "It may take some time to figure out, so Adam asked Xani not to go with him, but Mina's there for support…and to find some space for herself."

Jonah saw from Cindy's face that it was a much more somber endeavor for Mina than her words conveyed. "I need to go after her," he said urgently. "Or, least let her know that I'm back."

"Before you do that, perhaps we should take about your experience," Cindy suggested. "You died in a pool of sludge, apparently. What do you remember after that?"

Jonah had to think for a moment. "I woke up in a desert setting of some sort, with the ghost of one of my ancestors keeping me company. She left, and I was joined by Lucifer and Gabriel. They told me that Miranda was no more, and that her energy was collected to restore me, or something like that. I spoke briefly with Gabriel, as my reconstruction finished, and we talked about whom I needed to visit in Boston before coming here, and how best to transport me there."

"Miranda, as in Miranda White, the Garrison Brother's head witch?" she asked.

Jonah found it curious that, out of everything he had said, it was the mention of Miranda that had struck Cindy as interesting. "You knew her last name? I only found out hours before I died."

Cindy lowered her eyes. "Lucifer came by the Lotus last night, presumably after Mina and Adam were on their way back from Boston, and told me that Miranda would no longer be a cause of concern, but he was sparse with the details."

Jonah was still shocked that Mina and Adam were already gone, after being back for less than a day. Then, remembering Cindy's earlier point about Adam needing help, he understood their urgency. "Aside from Adam's condition, how did they seem?"

"You know them—they don't say shit without being badgered first, and even then, Mina wouldn't share much with me about what happened." Cindy paused and seemed to study him for a moment. "I noticed you got her a ring?"

Jonah smiled, gratified that she had worn it long enough for others to see. "It was my grandmother's ring, and my mother's engagement ring. I haven't had time to find a proper—"

"Just stop," Cindy said gently. "Mina's not about the money, otherwise, she would've stayed with Malcolm. She showed the ring to me last night, and she was still wearing it when she left. On her actual ring finger," she added, plucking Mina's gold chain out of her desk pen cup. Mina's engagement diamond and wedding band from her time with Malcolm still dangled from the fine rope chain, as they had for the past four years. "She's finally ready to let go of some parts of her past," Cindy said, "but she's holding onto you."

"I need to see her," Jonah said. "How long ago did they leave?"

"A few hours," Cindy shrugged without urgency. "And it'll be a few hours more before they land, so you have some time to plan out your approach, and what you're going to say, to her and to her family."

Cindy had a point. Jonah had expected to just come back and pick up like nothing had happened, just as he had done when he went to say good-bye to Connie and Teddy and let them know he was going to New York, but in his aunt and uncle's case, nothing *had* happened. As far as they knew, there was nothing suspicious about his absence and his decision to leave.

But Mina and her family did know what had happened to him, at least as much as Cindy did.

"Have you slept since your resurrection?"

Jonah shook his head. "No, actually. Apart from the time when I was…*dead*, I don't think I've slept since Sunday, and that wasn't really…" He was going to say "a full night's sleep," as he and Mina had spent their night together more awake or semi-conscious than actually asleep, but he stopped at Cindy's curious, knowing grin and finally said, "restful."

"You're such a gentleman, it's adorable," Cindy smiled. "Let me recommend that you take a nap before you make any rash decisions. Give your subconscious mind a chance to analyze what you've gone through,

12

maybe have something to eat. Mina and Adam are off-line, anyway, so there's no need to rush."

Mina picked up her head from her cushioned headrest and dabbed at her lip to make sure she hadn't been drooling in her sleep. She was more tired than she realized, and the droning white noise of the airplane had helped to knock her out soon after takeoff. She glanced out her window at the darkened sky, with just a sliver of the dying sunlight vanishing over the horizon.

"We have a couple more hours," Adam said quietly, in the aisle seat next to hers. "Do you need to stretch, or anything?" He caught the attention of one of the flight attendants and mimed a silent request for some water.

"No, I just had the strangest dream," Mina said, shaking her head. She had dreamed that Jonah was still alive, but when she saw him out of her periphery, he looked different. It had made little difference, as in the dream, she was so deliriously happy to have him back that she accepted him in whatever form he wanted to take.

The flight attendant delivered their water, and Mina finished hers quickly, as she overheard the flight attendants talking about their plans for Thanksgiving and what they thought their significant others were planning to get them for Christmas.

Adam gave her a meaningful look. "The holidays are coming."

"I'm not feeling very festive," she said, swirling the shrunken ice cubes around her cup.

"What do you want for Christmas, *mei-mei*?"

I want Jonah back. "How about world peace?"

"I was thinking more like an appliance or a gift certificate to a spa," Adam said.

"I'll settle for no one else getting hurt or getting their heart broken," she said, looking at him with some concern. Adam seemed too placid and normal, given what he had recently endured. "What about you? Should I find you the number for a therapist? It's not every day that someone punches holes into your brain."

Adam poured some untouched water from his full glass into Mina's and toasted her. "It's not every day that you watch someone you love die a horrible death, either."

"Jonah gave his life for both of us, so maybe a family therapy session is in order," she said.

"Depending on how this visit with Mom and Dad goes, we may need one, anyway," he muttered, voicing the same concern that she felt. "You didn't have to come with me, really. Whatever happens with me, it's something that I'll need to sort out, personally."

"We both have things to discuss with Mom and Dad," she said, finishing her water. "This visit is overdue, for all of us."

Cindy brought Jonah a blanket from the closet and left the office to let him fall asleep without an audience. Morgan and Xani were still at the counter, watching her expectantly, but she detoured briefly into the kitchen to make sure that Gia wasn't hovering behind the kitchen staff, either literally or figuratively, before she returned to the bar.

"Is it definitely Jonah?" Morgan asked.

Cindy nodded, "As far as I can tell. I told him to get some rest, so he can settle into his new body." From what she could see and feel of his strong, rangy frame, nothing was out of place, from the top of his silver-threaded black hair and his ice-blue eyes to his long, lean fingers—a musician or artist's fingers? Funny how she had never asked Jonah what he used to do for a living…

"What do you mean, 'new body'?" Xani asked.

"Jonah's body was obliterated when he died," Cindy said, returning to the conversation. "Given the way he perished, it would've been far easier for the powers to construct and customize a new body, than to try to recover and piece together his remains. Oh, that reminds me." She scooped a few ice cubes into a glass and poured some fresh water from the tap. "He's going to be dehydrated for a while."

"I can take that to him," Xani offered. "I sort of killed your moment with Morgan earlier, so I should probably give you some couple's time back," she mumbled.

"Thanks, sweetie," Cindy said, "but I should keep an eye on him myself. There's something else at work here—people aren't resurrected like he was, without reason. The fact that Lucifer and Gabriel seemed to be in agreement about it is even more suspicious."

"When are we going to tell Mina and Adam?" Morgan asked. "They deserve to know that he's alive and well."

"'Alive,' yes," Cindy said. "As for 'well,' that's to be determined."

"What do you think could be wrong with him?" Xani asked.

"I'm not sure. Might not be anything," Cindy said, swirling the ice cubes in the glass. "Of course, the day I want to pick Gabe and Luci's brains, they're nowhere to be found."

They were distracted by the sound of breaking porcelain on the office's tiled floor. Morgan reached the office first, but Cindy slipped past him to see what had happened.

Jonah was pale, glassy-eyed. "Where's Mina?'

"I told you already: she's not here," Cindy said patiently, picking up the chipped teacup where Jonah had thrown it. It was tough stoneware, with only a piece of the lip broken off.

"I had no voice, and I was weak and alone," Jonah rasped, almost plaintively. "I need to find her."

"You were too weak to talk, but you were strong enough to pick up and hurl a mug across the room?" Morgan asked, picking up the broken shard.

"He's feverish, maybe delirious, so I wouldn't expect him to be entirely rational right now," Cindy said, touching Jonah's forehead and cheek. "Here, drink this slowly," she said, holding the glass of ice water for him.

"What's in this?" Jonah asked, taking a cautious sip.

"Eye of newt and frog's breath," she deadpanned. "Just water, you moron." She let him hold the glass when he seemed more coherent. "Morgan, can you please bring me some valerian and turmeric?"

"From the bar, or the kitchen?" Morgan asked.

"Valerian's with the herbal teas, turmeric's in the kitchen spice pantry."

"You got it," Morgan said, ducking out.

"I wasn't like this when I was in Boston, I swear," Jonah said, taking slow sips.

"I believe you. But I don't imagine that you went anywhere like here, when you were in Boston, that could reveal your inner influences."

"What kind of influences?"

"I think you're something of a Trojan horse," she said. "Not by your own design, of course, but devils and angels don't generally agree to resurrect someone, let alone so quickly and with a reconstructed body, so before you see Mina again, we need to figure out your purpose."

"And I thought I was just here for her amusement and distraction," he muttered.

Cindy laughed. "Maybe you're that, too, but I have a feeling you've got something else going on. You don't remember anything else that Luci or Gabriel said that struck you as odd?

16

"Aside from Lucifer caring about Mina's opinion of him, no," Jonah said. "Why *does* she matter to him?"

Cindy shrugged. "That's something that predates my involvement. I only met Lucifer when he started visiting the Lotus, and the two of them already had a history." She noticed Jonah's concerned scowl. "Not that she would ever let herself get entangled with him. Whatever his interest is, she's never reciprocated."

"You're sure about that?"

"It'd be easy for Lucifer or Gabriel to find any of us outside the protection of the Lotus, if they were really intent on manipulating us, but Mina's never shown any signs of being under the influence of either of them," Cindy said. "And yes, I watch Mina very carefully for that—it's in my best interest to notice if she's compromised by one power or another. She's one of my best friends, but she's also the Lotus's main source of protection."

A knock sounded at the office door, and Morgan returned with a cup of hot water from the bar, with a mason jar of loose valerian tea, and the young fae girl, Gia, who carried a tray with a glass spice jar of turmeric, as well as small dishes of sliced fruit and olives and cheese cubes.

Gia set the tray down on the desk with sly glances towards Jonah.

Jonah stared for a moment, and Cindy realized that he noticed a resemblance between Gia and a younger Mina, when the latter used to wear her black hair short like Gia's. Gia braided and pinned a couple of longer locks to keep them away from her face, but there was enough of a shared semblance to catch his eye. Moreover, the fae teen had borrowed her sleeveless and backless shirt from Mina's closet, one of the few garments that allowed Gia's diaphanous wings to remain unfettered.

"Jonah, this is Gia, Galen's daughter," Cindy introduced. "Gia, this is Jonah Gideon, who helped rescue your father from captivity in Boston. And Mina's fiancé," she added pointedly, noting Gia's obvious interest in the broodingly handsome Jonah.

"It's very nice to meet you," Gia said, with a slight curtsy. "Thank you for saving my father."

"It was my pleasure," Jonah said with a nod. "And it's very nice to meet you, as well. Please tell him that I said 'hi.'"

Gia giggled, sounding like a twitter, and left the office as quietly as she had entered.

"She's fifteen," Cindy warned, seeing Jonah's eyes following her out.

"Not interested, just curious," Jonah said lightly. "'Fiancé'?"

"I was going to ask the same thing," Morgan said, looking back and forth between Cindy and Jonah. "When did that happen?"

"Mina told me she had made her decision in Boston," Cindy said to Jonah. "Before all this shit happened: before you died, and before she took her revenge on Ashu'ral by scrambling his brain… She's still yours, but first, we just have to make sure you're the same man she wanted to marry."

Walking from the car, across to their parents' rowhouse, Adam felt Mina's hand on his arm, and a napkin pressed into his hand. "What?"

"You might want to get that lipstick off your cheek before we see Mom and Dad," Mina suggested. "Left cheek. No, other left. *Your* left." Laughing, she took the napkin back and scrubbed his cheek clean. "Shit, I want to know what brand of lipstick Yumi uses. That stuff has some staying power."

"Am I being paranoid, or was someone taking pictures when Yumi was greeting me?"

"I'm amazed you could notice anything, the way she was climbing all over you," Mina said. "People are always taking selfies and reunion shots at the airport, so who knows? Maybe you showed up in someone's background. Does it matter?"

"Xani and I haven't had the discussion about old lovers and partners, yet," Adam said. "Not that I recall, anyway." His memory of his time with Xani was still hazy, and to his dismay, he remembered his years-old on-and-off relationship with Yumi Taira much more clearly.

"You only have to worry if, somehow, Xani sees a picture of you and Yumi together. There's nothing you can do about that, and you have nothing to feel guilty about, so forget about it for now," Mina said, as she unlocked the front door with their keycode.

"Mom! Dad!" Adam called, hearing his voice echo through the empty foyer. "Maybe they stepped out."

The house felt larger than it measured in square footage, as their parents kept the furniture spare and unfussy throughout, for as long as Adam could remember. As a child, he recalled it as being cold and colorless, except for the living room, where he and Mina spent most of their childhood years playing, before they had moved to New York.

Adam and Mina dropped their bags by the stairs and proceeded to the sitting room, each taking position on one of the matching blue brocade Queen Anne sofas facing each other. Just as they settled into their seats, their mother entered, as quickly and silently as though from thin air, and both children rose to their feet to give Selina Xing a greeting hug. "Your father will be along shortly," she said, waving them back to their seats. "How was your flight?"

19

"Fine, thanks for arranging the tickets," Adam said. "Did you send Yumi to greet us at the airport?"

"I couldn't make it to the airport myself," Selina said, "so I thought you would want to see a familiar face when you landed."

"*Ma-ma*," Mina interjected. "You could've sent someone else besides Adam's old girlfriend."

"Oh, did you used to go out?" Selina said innocently, looking at Adam.

Adam dropped his eyes. He had gone out a few times with Yumi Taira more than ten years ago, when he was still in college and Yumi was interning for his father's company, but they had been discreet to avoid any conflicts of interest or accusations of favoritism. They had drifted apart over the years, but Yumi still worked for the company, and she was still as gorgeous and demonstrative with her affection as Adam recalled.

"You know I'm already with Xani," he said.

The quick, light rhythm of their father's footsteps echoed across the marble floor. "It was just an airport pickup, son, not an attempt to meddle in your private affairs," he answered on Selina's behalf. The handsome face of Lin Xing greeted them at the French doors between the foyer and sitting room.

Looking at his father felt sometimes like a very optimistic glimpse at his future self, as Adam had inherited his dad's strong frame, cheekbones, jawline and full, almost blue-black hair. Adam only hoped that he would age as well.

"*Ba-ba!*" Mina greeted, rushing towards their father to throw her arms around his neck, and he hugged her back with a sighing laugh.

"Oh, you *do* remember who I am," he joked. "You changed your hair?"

Mina felt the ends of her shoulder-length black locks. "I'm growing it out. Does it look alright?"

"You hair always looks fine, Min-Min, even when it's an unnatural color." He tapped the tip of her nose. "You look more like your mother every day."

"I should be so lucky," Mina said, walking with their father to the center of the room, where he and Adam exchanged a brief hug. "How was Malaysia?"

Their parents exchanged a meaningful look, as they took their seats next to each other, before their father answered, "Good. It was a productive exchange, and everyone walked away with something they wanted."

"I'm sure." Adam tried to suppress his scoff, but he still felt Mina's elbow against his rib.

Lin Xing simply smiled. "What have you heard?"

Adam shook his head. "It's not my place to question your business decisions, Dad," he said.

"No, of course not, but I would welcome your commentary, nonetheless," his father said.

"I'm just curious about how you bargained for my reinstatement—actually, promotion—at Global Pacific." When he had received the call earlier in the week from the head of the Research Department, personally inviting him back, Adam had recognized his father's will at work. "What was your leverage, or was there something you agreed to give up?"

"I simply agreed to refrain from buying up more of their stock before the end of the year," he said. "The company is currently undervalued and will be reevaluated at the start of the first quarter, and the stock is scheduled to split soon after its earnings report, so my seat on the board remains secure."

Adam looked at his mother, then back at his father. "You never mentioned that you were on the board of my company."

"*Your* company?" his father grinned. "I wasn't on Global Pacific's board, until you started working there. I did some research and saw its potential, more or less, and decided to invest in the business," he said nonchalantly.

21

"I didn't want to make my board position public, and risk interfering with your function there."

"But that's exactly what you've done, by negotiating for my return. Why?" Adam asked. "You want to keep me chained to a desk?"

"We want to see you succeed," his father said. "And yes, we want you to stay out of trouble."

Adam glanced at Mina. "What about *mei-mei*? Now that I've been the kind of danger she's in, all the time, I can't stand by and watch her struggle through it alone."

"She will no longer be troubled by the likes of Miranda White," their father sniffed.

Mina looked at their father. "How do you know that?"

"I have assurances," their father said dismissively. "As for other possible threats, Min-Min has easily managed them in the past, on her own. And really, Adam, you wouldn't be as useful to her, as you've been in the past, until your faculties have all returned, would you? Whereas your current limited function would still be perfectly adequate for the job you've been offered."

Adam clenched his jaw briefly. "You'd rather have me working in an office at Global Pacific, than helping my sister?"

"We would rather have you be a success in your own right, without needing anyone else's aid at all," their father said caustically.

"I never asked for preferential treatment," Adam said sharply.

"It comes with your name, my son," their father said, "whether you want it or not."

"I don't need a handout, and I don't need this job." Adam shook his head and got to his feet. "What else did I expect, coming out here," he muttered. "We could've had this same discussion over the phone and saved you the airfare. Excuse me," he said to Mina and Selina, as he stalked from the room.

✧✧✧

Lin steeled himself for his wife's rebuke. "Our son is a grown man," he preempted, "who should have a thicker skin."

"But you know that he's proud, like you," Selina said. "You could've handled that differently.

"He could learn a thing or two from Mina on how to stay in a fight, instead of running away."

"I don't consider my toughness as much of an asset as you seem to," Mina said. "My skin has thickened to ensure my survival—"

Selina cleared her throat, and Mina cut her comment short.

"Your toughness will help speed you through this mood of yours," Lin said. "You are too old to still be unmarried, and too young to stop looking. If you need your mother or me to find candidates for you—"

"No!" Mina snapped, shaking her head vehemently. "No, thank you, *ba-ba*," she said, more calmly and graciously, "but I'm not ready for that. I'm not sure if I'll *ever* be ready for that."

Lin frowned at her downcast expression. "Did someone hurt you?"

"No, *ba-ba*, it's not like that…"

Lin reached out and grabbed Mina's left hand, as fast as a snake strike, to see her ring. "Who gave this to you?" he demanded, looking at the stone. "It's a paltry thing…"

Mina snatched her hand back. "And it's never leaving my hand," she resolved. "You don't need to know who gave it to me. It doesn't matter anymore."

"Clearly, it matters," Lin returned, heartened by the embers in his daughter's eyes—he hadn't seen it since her arrival, and he was glad that she still had her spirit. "If it didn't matter, you wouldn't still be wearing it, would you?"

23

Selina reached out, more gently, to stroke Mina's shoulder. "You need time, that's all. You're in pain, and it is too fresh and raw for you to think very clearly."

"You're right, *ma-ma*," Mina said. "I do need time. I can't talk to either of you about this right now. I'll go check on Adam."

Alone in the sitting room, Selina and Lin listened to their children conversing in the kitchen, mostly in rapid-fire English, with the odd Chinese phrase interspersed, in whichever dialect they chose in that moment.

"For a clever businessman, you are not nearly as gifted when speaking to your own children," Selina said. "You forget how Western they can be, in their emotionalism and their independence."

"I haven't forgotten," he said. "I merely hoped that they would take less after my temper, and more after your poise and pragmatism."

"You're trying to argue with children," Selina reminded. "They lack your perspective, experience and connections, and moreover, Mina finally let herself fall in love again, only to lose him tragically, so be patient with her. She will be herself again, soon."

"I know about this Jonah Gideon," Lin said. "Her former husband's cousin, as I recall? Is he the one that gave her that…that trinket?"

Selina smiled mildly at his sneering tone. "If you recall him, then you know he was a good and dutiful man," she said. "It was a fine match, even though it was a love match, and they would've been happy. I believe he loved Mina, otherwise he wouldn't have sacrificed himself the way he did."

"To foil Miranda White's plot, yes, I'm aware," Lin said impatiently. "I'm also aware that angels and devils had conspired to restore his life."

"Really," Selina said bemusedly. "Why would they do that?"

24

"Excellent question, dearest," Lin said. "Perhaps we can ask him when he comes here, which should be soon. Until we know, and until Mina is no longer weakened by her grief, we need to keep them separate. It will be painful for her not to know, but it's better than to have him betray her later, if he's not what he seems."

"How did you know of his resurrection?"

"Aciré Hart alerted me after his visit to collect his things from the State Street office," Lin said. "She confirmed that it is Jonah Gideon, at least in the physical sense and of what she could determine during their meeting. What lurks in his mind, and where his loyalties lie, remain to be seen."

"And she is certain that he is on his way here, not staying in Boston?" Selina asked.

"She helped arrange his travel to New York, actually. It is my supposition, though, that he'll find his way to California once he sees that Mina's not there. If your instincts about him are correct, that is," he teased.

"He'll come for her, sooner or later," Selina said. "When he arrives, I wish to speak with him."

"Shouldn't we both have a word with him?"

"No, husband, that would overwhelm him, I think," she said indulgently. "Just tell me when he's close, and I will coordinate a meeting with him."

Chapter 2

Jonah slept uneasily through the night, waking intermittently from troubling or disturbing dreams. He eventually stopped trying to sleep after the last nightmare, where he was visited by the spirit of Miranda White, young and resplendent in a pristine, flowing white gown. She almost looked angelic, except for the cold emptiness in her dark eyes and the cruelty of her smile.

I had considered keeping you for myself, she had taunted him, *to discover how you would feel inside me, but I think I like being inside you even more.*

You're dead, Jonah had retorted. *You have no power or substance.*

As long as you remember that I am a part of you, I will continue to haunt you, she had laughed. *As long as you live, so will I.*

And that was the last thing Jonah recalled from his dream, so that last statement followed him into his conscious state. Jonah turned on the bedside lamp, hoping the discomfort of the sudden light would jar him fully awake, but it was actually the knock on the door that snapped him out of his semi-sleep.

It was the sound of the rap on the heavy oak door, coupled with Mina's scents, that reminded Jonah that he was in a safe place: in her apartment, her bedroom, her bed. He tossed the covers aside reluctantly to answer the door, and looking through the peephole, he still had to think for a moment on whether to open the door. He glanced down at his t-shirt and loose sleep pants and decided that he wasn't really dressed for visitors, but whatever... He eventually turned on the living room light and opened the door to his late-night guest.

Xani had a general fretfulness about her, and she seemed lost in her own thoughts as she came inside, barely glancing at him.

"What time is it?" he asked.

"Two in the morning," Xani said. "Sorry to wake you, but I was too wound up to go home."

"No, it's fine. My dreams were shit, anyway," he said. "What's the matter?"

"I'm worried about Adam," she said, wringing her hands. "He didn't seem like himself when he left, and now I think I made a mistake in not going to California with him." She looked at him with a kind of desperation in her jade-green eyes. "You were one of the last people to speak with him before he and Mina came back to New York."

"That's true, but our conversations were more frustrating than anything else," Jonah confessed. "Half the time, he wasn't entirely sure of who he was or why he was there, so I did most of the talking."

"He didn't seem to remember much of the past few weeks," Xani said.

"He didn't recall much of his life at all, at first." He watched the worry deepening on Xani's face. "Look, a lot of time passed after the last time I spoke to him, and he was recovering quickly, so I'm sure he's come a long way since then."

"I want to try to make our relationship work," Xani said, "but what if his new memories and his new life don't include me? We can't recreate everything that happened to bring us together, but what if that was kismet, and that connection is lost?"

Jonah crossed his arms. "You're not the clingy or worrying type, so what is this *really* about?"

Xani hesitated for a moment, then brought up a picture on her phone, that she showed to Jonah. "This was taken tonight, outside the airport in San Francisco."

It was a photo of Adam, locked in a kiss and embrace with a pretty young Asian woman—presumably, as the woman's features were partially obscured by the camera phone angle—but his face was clearly visible. It wasn't a selfie, but a shot taken from a distance.

"I see." Jonah passed the phone back. "I can understand why you're upset, but this is one photo, completely without context," he said dismissively. "Who sent it to you?"

"I don't know," Xani said. "It's not a number I recognize."

"Then ask him about it when he returns," Jonah suggested. "There's no point in agonizing over it until you hear his side of it. He's on the other coast, so you can't do anything about it now, anyway."

"I can't, but you can," she said. "I know you're planning to go after Mina, so when you get there, can you just check on Adam for me, please?"

He wouldn't spy or snoop on his friend, but it wouldn't hurt to talk to him, and make sure he was feeling better, and more like himself. "Sure."

"Thank you!" Overcome by her relief, Xani wrapped her arms around Jonah's shoulders and kissed his cheek, and instinctively, his hands curled around to the small of her back.

He had never noticed the silky warmth of Xani's skin, and for an instant, he wondered why he had never tried to hold or kiss her before. She seemed surprised by the appeal of his touch, also, as she braced her hands on his shoulders—not daring to move any closer to him, but not quite pushing away, either.

"This is wrong," she breathed, sounding as though she was trying to convince herself.

To some part of Jonah's subconscious, it didn't feel wrong at all, but his rational mind reasserted itself, and he peeled his hands away from Xani's waist. "I'm sorry," he said, even as he fought the instinct to push Xani against the wall and feel the rest of her luscious skin.

"Me, too." She nodded but was slow to step back from him, at which point he realized that she had pinned *him* against the doorframe. "I shouldn't have come here."

Jonah looked at her, to test his resolve, and his passion had dissipated as quickly as it had swelled. He opened the door for Xani. "I'm planning to leave tomorrow, so I'll have answers for you soon," he said.

"Thank you," she said, more subdued. As she passed him on her way out, she looked at him a last time. "You *are* different. I can't tell exactly what it is, but there's a kind of darkness about you that wasn't there before."

"It doesn't frighten you?"

"No," Xani said bemusedly. "We all have light and dark forces inside us, but I know that, whatever is happening to you, you'll find a way to keep it in balance and use it to your advantage."

"How can you be so sure?" he asked, leaning against the door.

"Because you have Mina waiting for you," she smiled, "and if you can come back from death for her, you can overcome anything."

After spending a few more fitful hours in Mina's bed, Jonah gave up trying to sleep and got dressed in a t-shirt, sweatpants and sneakers. He left the apartment and rushed downstairs to get an early start on the day, planning on getting in a quick run, just to test the stamina and limits of his still-new body. He knew that technically he was the same, but Cindy's assessment of him and his brief encounter with Xani the night before left him doubting his own soundness.

The ground floor duplex door opened unexpectedly, and Galen greeted him with a warm smile and a bow. Jonah hadn't seen Galen since they had parted ways in Boston, when he and Mina had seen him safely to the wharf for his journey to reunite with his children in New York. The fae looked healthier, stronger and undoubtedly happier.

"I was wondering who would be in such a rush at such an early hour," Galen grinned. "You look good for a dead man, Jonah."

"I wouldn't know. It's my first resurrection." Jonah took the fae's extended hand. "It's good to see you again, too, Galen. I'm glad you're settling in comfortably."

"Everyone has been more than kind and generous," Galen nodded. "It's almost too tempting to stay, but I've told Cindy that we'll be out of her way once our contacts in the Caymans have set up our new life: our documents must be forged, and a paper trail created."

"I'm sure you're not in anyone's way. You don't seem the type," Jonah said.

"You haven't met the others," Galen laughed. "Why don't you come in, if you have a moment to spare?"

Jonah entered the duplex for the first since he left New York previously, and it was no longer the cold, bleak space he recalled during its vacancy. Mina had occasionally checked the duplex after the previous tenants had moved, to ensure that no squatters or vermin had taken up residence, and Jonah had enjoyed accompanying her when he was still in his husky form; his canine senses picked up odors accumulated over the decades of the families that had resided there, from old-fashioned perfumes and cosmetics in the bedroom to spilled sauces, creams and libations in the living and drawing rooms. He had imagined lavish parties and family gatherings that must have taken place in that spacious apartment.

Now, with just Galen and his children occupying the duplex, there was still a festive and lively atmosphere, with children's toys and clothing tossed where the previous tenants had once arranged their decorations, *objets d'art,* and furniture. The children looked up from their half-finished breakfasts at a visitor's arrival and swarmed him at once.

Swarmed in the literal sense, as all three of the dark-haired children boasted lacy wings that carried their weight easily, as they buzzed around Jonah and landed in a semi-circle around him.

"Children, don't crowd," Galen said. "This is Mister Gideon, a friend of Miss Cindy and Miss Xing."

"Mister Gideon," the boy marveled, looking directly up at him. "Dad said you fought as fiercely as a werewolf!"

Jonah grinned. "Your dad is pretty tough, too. We made a good team." He crouched to look at the toddler girl shuffling her feet and flitting her wings nervously. "I heard you just had your wing-sprout. I can tell you practice a lot."

"It's like a human infant going from crawling to cruising to running, in the span of days," Galen said with a tired but proud smile. "This is my youngest, Fern. Fallon is six, and you've met Gia, I believe."

Gia extended her hand with a coy smile, and on impulse, Jonah took her hand with a bow and kissed her knuckles. The younger children giggled at the funny human gesture, and Jonah noticed a pink blush flood Gia's golden-ivory cheeks, as he released her hand.

"Children, go finish eating," Galen said. "And Fallon, wash Fern's bowl, please." Before Fallon could voice his protest, Galen reminded, "Gia has to get dressed and go help Miss Cindy at the Lotus, so I'll need you to pick up before lessons."

31

Jonah watched the children return to the counter to finish their breakfast, and he sensed Galen's eyes on him. "Your children are beautiful and well-behaved, Galen. You must be very proud."

Galen nodded. "They mean everything to me." He led Jonah to the living room area, out of the children's earshot. "I know you to be honorable and honest, but I need to voice a request, and I hope you don't take it as an insult."

"What is it?" Jonah asked, intrigued.

"I would appreciate if you didn't seduce my daughter," Galen said plainly.

Jonah was stunned at the accusation. "What?"

"I know my Gia is beautiful and flirtatious, but she is only fifteen—"

"Galen," Jonah interrupted, "I swear I'm not trying to seduce your child."

Galen waved Jonah to take a seat on the sofa. "You may not be trying, consciously, but I would guess that you are now acting and thinking in ways that would've never crossed your mind when we first met. I honed my skills for years in service to Ashu'ral, and I can sense earthly and supernatural influences at work. You, my friend, are definitely compromised."

"When I returned to the Lotus last night, Cindy suspected that I was different, too," Jonah said.

Galen raised his brow. "The protection wards around the Red Lotus distort the effects, so if Cindy still sensed a change about you, then it's significant. Would you mind if I tried something?"

Galen went to a sideboard and pulled out an assortment of jars and bottles that Jonah recognized as coming from Mina's stores. "Mina was generous enough to give me permission to raid her supplies, and I'll reimburse her when she returns."

Jonah recalled the couple of times that Mina had used her elixirs and draughts on him, and he didn't recall either experience being pleasant, but Galen seemed unconcerned, as he combined his concoction of herbs in something that looked like a molcajete used to mash up avocado and molé sauces. He returned to the sofa and balanced the mortar on his lap, as he finished pulverizing the paste. Almost like a garnish, Galen pricked his finger on the tip of a scalpel-like blade and dripped a couple of drops of his blood into the mix.

"Hey, you don't expect me to consume that, do you?" Jonah asked, peering into the stone bowl. It smelled grassy, with a minerally, liver-y accent.

"I've seen what humans eat—this would hardly be the most toxic or distasteful recipe you've tried," Galen said, glancing aside at him. "But no, I don't expect you to eat or drink it."

"So, what do you—"

Before Jonah could comment, Galen reached over and smudged a thumbprint across his forehead. Jonah yelped at the searing pain of the contact, and he fought not to rub it off—with his luck, any such attempt would have just meant pain for both his head *and* his hand. "Fuck, that's like napalm!"

"So, I've heard," Galen said mildly. "Hold still, I still have to smudge your eyes."

"Fuck that!" Jonah exclaimed, backing away, his eyes already watering. He regretted complaining about any discomfort from Mina's concoctions. "Does this stuff leave a scar?"

"No, it washes off with soap and water. Come back here, coward," he reprimanded lightly, "before I have to amend my account of your bravery to my children. I need to mark you, in order to read you."

Jonah leaned forward and braced himself, nodding gratefully to Galen for the dignity of a rolled-up washcloth to bite down and distract himself from the stinging. He reminded himself of the second before his death, with Mina's face the last image he saw, as the flaying, broiling foulness consumed him from the bottom up, and his mind registered his impending demise for that fraction of a second before it happened—Galen's "unholy molé" didn't seem all that bad, by comparison.

Jonah closed his eyes and felt Galen gently dab his eyelids, spreading the scorching pain further. Unable to avoid the physical agony, Jonah withdrew into himself to attempt a moment of introspection. Cindy, Xani and Galen were right—things seemed different now, and he felt urges and had thoughts that were much darker than what he had before: not evil, per se, but morally ambiguous, in a sense.

"How conflicted do you feel, Jonah?" Galen asked.

Jonah eased his eyes open a sliver and spit out the towel. "More so now than I used to feel, before I died. I used to be a peace-loving type, until my situation changed."

"Well, I can tell that's bullshit," Galen dismissed. "Your body and aura show the scars of your physicality. You'd seen your share of fights and punishment, even before you fell in with Mina and her company."

"I wouldn't pick a fight, but if I found myself in one, I'd defend myself," Jonah clarified. "Otherwise, I used to keep to myself and not stick my nose where it didn't belong. That's what I meant."

"And now?"

"Now, I feel…" He struggled to find the words. "I feel restless. I feel like I need to bring the fight to others, to prove myself." He thought about what that meant. "To show that I'm worthy of Mina."

"To show whom?" Galen pressed. "Mina doesn't need anything else from you, and from what I can tell, her friends and family seem to like you well enough."

Who else would have a stake? Who had orchestrated his resurrection? *Lucifer and Gabriel.* "Angels and devils," he muttered.

34

Galen rolled his eyes. "Aren't they the worst? You feel their push and pull, don't you? The air around you is thick with strife—they worked in tandem to bring you back, so it makes sense that they both have an agenda for you. Unfortunately, it's not a single, shared agenda—that would simplify things for you greatly."

"I'm going over to the Lotus," called Gia, donning her borrowed trench coat over her tucked wings, and pulling her short dark hair into a stubby pigtail. "The elves said they want me to help peel a hundred pounds of onions—I really hope they're joking, else my skin will reek of them by the time I'm done." She paused. "Reek of onions, not elves."

"You have to pay your dues if you're serious about working there," Galen laughed. "I'm proud of you for sticking with it."

"Thanks, Papa," she smiled. "Will I see you there later, Mister Gideon?" she asked, seeming not to notice Jonah's furiously watering eyes or the unappealing, muddy streaks on his face and eyes.

"Maybe," Jonah said, hoping to sound curt and dismissive, but Gia merely smiled shyly as she turned on her heel to go. He almost dreaded to see Galen's reaction, but the fae simply shrugged.

"You're being more mindful, and there's little else you can do, really," Galen said. "You can't control the responses you elicit from others. Keep your hands to yourself, and I'll have to remind my daughter to do the same."

With her morning mug of tea in hand, Mina walked through her parents' house, which she hadn't visited since shortly after her divorce, to note the changes of décor and furnishings that had been made since her last visit. Selina had an eye for sleek lines and muted hues, while Lin was more earthy and colorful in his tastes, but somehow the combination worked harmoniously in their home. It felt sometimes like a museum to Mina, and she had learned from an early age to move nimbly around fragile antiquities—not the easiest skill for a rambunctious child to master—but her practiced reflexes and precision helped her stay alive in her profession, especially when facing off against stronger adversaries.

Mina wandered into her father's study and saw the small gavel that was gifted to him by a prominent local official. Lin Xing was always receiving gifts and tokens from his associates, and he was known to be equally generous when reciprocating. The gavel caught her eye, as it reminded her of Erik Farrier's enchanted hammer that she had borrowed to break Ashu'ral's body and mind. She wasn't proud of what she had done to the demon, but ultimately, she felt justified in her actions, in ensuring that no one else would ever need to suffer as her brother and Jonah had.

Mina glanced at her father's blotter and saw a scribbled note logging a message from Aciré Hart to her father. As Lin Xing dealt mostly with Bullfinch and Farrier for his business matters, it was unusual for the third partner to reach out, but not unprecedented. Mina was curious, though, about what Aciré would have to discuss with her father that couldn't be relayed through one of the other partners.

Mina felt a buzz in her pocket from an incoming text on her phone, from Aciré, to check in and ask for a couple of minutes to "go over stuff." Mina chuckled at Aciré's vague phrasing—as Mina's friend and personal counsel, Aciré knew her preference to discuss details over the phone, rather than overshare on text messages.

On her way back to the kitchen with her empty mug, Mina called Aciré back, noting the time to make sure that it was still early in Boston, to avoid interrupting her during a lunch meeting or client call. She didn't expect a long conversation, probably just long enough to go over some outstanding details regarding the settlement of Malcolm's will.

"Good morning, Mina," Aciré greeted warmly. "How's your visit going so far?"

"Uneventful, and it felt weird sleeping in my old room last night," Mina said, setting her empty cup in the sink. "What's up? Do you need my bank account numbers or signatures on anything?"

There was a pause on Aciré's side. "Did your father mention anything to you last night or this morning, that you may have questions about?"

Mina was confused. "We talked a little last night when we arrived, usual parent-child conversations. What's this about?"

"Oh," Aciré said shortly. "Never mind, then."

"Aciré," Mina said warningly.

"Client confidentiality, girlfriend. You know how that works," she said. "But while I have you…"

Mina and Aciré went over the cash transfer instructions, verifying accounts and beneficiaries, before Mina asked about Malcolm's parents. "How are they doing? Have they been told about Jonah's death, yet?"

"No, I haven't spoken to them about it," Aciré said carefully. "He's not officially missing."

"And when it becomes official, are we supposed to just let them believe that he's just disappeared?" Mina frowned. "At some point, they should be told the truth, even if they won't understand the circumstances."

"I don't disagree," Aciré said diplomatically. "But it's not my decision to share or withhold any information, at this time. If you'll excuse me, Mina, I have a client waiting on me outside. Promise me you won't call Malcolm's family on your own, okay?"

"Yeah, sure. I'll talk to you soon." As Aciré hung up, Mina pondered: whose decision was it?

Lin came into the kitchen. "A phone call, this early? It's not even eight o'clock."

"Just going over a couple of things with Aciré," Mina said vaguely, going to the refrigerator to pick something for breakfast, and to avoid her father's incisive eyes. Grass jelly, tofu, boiled eggs, fruit… Mina took her time making her choice and eventually took out a container of butter, flinching when she saw her father still at the island counter, watching her. "It was nothing, Dad. It was a brief call."

Her father knew her too well and divulged nothing, either through his expression or his reply: "What did she say?"

"She wanted to confirm some account information with me," Mina said. "What else could we possibly have to discuss?" she asked lightly.

Lin's expression turned serious, but still patient. "Min-Min, you know your mother and I will always want the best for you, and always try to keep you safe. If we don't share everything with you, it's only because the timing isn't right."

Mina sawed off a piece of sourdough from the loaf on the counter and popped the slice in the toaster. "I know, but if I'm here, I want to contribute and understand, especially if it's something to do with me." She took a plate from the cupboard and the butter spreader from the drawer, without having to think about where anything was. "Aciré didn't tell me anything, by the way. Is she waiting for you to give her permission?"

Lin gave her a mischievous, wry smile. "What do you think?"

Mina set her dish down and hid her face in her hands tiredly. "*Ba-ba*, please! I don't have it in me to play these kinds of games right now. Can't you just tell me what you're keeping from me?"

Lin regarded her with a pitying gaze. "No." He took her piece of crisped sourdough from the toaster and turned to leave the kitchen. "If you can't ask without that whining tone in your voice, then you're not ready to hear it."

Mina fought the instinct to pout, but internally, she still felt like a scolded child, being chastised for attempting to meddle in grown-up matters. As was usually the case when she was young, her father was acting as the final authority on what she could be allowed to know and do for herself.

"That's fine, *ba-ba*," she said, managing to steady her voice. "I didn't come home expecting your sympathy or support. I've learned to manage without them." She sliced another piece of sourdough for the toaster and washed her empty cup in the sink, along with several other pieces of glassware and cups that had been left; it was a habit she had acquired over the years of living alone, to wash things as they were dirtied, to minimize the clutter in her small apartment.

By the time she dried her hands, Lin had left the kitchen, not that Mina had expected him to stay. It was fine, as she had spent the idle minutes while she was washing dishes also mentally reviewing her brief talk with Aciré. Given her father's steadfast evasiveness, and Aciré's similar secrecy, it was a natural conclusion that her father had directed her attorney and friend to keep silent.

Aciré wasn't even allowed to tell Connie and Teddy that Jonah was dead. *'At this time'*—why?

Shit, does Dad know something about Jonah that he's keeping from me?

Mina buttered her toast and ate absent-mindedly, thinking of her father's intentions; he was challenging her to circumvent him to get what she wanted. She grinned, realizing that her father had purposefully riled her, to shake her out of her funk and stop feeling sorry for herself. It worked like a charm.

With her last chunk of sourdough toast clamped between her teeth, Mina washed her plate and butter

39

knife and grabbed her jacket on her way through the living room. The front doorbell chimed, as she went to leave, so she opened it without a thought.

Yumi Taira stood in the doorway, clutching a large white envelope to her chest. She smiled with amusement at Mina's disheveled hair, her jacket awkwardly half-on and a hunk of sourdough still clamped between her teeth. Mina pulled the toast out of her mouth and finished shrugging into her jacket. "Hi, Yumi."

Yumi, of course, looked perfect. When they were younger, Mina had always admired Yumi's doll-like features with a sense of awe, as she seemed too pretty to be real, but as the years went by, the novelty of Yumi's flawless, ageless beauty began to wear, and Mina was relieved that Adam had avoided further involvement with her. As he had continued to grow and mature, Yumi was always the same.

"I'm still getting used to seeing you again, Mina," Yumi greeted with a cute, rosy smile. "It's so nice that you've come to visit, after being gone so long."

It was not-so-subtle dig at Mina's scarce presence in her parents' lives, when traditionally, it was the daughter's role to stay close to home to see to her aging parents' needs. "Yes, it's a good thing that my parents don't mind having me underfoot this week," she said lightly. "I'm sure they'll be relieved when I head back to New York."

Mina stood aside and let Yumi inside. "Is that for my father?" she asked, pointing to the envelope.

"Yes, he asked to get a hard copy as soon as the report arrived, and since I signed for it this morning, I thought I'd drop it off in person, rather than make him wait till he got to the office," Yumi said, tucking a long, silky black lock behind her ear. "Is Mister Xing here?"

Before Mina could answer, Selina came to the foyer. "Miss Taira, what a lovely surprise."

Yumi bowed deeply to Selina. "Good morning, *Xing-sama*. I'm sorry to intrude so early this morning."

"Not at all," Selina said. "Have you eaten yet this morning, or would you like some tea?"

"No, thank you," Yumi said, with another bow. "I just wanted to give this to Mister Xing, and then I'll return to the office."

"How very thoughtful of you. Come, you can wait in his study," she said graciously, gesturing Yumi towards Lin's home office, then stopped. "Mina, are you going out already? So early?"

Mina relaxed her jaw when she realized she was chewing her sourdough a bit aggressively. "I have some personal business to take care of. I'll probably be back before you even notice I'm gone."

Lin met the women in the foyer and quickly assessed the situation. "Is that the report, Miss Taira? Thank you for bringing it by—I'll look it over before the ten o'clock meeting. Please call Mister Bullfinch when you get back to your desk and confirm that he has a copy, as well."

He took the envelope from Yumi and nodded in a way that was dismissive without being rude, and ushered Yumi to the door. Once the door closed behind Yumi, he tucked the envelope under his arm and headed towards his study. "Now that that's settled, let me get out of the way. Don't let me interrupt your mother-daughter time," he said, shutting himself into his office.

"Don't be petty, little one," Selina said, noticing Mina's continued surliness.

"I'm not," Mina pouted. "Just because Yumi's prettier, or is more dutiful, or…" She took a stab, based on what she had noticed about the flawless Miss Taira. "Or a *huli jing*, like you. Technically, *kitsune*, if she came from Japan."

Selina smiled and smoothed down one of Mina's errant locks. "She may be of my kind, but you are my own. You are part of me." She reached over and brushed a sourdough crumb from the edge of Mina's lip. "You have a good eye. How can you tell what Yumi is?"

"Partly instinct," Mina answered. "Plus, she always looks perfect, she hasn't aged or changed over the past ten years, and she's trying to make herself a fixture in your lives."

"She is *kitsune* without family or clan here to protect her," Selina said. "Of course, she wants to secure her position," she said, wrapping her hand around Mina's waist, "but that doesn't mean that she'll ever take yours."

Mina flashed her mother a look of defiance. "Not Xani's, either. That was unkind of you, to send Yumi to meet us at the airport. You must have suspected how she would behave around Adam, if she's seeking your favor."

Selina laughed lightly. "I merely asked Yumi to meet you; I didn't tell her to give your brother such an enthusiastic welcome. I certainly didn't ask anyone to take a photo of them together to post online."

"What?" Mina exclaimed, stepping away from her mother.

"It wasn't Yumi's doing, either, but even if it were, it would be perfectly innocent," Selina said. "Yumi didn't know that Adam has someone in New York."

"No, but you did," Mina frowned. "You didn't think to tell Yumi about Xani, or warn me or Adam beforehand of what you were planning?"

"Of course, I thought about both," Selina said, "and I opted not to."

Why the fuck not! Mina wanted to cry, but she noted Selina's cool, confident demeanor. "You're up to something."

Selina bobbed her head noncommittally, as she strolled towards the kitchen, with Mina in tow. "I'm always up to something, little one." She opened the refrigerator and pulled out a pitcher of unsweetened

42

jasmine tea. "Your father and I couldn't possibly let you live on the other coast without checking that your friends and companions are worthy of your time and effort."

"Xani's seen the picture already, hasn't she?" Mina shook her head, feeling terrible for her friend. "She doesn't deserve this. She cares about Adam, and even offered to fly out with him."

"It's to her credit that she didn't," Selina said, pouring out two glasses of tea, one for herself and one for Mina. "Sometimes, love means letting go, keeping a distance, and trusting that your loved one will return of their own accord." She clinked her glass with Mina's and took a sip. "The same philosophy applies to children, too, by the way."

"What you did wasn't fair, to either Xani or Yumi," Mina said. "Or Adam, for that matter."

"It would be more unfair to let them live in ignorance, with their dynamics untested and stagnant," Selina said. "This is how we learn resilience, Min-Min. It's why you were ready to burst out the door to hunt down the answers that your father refused you."

"You know what he's keeping from me, too, don't you?" Mina asked.

"Of course," she said, taking Mina's empty glass from her. "And I won't tell you, either. Trust me; it'll be far more meaningful once you've gained some perspective first. Go, have fun. Tell the selkies at Pier 39 that I said 'hello'."

Chapter 3

As he passed Micah on the way through the front door, Jonah's eyes took a moment to adjust to the red and orange pumpkin lights inside the Red Lotus, not yet open for business. He scanned the empty lounge briefly to see if Gia was about, but he only saw Cindy behind the bar.

"Don't you ever go home?" he quipped, glancing at his phone and noticing that it was barely noon. He knew that she had an apartment somewhere in Manhattan, but lately, it seemed that he only ever saw Cindy at the Lotus.

"And miss the chance to see your beautiful face? Not a chance," she said. "Besides, I'm expecting a couple of VIPs before hours, so I have to make sure everything's neat and tidy. What can I get you?"

"Just water," he said, wondering why Cindy still bothered asking. She was aware of his dietary restrictions due to his canine nature, still integrated into his being despite his resurrection. "Galen made me some savory oatmeal for breakfast, to reward me for being cooperative during his examination of me."

Cindy arched her eyebrow, setting the glass in front of him. "And how did that go?"

"It wasn't fun, but it confirmed what you suspected, that Lucifer and Gabriel are pulling my strings, one way or another," Jonah said. "I wish I knew why."

"You can ask them yourself," Cindy said, pointing her chin towards the door, where Lucifer sauntered past

44

Micah breezily. She reached for a highball glass and listened for the devil's first drink order of the day, and Lucifer's crisp blond hair shone like gold, even under the muted lights of the bar.

"Oh, you're here, too," he said apathetically, glancing at Jonah. "Nothing for now, sweet Cin. This isn't an entirely social visit, after all."

"Thank you for accepting my invitation," Cindy smiled. "I wasn't sure it would reach you."

"I always hear when you call for me." Lucifer took a seat a couple of spaces to Jonah's left. "How are you enjoying your new body, Mister Gideon?"

"Still checking it over," Jonah said.

"With assistance?" Lucifer looked over at Gia, who had emerged from the kitchen with bowls of citrus garnishes for the bar's stock. He was subtle with his examination of Gia's young curves, but he didn't bother disguising his interest. "Good morning, Miss…"

"Off-limits," Cindy said tersely, taking the fruit from Gia's hands.

Gia smiled at Lucifer but saved her eyelash flutter for Jonah. "Can I bring you anything from the kitchen, Mister Gideon?" she offered sweetly.

"Maybe later, sweetie," Cindy said, shooing her back to the kitchen, then turning to Lucifer. "Okay, what did you do to Jonah?" At Lucifer's innocent glance, she elaborated: "You didn't have to make him hotter and tastier than he already was."

Jonah looked over, muttering, "That's not really my main complaint."

"It's all related," she said. "Well?" she asked Lucifer. "When you put him back together, you folded in something extra."

"Why would I do such a thing?" Lucifer asked. "I would fall further out of Miss Xing's favor, if a tainted or imperfect specimen was returned to her. I want her to be happy with the refurbished Mister Gideon, as much as

45

anyone. He'll even come with a lifetime warranty, subject to terms and conditions."

"He's not an appliance, Luci," Cindy said.

"Depends on how Miss Xing wants to use him," Lucifer remarked.

"Hey, I'm right here!" Jonah exclaimed. "Physically, I may be the same, but I don't think and feel as I used to. There's more that I want to do, and I have more nervous energy to burn."

"Sounds like a boost in your testosterone levels," Lucifer said mildly. "Some men enjoy feeling that kind of virility, but perhaps you're the more passive type. It may also be a psychological change resulting from your experience with death: you appreciate life more and want to live it more fully."

Cindy seemed to sense that Lucifer was holding back something. "I'm going into the office for ten minutes. The two of you can clear the air while I'm gone."

Only when Cindy shut the office door did Jonah speak. "You're in my head, somewhere, aren't you? I feel your influence, whether I'm conscious or not. Why did you alter me?" When Lucifer didn't answer right away, Jonah added, "I can tell because you don't loathe me as much, at least not as openly."

Lucifer turned to face Jonah directly. "Your instincts are correct, but you can relax: you're not a sleeper agent under my influence or possessed in any way. Nor are you powerful enough for me to bother with securing your allegiance, not like…" His voice trailed, allowing Jonah to fill in the rest.

"Not like Miranda," Jonah said. "Some of my reconstruction was sourced from her, so bits of her remain in me." He recalled his dream from the morning, where Miranda had mentioned living on inside of him. "And since she had pledged herself to your service, those bits are still tied to you."

"Good, you're not as dumb as you look," Lucifer said. "I was hoping to avoid a long-winded exposition."

"You could've released your hold, but you want us to stay connected. Why, to use me to stay close to Mina?" he scowled. "She may not want me anymore, if she senses that I'm not entirely myself."

Lucifer shook his head. "I meant what I said before: I want Mina to be happy with you, so nothing has been added or removed. But you're correct, in that I have a purpose for you." At Jonah's automatic grimace, Lucifer said: "Nothing diabolical, I give you my word. I have more talented resources to execute my more grisly and horrific errands, but occasions arise that require a little more subtlety and finesse."

"You need someone who can pass for human," Jonah said readily, a little disconcerted that he could track with Lucifer so easily. "So, what do I have to do? Spy for you, kill someone?"

"You're catching on," Lucifer grinned, leaning closer to whisper: "Here's the best part: it wasn't even my idea."

"Whose idea—"

Micah's booming voice echoed through the empty lounge, even at a whisper, as he greeted the black-suited, tan-skinned, dark-haired angel who had arrived.

"Gabriel?" Jonah flashed Lucifer a look. "You're shitting me."

"I shit you not, Mister Gideon," Lucifer said. "We angels and devils are sometimes of like mind, just at cross-purposes," he said, nodding a greeting to Gabriel, who took a seat at Jonah's right. "Mister Gideon is coming around, Gabe."

"He doesn't appear that way," Gabriel said, noticing Jonah's scowl.

"Not coming around to our approach, just in his awareness of our interference," Lucifer clarified.

"Please understand, Mister Gideon," Gabriel soothed, "my counterpart and I are often limited in how we can directly affect the actions and lives of humans, so periodically, we must engage facilitators to intercede. Miranda White and Jack McKay were but two examples of humans who needed to be recalled, I think you'll agree."

"Those two were assholes," Jonah agreed. "But you guys like balance, right? For every Miranda in play, there would be a genuinely good person who would also be 'recalled' when she was."

"Yes, and in that case, the balancing factor was you," Gabriel said. "The circumstances don't always align as neatly, and that is where you would come in, to help keep things equal."

"How's that?" Jonah asked. "It sounds like you're asking me to be your enforcer, or hit man."

"Nothing so unsavory, Mister Gideon," Gabriel said. "You won't be called upon to do anything against your nature."

"And we're not asking," Lucifer said glibly. "This is your price, for having a second chance to spend your life with Mina. It's not too steep, is it?"

"Depends on what you want me to do." He was willing to surrender and risk a great deal, but he also had to be worthy of Mina—that meant not doing anything that he would have to hide or keep secret from her. If that meant forfeiting his life a second time, then that would be his miserable fate, but he couldn't stomach the idea of beginning a relationship with Mina under a cloud of lies and deceit.

"I will leave you to discuss the details of his first assignment," Lucifer said, on his way to the front door. "I will need to catch up with Cindy another time; I'm late for another appointment."

"My first assignment," Jonah said distastefully. "Do I get gadgets or special equipment, or do I just have to use my bare hands?"

Gabriel laughed, making a soothing organic sound that reminded Jonah of rainfall or crashing waves. "You underestimate your skillsets and your autonomy, Mister Gideon. Lucifer may have recycled some pieces of your cousin Miss White for your rebuild, but I promised my Master that I would oversee the process, to ensure that you're worthy and useful to us all, equally."

"Great," Jonah sighed, inferring Gabriel's meaning—again, more easily than he would have in the past. "You did something to me, too."

"I'll leave those details for you to discover on your own," Gabriel said, with a kind, sympathetic smile. "This is your assignment, in the meantime." He pulled out an ivory-white notecard from his jacket pocket and slid it facedown across the bar to Jonah.

"Gabriel, you made it," Cindy greeted, returning to the bar. "Thank you."

"I was overdue for a visit, anyway," Gabriel said. "Plus, I haven't spoken with Mister Gideon since before his resurrection."

Jonah picked up the notecard with a sense of trepidation, and it took a second for him to register the headshot of the individual on the assignment card. His gut instinct was to tell the angel to go fuck himself, but as he read the details on the card, he shook his head in dismay. "No."

"What is it, honey?" Cindy asked, glancing disapprovingly at Gabriel.

"If not you, then we will need to find another to complete the task," Gabriel said. "A stranger who would be more menacing to such a tender soul." He got to his feet. "It is your decision, Mister Gideon, and as you are new to this arrangement, you are allowed a pass, just this once. But it will only become more painful, the longer you delay, for both you and your charge."

Gabriel nodded to Cindy and Jonah and left without further comment, leaving the two of them in awkward silence for a moment, as Cindy prepared the stemware for the bar and Jonah continued to stare at the notecard.

"I don't think I can do this, Cin," Jonah said, turning the card around to show her the details.

She smiled compassionately with barely a glance at the card. "You know it just looks like a blank card to me, right? It's only meant for your eyes."

"Shit," he muttered. "Ever have one of those days when you wish you were never resurrected?"

Cindy chuckled. "You're a good man, and I trust you to do the right thing, whatever your burden."

"I was afraid you would say that," he said, slipping the notecard in his pocket. "Wish me luck."

She leaned over and gave him a lingering kiss on the cheek. "Just a touch of fae dust."

"Thanks." He took a deep, fortifying breath and exchanged a nod with Micah on his way to the door. "Any advice for me, Micah?"

"Nah," the mighty jinn flashed his brilliant smile, holding the door for him. "Just be yourself."

Adam awoke with a start, as he recognized the figure of his mother sitting at his turned-around desk chair, silently watching him with her chin propped on his head-rest. "Jeez, Mom!"

The blinds were open, but the light wasn't blinding, so it was still early, but his mother was dressed for the day, already: loose sweater over slender jeans, with a long silk scarf coiled loosely around her neck. "You usually don't sleep this long, do you?"

"No, Mom, I don't," Adam said, sitting up in bed. "What time is it?"

50

"A little after nine. Your father's at work, your sister's out exploring. What do you have planned for today?"

"I think I need my head examined," Adam murmured, getting out of bed. "I should be happy that you and Dad care enough to find me a secure, cushy job, but I can't help feeling that you're doing this because you don't trust me the same way you trust Mina."

Selina turned around in the desk chair gracefully. "Of course, we trust you. But you have to admit: you're not as accustomed to dealing with the supernatural as Mina is, and you have to consider that this may not be your path."

"How would I know that, if I've only been dealing with witches and demons for a few weeks? Mina's been at this for years."

Selina got to her feet and tucked the chair under the desktop. "It's also possible that you're reacting emotionally to the way that you were let go from Global Pacific, and you're overlooking the opportunities that this second chance provides," she suggested. "If you don't have anything pressing, why don't you put on something neat and visit your father at his office? He may be more conversational this morning than he was last night, and he's always proud to show you off."

Adam smiled at his mother's persuasiveness. "It would also help ease me back into the trappings of corporate drudgery, wouldn't it?"

"Maybe, or maybe not," Selina said lightly, going to the door. "You won't know until you get there."

Adam browsed his closet for a proper, business-casual work outfit, and even found a pair of shoes that still fit him. He had forgotten how many of his work clothes he had left at his parents' house over the years, during brief visits while going to or returning from business trips. Just as surprisingly, his slacks felt looser in the waist, while his shoulders and chest felt snugger;

his mind was still a mess, but physically, he never felt better.

After a breakfast of sourdough toast and soft-scrambled eggs—which Selina lovingly prepared and watched him eat, to the last crumb—Adam took advantage of the mild San Francisco weather to walk to his father's high-rise downtown office, enjoying the gentle California sunshine on his face.

"Mister Xing, welcome back to San Francisco," greeted the security guard with a broad smile.

"It's been a while, Tony. Am I still in the system?" he joked, glancing at the lobby computer.

"Until your father sells the building, or until I retire, whichever comes first," the guard said with a wink, passing a security badge to Adam.

Adam cringed at his photo on file, which was printed on the security tag. "Damn, this picture's at least five years out of date. I haven't used that much product in my hair in ages."

"Aww, don't complain; you still got your hair," Tony laughed, rubbing his hand over his shiny bald pate. "Besides, you'll always look like a kid to me, Mister Xing. Have a good day."

Upstairs on the forty-second floor, the employees and officers of his father's eponymous company treated Adam with similar respect and warmth. He looked at the company sign, which was simply the Chinese seal calligraphic symbol for their family name, translated into English underneath, in bold block letters.

"I could have the sign changed to read 'Xing and Son,'" Lin joked, clapping Adam on the shoulder. "The English part anyway."

"No, that sounds like it would be a mess of paperwork," Adam demurred. "Besides, what if Mina decides she wants to participate in the family business?"

Adam walked alongside his father, matching his long, easy stride, back to Lin Xing's corner office. Lin shut the door behind Adam and gestured him to a guest armchair. "This company started with me, and it will most likely die with me. I can see that neither you nor Mina have any appetite for my line of work."

Adam admired the view from his father's window before he circled around the desk to take a seat. "You're not expecting me to accept the position at Global Pacific, are you? Why did you have them make me the offer, then?"

"Because once in a while, you need a reminder of who we are," Lin said without hubris, as he took his chair behind the desk. "I meant what I said to you last night: we want you to be successful in your own right. But as you gain notoriety and renown, it will be more difficult to know who sees you as a means to their own ends, and who wants you for yourself."

"Global just wants me because I'm another connection to you," Adam said.

"Probably," Lin smiled. "But it doesn't matter which way a door swings open—once it's open, it can be used in either direction. If you were a different kind of son, I would have you climb the ranks there, and we would eventually merge Global Pacific's operations under the Xing name."

"'Then, we can rule the galaxy, as father and son,'" Adam intoned with a semi-closed fist, in his best James Earl Jones voice.

He wasn't sure that Lin would get the reference, but his father laughed. "Better Darth Vader than Emperor Palpatine, I suppose. You get my point, then. I didn't raise you to be my puppet or pawn."

"I just have to avoid becoming someone else's," Adam said grimly. He made an effort to smile when a knock sounded at the door, and Yumi Taira entered with a tray of Japanese-style teacups and a cast-metal teapot, as well a couple of bottles of water.

53

"Thank you, Yumi. You can set it here on the corner," Lin said, clearing some papers from his desk to give her some space, and glanced at Adam. "You're staying for lunch?"

"Sure, why not," Adam said. "Mission burritos from the taco truck?"

"It wouldn't be my first choice, but you're the guest," Lin sniffed. "Reschedule our one o'clock call with Chicago, please," he directed Yumi. "I trust that you also have everything for the two o'clock meeting and don't need me hovering?"

"It's always nice to have you there, sir, but I think I can manage," Yumi said graciously. "It's just to go over the event schedule for the first quarter, so I'll forward you any concerns raised, and any open items for follow-up."

Adam didn't miss Yumi's coy, sideways glances at both himself and his father, and he briefly wondered if she was naturally so flirtatious with every man she encountered, or whether she reserved her special attention for the two of them.

"Are you spending the day with us?" Yumi asked. "In case you wanted me to reserve one of the conference rooms."

"No, thanks, this was last-minute, and I'm not staying too much longer," Adam said, flashing a look at his father.

"Oh," said Yumi disappointedly. "Well, if you need anything at all, I'm just around the cubicle wall to the right."

Adam waited until Yumi had shut the door behind herself and disappeared past the frosted glass windows before speaking. "She doesn't seem to have changed much from when we used to date."

Lin poured out some tea and grinned. "You used to do much more than date, as I recall."

Adam felt his face redden. "Well… wait, you knew we slept together?"

"I wasn't entirely sure, until now," he said slyly, passing Adam a bottle of water. "Considering your feelings for Yumi back then, I'm astonished that you managed to keep your relationship a secret."

"I had a feeling that Mom wouldn't approve," Adam said, taking a sip from the bottle. "It seemed better to stay quiet."

"Your mother knew, but she appreciated that you didn't make a fool of yourself. I appreciated your discretion, too," Lin said, taking a sip of his tea. "Do you remember the Chinese character for 'argument'?"

"It's two of the symbol for female, side by side," Adam answered easily.

"And the one for 'tranquility'?"

"A single female, under a roof," he said.

"Yes. Setting aside the misogynist undertones, there is some merit to that perspective," Lin said. "Your mother deserves to feel secure in her own home, to know that she always has our love and will never be replaced."

"That would never change, even if I've fallen in love with someone," Adam said, smiling at his father's unwavering fidelity to his mother.

"And have you fallen in love?" Lin asked in earnest.

Adam had said it so naturally, without thinking, that he had to retrace his train of thought. "Yes, I suppose I have," he said quietly. "That must sound very sentimental and mawkish." Especially to his father, whom he had rarely seen act emotionally or spontaneously towards his mother.

"It's human to feel that way. It's a luxury of our modern times, that you can live by your emotions, at your own pace," Lin said, almost wistfully. "Did your mother ever tell you how she was weaned, when Jin Mudan was young?"

Adam shook his head, surprised to hear his father refer to Selina by her *huli jing* name. "I think I would remember that."

"Her mother pushed her away from her teat, then snapped and snarled at your mother when she tried to feed again," Lin said. "Your grandmother eventually bit your mom hard enough to break her skin, to make the point that she was no longer welcome in her den: she needed to fend for herself, or starve."

"How old was she?" Adam asked, trying to picture his mother as a young fox pup.

"She had just finished her tenth winter in the den—it's an entire lifespan for a natural fox, but it's a typical childhood for *huli jing*, so she'll tell you that her mother was right to force her out. Your grandmother was coming into heat again and knew that any male in the area would either try to mate with your mother—even though she was still a juvenile—or try to kill your mom to ensure that there was no sharing of resources or attention."

Adam was astonished that his father spoke so easily about his mother's experience. "How long did you know Mom before she told you about her childhood as *huli jing*?"

"I knew about her nature from our first meeting, but it was a few years before she trusted me enough to share details about her youth," Lin said. "But my point in sharing that vignette is to frame your mother's fierceness a little better. She's had to struggle for everything that is hers, and now that she feels safe, she has little tolerance for anything or anyone that she senses as a potential threat."

"Does that extend to me and Mina, too? Her protectiveness, that is," Adam clarified.

"Well, she certainly doesn't see you as a threat," Lin said wryly. "But yes, she sees you both as an extension of us, as our future, so you must be carefully guarded. Jin

Mudan and I will fade in time, so we must ensure that you're able to take care of yourselves without us, but your mother has a harder time letting go than she will admit."

With the rest of the photo-snapping tourists, Mina watched the sea lions lounging and sunning themselves on the docking rafts off the side of Fisherman's Wharf. With a stiff breeze blowing off the water against her, she wrapped the unzipped edges of Jonah's heather-gray hoodie more closely around herself. When the sun started feeling a little warm on her face, she ducked under an awning and checked her phone—it was still early, but she was surprised not to get any calls from New York, to check on her and Adam, not even from Cindy.

"You look disappointed, kid," said a low, lyrical voice from one of the souvenir vendor carts.

Mina recognized the voice, although she hadn't heard the drawl in over ten years, the summer before she started college. "How are you, Cole," she greeted. She looked up from her phone and met the stormy hazel-gray eyes of her old friend. With his long chestnut hair still sleek and shiny under the brim of his cap, he didn't look as though he had changed at all over the past decade. "It's not my morning, it seems."

"The morning's not yet over, darling," the man grinned broadly, the dappled sunlight reflecting off his smooth skin. "Come, tell old Cole what's bothering you," he coaxed, holding his sun-tanned hand out to her.

To her seasoned eyes, Cole's velvety tan skin was a clear indication of his selkie nature, but most people just saw a bewitchingly handsome man with a smooth, drawling accent. Mina smiled at his playful wink and let him wrap his hand around her shoulder. She knew Cole too well to be taken in by his charms, and he knew her family too long to toy with her past a casual flirtation.

"So much has happened since we last talked, I don't even know where to start."

She looked at the gaudy, cheap souvenirs that Cole had displayed on his cart: keychains, refrigerator magnets, shot glasses, toddler-sized t-shirts, and of course, the ubiquitous cast-metal San Francisco trolley car models. "How's business? And the family?"

"Business is grand," he said, attracting passersby to his kiosk cart with his disarming smile, and Mina noticed that the vast majority of them were women. "And the family... Well, they're out and about, as always."

"You selkies aren't causing trouble around here, right?"

"I think you would've heard, if California sea lions were rioting on the Wharf," Cole smiled. "There are plenty of fish and crab for all, so there's no need to squabble."

"I'm glad to hear it," Mina said, standing aside to avoid blocking the browsing shoppers. "My mother says 'hello,' by the way, to you and your kin."

"She's so sweet, your mom," Cole sighed. "So, what's up with you? You seem a little preoccupied."

"A little," Mina admitted. "I'm trying to get some news about what's happening at home." At his brief, puzzled glance, she clarified: "*My* home. New York. My friends are usually better about staying in touch and telling me if anything is wrong."

"Then, either nothing is wrong, or they're trying not to trouble you with matters that you can't fix," Cole said. "There is such a thing as knowing too much, or too soon."

"Do you know what's happened?" she asked, wondering if the Pacific and Atlantic selkie clans shared gossip.

"No, but I know you," he said. "And you have good taste in friends, so trust them."

He turned to a young woman, giggling and fawning with her friends over a basket of glass-eyed sea lion pup plush animals. "Normally, eight dollars each, but I can let three of them go home with you lovely ladies for twenty." The sale was breathtakingly quick, but the trio of young women were so enamored and flattered by Cole's sunny personality and laughing hazel-gray eyes that they almost bickered over who would have the honor of paying him.

"You're a natural at this," Mina said.

"I get to be outside and talk to pretty girls all day, what's not to like?" he smiled, then finally noticed Mina's black sleeveless U2 concert t-shirt under her oversized gray hoodie. "You never struck me as a classic Irish music fan, Mina."

She glanced down at the red, black and white logo over her left breast. "Actually, the shirt belonged to someone else. The sweatshirt, too," she said, remembering how she had acquired them from Jonah.

"Jeanie Mac, did someone hurt you, darling?" he murmured in a heavy, deliberate brogue at her solemn visage, noticing the ruby on her ring finger. "I can drag him into the bay, sink him below the waves, and leave nothing but his sorry soul for the devil to take."

Only Cole could make a murderous threat sound so lyrical and lovely. "That's kind of you, but he's already passed. I'm not sure where his soul ended up, but I haven't been visited, so that's a good thing, isn't it?"

He touched her hand. "I'm sorry that you lost him. It doesn't sound like there's anything to be done about it, so be careful not to lose yourself, too. You still have people who love you and need you, so make sure you don't forget about them. Count your blessings, while you can."

"You mean my parents," Mina said. "It has been a while I've stayed with them, so Adam and I should make the most of our time, while we're here."

"There," he nodded. "Your parents will see you less and less, as the years pass, and family time is always precious." The sea lions barked and crooned from the barges, delighting the tourists, and Cole grinned at the spontaneous, joyous cacophony. "Even the mad moments. Especially those."

Jonah stood in front of the old oak door for the second floor apartment for a couple of minutes before he dared to knock. This was, by far, one of the hardest visits he'd ever been obligated to make, and he still wasn't entirely sure that he had the fortitude to follow through on what was required of him, or the steps for how to go about it.

Jonah had a glimmer of hope that perhaps no one was home, and that he had a brief reprieve, but the door opened, and Millie Krantz's glowing face smiled up at him.

"Jonah!" she beamed, the creases around her eyes and lips deepening with her grin. "You're back in New York, already! It hasn't even been two weeks, has it?"

Jonah smiled sheepishly, holding out a small ballotin of chocolate-covered cherries that he had picked up from the corner bodega. "I guess I couldn't stand to be away from you, Missus Krantz."

She waved her hand with a giggle. "Oh, you tease! Come in, come in," she said, accepting the box.

Jonah entered Millie's neat, cozy apartment, full of souvenirs and reminders from earlier times: old television with an adjacent stereo system, fitted plastic covers for the upholstered furniture, and ceramic trinkets and figurines encased behind glass. All of it clear of dust, none of it produced within the previous ten years.

He hadn't noticed it the same way when he had last visited as Mina's husky, as he had been more captivated by the spectrum of odors that he realized in hindsight had reminded him of his aunt and uncle's house in Boston. Now, back on his own two feet, Jonah felt a little saddened to see that Millie lived within a snapshot of an earlier era, stuck in her life before Arthur Krantz's passing.

And that was the key, as evidenced by Arthur's ghost following and observing close behind Jonah, curious about his reason for visiting.

"How are you feeling these days, Missus Krantz?" Jonah asked, recalling the details from Gabriel's card: *Terminal, estimated 36 hours, 12 minutes.* "When I left New York, you had a little health scare, I recall."

"I feel fine," Millie said serenely. "My daughter came to stay with me a couple of days, and she checks on me every day. In fact, I had finished a lovely chat with her on the screen when you knocked," she said, gesturing to the tablet sitting on her kitchen table.

You're in constant pain for every waking minute, Millicent, Arthur chided gently, beyond Millie's hearing, but not Jonah's. *You should be taking the medicine—it can't cure you, but it'll make your days go easier.*

"I hope you don't mind if I start on these," Millie said shyly, tearing the thin cellophane on the box of candies. "I adore them. How did you know?"

Jonah had recalled accompanying Mina when she had picked some up for Millie, but he had been wearing a leash, then, so... "Mina," he said shortly. He noticed Millie's trembling hand, as she struggled to extract one of the nested chocolates from the box, and he fought the urge to reach over and help her.

Instead, he set his hand on hers and suggested brightly, "You know, it seems so uncivilized to eat out of a box. Let's do this properly." He went to the kitchen and brought back a decorative saucer and a napkin, as well as a mug of tea that Millie had left behind on her counter.

Jonah returned to the table and served Millie with reverence, setting down her mug of tea in front of her, then setting down the saucer, lining it with the napkin, and setting three chocolate cherries on top of the napkin. All the while, he was conscious of Arthur Krantz looking over his shoulder, and Millie's lips quivering with emotion.

"I don't have very long," she confessed quietly. "I have already said my piece, and I don't want to be a burden to my daughter. She told me that she's looking for a facility by where she lives down south, but this is my home, and those places are so expensive… Oh, why am I bothering you with this?" She took a chocolate, grasping it more easily, and popped it in her mouth.

Don't apologize, Millie, Arthur said. *He's here to help you.*

"I don't mind, Missus Krantz," Jonah said, glancing at Arthur for his cryptic remark. "Sometimes, it helps to talk to someone, to sort things out by getting them out in the open. What is it, if I may ask?"

"Cancer, mainly," she said, taking another chocolate. "It started in the lungs, got into my blood, and spread everywhere else. It's a blessing, really, that it spread so quickly, to not drag this out longer than it needs to be."

"What did your daughter say, when you told her?"

She didn't, Arthur said.

"You didn't tell your daughter?" Jonah followed up in surprise.

Millie looked amazed that he knew that, but she was unapologetic. "It's my life, and my decision. I chose not to give her another burden, and another cost, to concern her. I don't want her to worry that every conversation we have could be our last."

"You're very brave to do this alone," Jonah said. "Have you told anyone?"

Millie wrung her hands. "I told Mina, when she took care of me at the hospital. I made her promise not to tell my daughter, Rebecca. You're a very good listener, just like Mina. Has anyone ever told you that? There's something about you that inspires confidence."

"Thank you. It's my turn to be honest with you," Jonah took her small, thin hands between his. "Millicent Agatha Krantz, I've been sent here to ease your suffering."

"What does that mean?" she asked, slightly frowning. "You're not a doctor, or faith healer…"

"No, Ma'am," Jonah said, shaking his head. "I'm not here to cure you."

Tell her you're here to provide mercy, Arthur said, and Jonah felt the spirit's energy on his shoulder, like a tap, before Arthur crouched next to Millie to look up at her face. *And that I'm here with her.*

"Arthur says to tell you that I'm here to provide you mercy, and that he's here with you," Jonah said, feeling his voice catch at her look of happy surprise. "He's here with you a lot, actually. He misses you so much that he's never moved on from here."

Arthur shot him a surprised look, and Jonah shrugged. "It's true."

"You can see him? You can talk to him?" Millie marveled.

Jonah nodded. "As clearly as I see you."

"What kind of mercy are you offering?" Millie mused, then frowned. "Are you here to kill me?"

"I'm here to take away your pain, Missus Krantz, not to cause you more," Jonah said soothingly. "As you said, it's your life, and your decision. If you don't want me here, I'll leave." As he made the offer, he realized that he didn't want to go anymore. He wanted to give Millie Krantz the opportunity and dignity to choose her own terms and moment for departure.

Please don't leave, Mister Gideon, not yet, Arthur said, trying to touch Millie's face, and his ghostly hand passed into her cheek. *It hurts to see you in pain every day, my pretty girl, but I'll stay with you until it's your time.*

"He knows you're suffering," Jonah said. "He watches you struggle every day."

"Oh," she sniffed. "He was always like that, always bothering me when he saw that I was upset, following me until I told him what was wrong. Except I can't talk to him, anymore," she said sadly.

"You can just talk. He hears every word you say to him, believe me," Jonah said.

"How is it that you can see and hear him?" Millie looked at him closely. "This bridge that you have to the other side, Jonah: have you crossed it yourself? You seem different from the last time I saw you."

"You're asking if I've come close to death before?" Jonah asked, not entirely surprised by her question, given her unique situation of living below Mina's apartment, and above Galen and his family. She had undoubtedly seen and heard her share of otherworldly phenomena. "I have, Missus Krantz. There is nothing to fear on the other side, if you're at peace with what you've done during your time here."

"This is too much excitement for me," she said, pushing back her seat. "I think I need to lie down."

Getting unsteadily to her feet, she took Jonah's hand for balance and shuffled to her couch, and the effort was obvious, judging by her grimace.

"Every day seems a little longer and more arduous, but emptier. Does that make sense?" she asked wearily, lying back on the couch and propping her feet up.

"It does, Missus Krantz," Jonah said, letting Millie hold onto his hand with a surprisingly tight grip.

"I'm glad you're the one to see me off, Jonah," she said, closing her eyes.

"Me, too," he said, quietly, not sure what else he was supposed to do.

Me, too, echoed Arthur, perching at the edge of the couch, stroking his fingers across Millie's head. *Thank you.*

Gradually, as her hand softened its grip, Millie's features slackened, and her breath slowed until it stilled altogether. She passed with a relaxed brow, and a relieved, serene smile on her lips, and her fingers slipped from Jonah's hand. Arthur leaned over and kissed her lightly.

I'm still here, Millie, he whispered.

For Jonah, it was like watching a butterfly freeing itself from its chrysalis: the bright and beautiful essence of a reborn creature, rising from its ungainly spent shell. Millicent Krantz's spirit rose from her body and cried with joy at being reunited with her beloved Arthur, and the ghosts entwined and twirled around Jonah, celebrating with their first dance in many years—free of pain, and free of longing.

Jonah held the hands of Millie's physical body one last time and rested them on her belly, giving her the appearance of still being asleep. He nodded to Arthur and Millie Krantz to take his leave, letting everything else in their apartment stay as it was, making sure that the stove burners were all off, before he let himself out of Millie Krantz's apartment, for the first and very last time.

Chapter 4

Cindy said nothing, as she saw the two men enter separately. They both seemed preoccupied and distressed, presumably for different reasons, but she sensed a link between them, aside from their casual friendship. Morgan showed his emotions openly in his sad expression, but Jonah was more stoic, which concerned Cindy more.

"Gia, sweetie," she called to the girl straightening the chairs, "can you please tell the elves that I need one of the 'X'-marked pints in the deep freezer warmed up? Thanks."

As Gia headed into the kitchen, Morgan stepped to the counter, and Cindy greeted him with a kiss. She stroked his wild red locks. "What happened, babe?"

Morgan looked at her with pained green eyes. "I just came from Mina's building. The paramedics were there, but they were too late. Missus Krantz…" He couldn't even bring himself to say what Cindy already knew: Millie Krantz was found dead in her apartment.

As Cindy came out from around the bar to give Morgan a comforting hug, she looked over at Jonah, who had heard Morgan's news but seemed to have a more subdued reaction.

"Did you know?" she heard Morgan ask, and as she straightened, she realized that his question was directed at her. "That she had died?"

"I had a suspicion that something had happened," she said, returning to the bar. "I called to check on her, then asked Galen to go knock on her door when she didn't pick up. When he had no luck, I called the precinct," she said. "The captain sent a car over for a wellness check, and he just called me before you came in."

Cindy recalled the update: no forced entry, no sign of foul play. They would wait for the medical examiner's report, but it had all the indications of a natural death, most likely from a ruptured cerebral aneurysm or from her cancer. The captain's hunch: Millie Krantz had simply lain down on her couch and passed away peacefully in her sleep.

"She seemed fine when I dropped off some things with Galen last night," Morgan said, still shell-shocked. "She was reading a bedtime story to Fern and Fallon, and they were snuggling under a blanket with her."

Cindy preferred to remember Millie that way, rather than dying alone in her apartment. "That sounds just like her. She enjoyed spending time with all of us fae, but she absolutely adored the children."

Morgan smiled wistfully, sharing the recollection. "I'm going to raid the kitchen and stress-eat until the elves kick me out," he dead-panned. "Can I get you guys something?"

Jonah shook his hand, and Cindy said, "Not for me, thanks." She snapped her fingers. "Actually, there should be a saucepan with something that I asked the elves to warm up. Can you please have one of them bring it out to me, please?"

"I'll see if Gia is free, if the elves are busy—"

"No," Cindy said, shaking her head resolutely. "I've asked the elves not to make her handle animal products."

"Okay...I'll bring it out, then," he said, disappearing into the kitchen and returning a minute later, as Cindy set down a couple of cocktail napkins on the counter in front of Jonah. "Is this it?"

"Thanks, babe," Cindy smiled, giving Morgan a kiss on the cheek.

"The elves started a batch of gelato this morning," Morgan said, "so they offered to let me taste-test for them."

"Sooo jealous," she teased, pulling an oversized glass mug from under the counter. "Save me some."

As she emptied the fragrant, savory saucepan liquid into the mug, Jonah looked longingly at the assortment of bottles behind the bar. "Yearning for something boozy?" she asked, serving him a glass of ice water, more ice cubes than water.

"You have no idea," he murmured, looking at the water dispiritedly. "Okay, maybe you do," he amended, looking at Cindy. "Sorry."

"It's alright, honey," she said gently, setting the steaming mug in front of him with a wink. "Off-menu item. Let me know what you think."

Jonah took a breath of the rich, meaty steam. "If I still had a tail, I'd be wagging it. What is it?" he asked, cupping his hands around the warm mug.

"Free-range venison bone broth," Cindy answered readily. "One of my Sasquatch patrons gave me the recipe once, and I keep some frozen for him, for whenever he comes in."

"You're not fucking with me, are you?" Jonah questioned, taking a scant sip.

"Oh, if only," Cindy bemoaned, leaning towards him flirtatiously, "but I think Mina and Morgan would take issue. I promise you, it's the real thing. Rendered from the stripped carcass of a three-point New Jersey white-tail buck. How is it?"

Jonah took another small sip and closed his eyes. "It's no substitute for dark chocolate or a single-malt, but it takes the edge off, thanks."

"Use the ice water, if the broth is too hot," Cindy said, returning to taking inventory of her bar stock. "You weren't gone for very long. Did everything go as you wanted, for your first outing?"

"It went as well as could be hoped," Jonah said, taking the blank-looking ivory notecard from his pocket and dropping it on the bar. "But I wouldn't say it was anything I wanted."

Jonah's timely arrival on the heels of the news of Millie Krantz's passing was too perfect to be a coincidence, especially prefaced by Lucifer and Gabriel's earlier "chat" with Jonah. "They made you a reaper, didn't they? A catalyst for souls to pass from this world to the next? That must've been Millie Krantz's information on the assignment card that Gabriel gave you earlier."

Jonah dropped his head tiredly. "It's one thing to take out enemies in self-defense, or to protect someone else in the heat of battle. I've never had to sit with a sweet little old lady, as she took her last breaths."

Cindy covered Jonah's hand with her own, as she leaned on the counter. "The alternative would have been for Millie to pass alone, or painfully and slowly, with no one to share her last moments."

"Or someone else could have been sent, who was a stranger to her," Jonah said.

"That's right," Cindy said. "For what it's worth, I think Luci and Gabe made an inspired choice when they selected you."

"I disagree," Jonah growled. "I'm going to need therapy soon, unless my life is revoked for my incompetence first."

"See, your compassion and caution make you perfect for this job," Cindy said. "You want to do things right, not easily or quickly. It's very sweet." Impulsively, she leaned closer and gave him a soft, gentle kiss to soothe his hurt. There was just a hint of venison gaminess on his lips, tempered by bone broth's rosemary and juniper.

Morgan returned from the kitchen, as they separated, with a tulip-shaped glass dessert cup filled with a generous scoop of something that looked like orange sherbet. He stole a spoonful of the concoction before presenting the rest of the cup to Cindy.

"Thank you," she smiled and kissed Morgan, tasting the sweet, tangy chill on his lips and tongue. "Yum. Mango, yuzu and tangerine gelato. Much tastier than feral deer."

"I'm pretty sure that's not on the dessert menu tonight," Morgan said, unaware of her meaning, as he slipped past her to grab the half-filled rectangular bottle of amaretto from the bar before heading back to the kitchen. Before Cindy could protest, he said, "The elves said they need it for the cookies to serve with the gelato. I'll bring you a fresh bottle from the back. You know this bottle will be done by the time the elves take their nips, anyway."

As Morgan disappeared into the kitchen, Jonah took a deeper drink of the bone broth, seeming more relaxed with every sip. "Does Morgan know you still flirt and kiss your customers?"

"I don't do that indiscriminately, honey," Cindy said, "just the friends I love and trust, who won't misread my affection. At the end of the day, my heart still belongs to Morgan. His voice is still the last one I want to hear every night, and the face I look forward to seeing most every morning."

"I'm happy for you," Jonah said.

"Thanks," she smiled. "I'm happy for you and Mina, too. Or, rather, I will be, when you're back together. Any idea when that will be?"

"I'm thinking that my handlers will need to weigh in, first," Jonah said humorlessly. "I can't just pick up and fly to California, if I have a deadline here."

"'Deadline', that's funny," Cindy said, looking to the door, where a broad-shouldered, blond-haired hulk of a man was engaged in a deep, rumbling conversation with Micah, matching the jinn's arresting timbre. Jonah seemed on his guard, seeing the two imposing men gesture towards him.

"It's okay," Cindy assured, "you're safe within the walls of the Lotus. Besides, this guy's a friend."

The rangy newcomer approached the bar. "Good afternoon, Miss McManus."

"Good afternoon," Cindy greeted similarly. "What brings you by during your lunch hour, Bullfinch?"

"I have something for Jonah Gideon," Jacob Bullfinch said, flashing a glance at Jonah. "I presume that's you?"

"Depends, are you delivering a subpoena or summons?" Jonah asked warily.

"No, but that's a fair question," Bullfinch said amiably, with his hand outstretched. "My name is Jacob Bullfinch, and I work with Aciré Hart. You can just call me 'Bullfinch.' Just to confirm: you *are* Jonah Gideon?"

Jonah relaxed at hearing the familiar names. "Yes," he said, shaking the offered hand. "Are you here on Aciré's behalf, or for one of your clients?"

"Both, actually," Bullfinch smiled, with a ruddy glow on his naturally-tanned cheeks. He took a seat at the counter next to Jonah and pulled out a business-sized envelope. "A few of my clients have a vested interest in your welfare, it seems. Aciré asked me to make your travel arrangements, since you would be flying from New York. Please make sure I didn't misspell your name or get your details wrong."

"I'm sorry to make you go through the trouble, but I have other commitments," Jonah said. "I don't know when I would be able to travel."

"I'm aware of your circumstances," Bullfinch said without concern, pulling out an assortment of printouts.

71

"This is your itinerary, and this is your ticket, for your flight to San Francisco. It is a full-fare, roundtrip ticket, so you can choose whichever return flight works best for you, but make sure you catch that outgoing flight today."

"I'm not sure you heard me," Jonah scowled. "I said—"

"I said I'm aware," Bullfinch said shortly, with his smile in place, as he slid a business card towards him. "When you arrive in San Francisco, you'll need to be properly outfitted, so your fitting will be done at that address; the tailor keeps irregular hours, so I would recommend calling ahead to schedule."

Jonah shook his head, annoyed at having his concerns dismissed. "Okay, whatever."

"Bullfinch, maybe you can tell Jonah which clients sent you," Cindy suggested gently.

"Of course," Bullfinch nodded and slid an ivory-hued notecard across the counter towards Jonah, next to the business card. "Lucifer and Gabriel send along their regards, as well as the details of your next assignment, in San Francisco."

Jonah stared at the cards for a few seconds before he picked them up. "I'm being sent to San Francisco?"

"The note card looks blank to me, but that's what Lucifer said." Bullfinch straightened in his seat, as Cindy set a napkin and a small snifter of brandy in front of him. "Thank you, Miss McManus."

Jonah scanned the details on the notecard and was a little relieved to see that his next charge wasn't anyone that he knew, but the individual seemed young and in perfect health: this one seemed more like an assassination. "In case I need to stay overnight, is there a hotel you would recommend?"

Bullfinch raised his brow, as he sipped his brandy. "Are you presuming that you won't be invited to stay with anyone?"

"The way my day is going, I'm not presuming anything," Jonah said. "I have no idea what to expect when I get to California."

"That's fair," Bullfinch said. "No worries, we can acquire a room for you, should you need one. My number is listed on the back of the envelope, but Aciré will also be reachable, if you need anything."

"If I need a car—"

"You're flying to San Francisco," Bullfinch reminded. "You *don't* need a car to get around."

"Are you saying that to manage cost? Do I have an expense account, by the way, or am I expected to pay out of pocket?" Jonah asked, just to see if he could annoy Bullfinch. "If it's a matter of my handlers not *trusting* me to operate a two-ton hunk of metal and glass, maybe they shouldn't have made me a reaper."

Bullfinch exchanged a thoughtful glance with Cindy, then turned back to Jonah. "First day on the job, Mister Gideon?"

"Is it that obvious?"

"Are you usually this truculent with people you've just met?" Bullfinch returned. "The work won't necessarily get easier, but you'll get more used to it, by the end."

There was a paternal, mentor-like kind of tone to his voice. "You're a reaper, too?"

Bullfinch bobbed his head side-to-side noncommittally. "I step in occasionally, as needed, but I served my term, so technically, those days are behind me. Nowadays, my main side hobby is necromancy, especially with non-human beings. It's how I met my girlfriend." He stopped and looked at Jonah. "Shit, do people open up to you all the time like this?"

73

Jonah finished his broth. "I've gotten used to it. How long did you serve as a reaper?"

"A hundred years," Bullfinch said grimly, then broke into a grin. "I'm kidding. It varies, depending on the term and the reaper's skills. I served for twenty years, on and off, and spent my free time working odd jobs and studying law."

Jonah looked at the papers a last time and stuffed everything back in the envelope. "I guess that's a 'no' on the expense account, then."

"From the financial portfolio I reviewed with Aciré, it looks like you can afford to pay your own way," Bullfinch said. "But apart from personal expenses, all your costs will be reimbursed, as long as you're not too extravagant with food or drink. Your patrons want your mind focused on the assignment, not on budgeting."

Patrons, ha. "Don't worry. I have dietary restrictions," Jonah said, "so I won't be ordering bottle service or *foie gras*."

"Ah, right," Bullfinch nodded. "You're the accidental shifter. I'm guessing you weren't an affable golden retriever or beagle when you were under the curse. German shepherd, maybe blue nose pit bull?"

"Siberian husky," Jonah answered, surprised by Bullfinch's insight.

"Of course, I should've guessed by your eyes and your snark," Bullfinch said. "Witch or demon curse?"

"Witch," Jonah answered. "Excuse me, but why do you care?"

"I don't, personally," Bullfinch said, "but my *other* clients are interested in my impressions, from a necromancer's perspective. I have some details from Lucifer and Gabriel, but I want to respect your privacy, as well, so I don't want to share more than you feel comfortable revealing."

Jonah considered Bullfinch's varied clientele, about who would care enough about Jonah's background to ask for such details… He then recalled something that Mina had said, about her working mostly with Aciré, while her parents engaged the other firm partners, Bullfinch and Farrier, more regularly. "Adam and Mina's parents?"

"Yes, they research all their investments thoroughly," Bullfinch said. "As their children's acquaintance, I'm sure you already expected that you'd be thoroughly vetted."

"You said you were a necromancer," Jonah said. "Doesn't that typically involve dead things?"

"And briefly, you *were* a dead thing," Bullfinch said casually. "Hence, the additional scrutiny."

Jonah blinked tiredly. "I'll tell you whatever you want to know."

"Well, it's less about what you reveal," Bullfinch said, "and more about what you hide."

As Jonah considered how much he felt comfortable disclosing to Bullfinch, Morgan darted out from the kitchen. "I have a client meeting across town in fifteen minutes. See you later?" He and Cindy exchanged a quick kiss, before he noticed Bullfinch at the bar. "Mister Bullfinch, hi! I'll send you the estimates to wire up the apartment in Long Island City before the end of the day, if that's okay."

Bullfinch nodded. "That'll work, Mister Crain. Thank you."

"Can I get you something from the kitchen?" Cindy offered, retreating towards the kitchen with her empty dessert glass in hand. "Maybe a raw marrow bone that the elves could spare from the stock pot, for Taquito."

Bullfinch laughed. "That's a bit much for a ghost chihuahua. Besides, Taquito may love it, but I don't think Izzy would appreciate my bringing a raw hunk of anything to her place. We don't have that kind of relationship."

"Not yet, but you could, if you play your cards right," Cindy teased. "Let me see what they have. At the least, you can bring Isabel some gelato." She left before Bullfinch could rebut.

Jonah got up from his seat. "I should get my things from Mina's apartment." He took a deep breath. "I don't even know what I'll say to her when I see her again."

"Does she know you're back?" Bullfinch asked.

"If she does, the news didn't come from me," Jonah said. "Cindy didn't feel it was prudent to tell Mina and Adam the news until I checked out, inside and out."

"And have you gotten the go-ahead?" Bullfinch asked. "From Miss McManus and company?"

"I don't know, actually," Jonah said, replaying recent conversations in his head. "This reaper development side-tracked me. Besides, if Mina knew I was alive," he said, flashing his phone, "she probably would've already texted or had someone else get in touch with me."

Bullfinch finished his brandy. "Maybe, unless her parents have her distracted. Give me your hand; I just need to see something." Jonah hesitated, and Bullfinch laughed. "You're not my type, dude."

"No, it's not that. Last time I complied with a simple request, I got smudged by a fae with a flesh-burning paste."

Bullfinch winced. "Yeah, I've had that done to me, too. *No bueno.* You're safe, I promise."

Jonah finally gave Bullfinch his palm. "What are you looking for?"

Bullfinch studied the contours and lines of Jonah's hand intently, as though practicing some type of palmistry. "Your shifting curse was cast by a witch and removed by a fae?"

Jonah nodded. "Cindy removed the curse, and it was recast, but it didn't take the second time." As he thought about the situation, he knew that wasn't exactly so: some effects, like his senses and his food restrictions, still lingered, while his feral instincts to fight and guard, came and went with his moods.

"Your mortality and soul are intact, but your identity isn't fixed," Bullfinch said, releasing Jonah's hand. "You actually have the ability to shift at will, if you wish, but you keep that part of you suppressed. Or, you haven't tried to, for fear of staying stuck that way."

"You're saying I can change back into a dog, whenever I want?" Jonah asked incredulously. "How can you tell that, by looking at my hand?"

"Because I've been in your place. I made some bad decisions and did my penance," he said wryly. "In my day, I was called *nagual* and other things, but I was basically a shapeshifter, like you."

"Uh-huh," Jonah said cynically. "'In my day'? You look about my age."

"Yeah, I'm not," Bullfinch said reservedly. "I don't know you well enough to tell you my age, but let's just say that Lin Xing and I go way back, so I have a personal interest in making sure that he and his family are safe. If that means that you need to go to California," he said, gesturing to Jonah's travel documents, "then safe travels."

Lin parted ways with Adam after their food truck lunch, with Lin returning to the office, while his son went to shop for a gift for his girlfriend, Xani. Lin wondered if Adam was looking for an excuse to stay out, to avoid Yumi's blatant overtures, and he admitted that Adam was probably right to follow his instincts, when Lin returned to the office to find Yumi wearing a more fitted blouse, with her long hair loosened.

Yumi was a professional and one of Lin's trusted direct reports, so she knew not to let her personal feelings interfere with her work, but her disappointment was clear when she saw Lin walk through the doors alone. She trailed him to his office and gave him an inquiring look.

"Adam went to find something for his girlfriend," Lin said, clarifying once and for all that his son was taken. "You changed your shirt?"

"I spilled some tea on it, right before the two o'clock video conference," she said with a dismayed frown. "It was a quick call, and I'll send you an email with the summary."

"Thank you," Lin said, glancing at an unaddressed red envelope on his desk blotter.

"That arrived while I was in the conference room," Yumi said, following his eyes. "I didn't see who delivered it."

Lin turned over the envelope and saw the dark red wax calligraphy seal holding it closed. "Thank you, Yumi. That will be all. Please close the door on the way out."

Lin took a seat before opening the envelope and fought the instinct to crumple up the note after reading it. It was less of a note and more of a summons, and Lin was not in the mood to play games with local thugs. Not when his family was being targeted by veiled threats, and definitely not when his children were in town.

Lin looked at his computer clock. It was barely three o'clock, and he had just about depleted his "daily allowance of fucks to give," to borrow one of his advisor Bullfinch's favorite phrases. Lin knew what his instincts were advising, but knew his wife would want to give her opinion, too. He scanned his emails a last time to check for anything urgent, then shut down his computer for the day.

His daily, after-work walk home was one of Lin's favorite parts of the day. Seeing the warm afternoon sunlight illuminate the streets of San Francisco, lighting his way home, was one of the reasons that he had decided to return to California, after trying out life in

78

New York for a few years. He enjoyed spending the five years in Manhattan—and apparently the children liked the bustling, grungy city enough to want to return there—but San Francisco had been his first safe haven upon arriving in the United States, and he and Selina considered it their home.

Selina. Quickening his step at the thought of her, he smiled with amusement at his wife's self-chosen name. While she had gone by the name "Selina Xing" for longer than one could guess by looking at her, she would always be his Jin Mudan, his Gold Peony. His true love, his faithful partner and the mother of his beautiful, intelligent children—

WHAAAAEEEHOOOO!

It sounded like the screeching, ear-blistering blare of an electric guitar that greeted him at the front door. Or a blender or chainsaw… Who could tell the difference?

The noise was coming from somewhere upstairs, and once he recognized the noisy rock music chords, he knew that Mina was home. Rather than straining his voice to try to call to her, Lin dropped his shoes by the door and climbed the stairs, followed the "music" to Mina's room, where the door was closed. He waited until the current song ended before he knocked on the door.

Mina came to the door promptly, and she quickly tossed her hairbrush on her bed, but Lin recognized the embarrassed flush in her cheeks.

"Playing at being a rock singer again?" he smiled, recalling how Mina used to spend hours hidden away in her room, blasting the American and British pop music from her stereo, lip-synching in front of her dressing mirror. At least, she still listened to traditional Chinese opera and movie soundtracks, too, but he often wondered if she did that to appease him, to show him and Selina that she hadn't entirely abandoned her culture and roots.

"It helps clear my mind," she said, and she did seem more relaxed than she had been that morning.

"Did you find the answers you were seeking?"

"No, *ba-ba*," Mina said. "But that's alright. I've decided to adopt a more philosophical approach to the situation: whatever I need to know, I'll find out in due time."

Lin chuckled. "Have you been speaking to the selkies again?"

"Just Cole," Mina said, and caught Lin's eye-roll. "He gave me some advice, that's all."

"He didn't offer to give up the sea and his seal-skin for you?"

"Why would he? He has plenty of willing candidates who would accept him unconditionally." Mina shut off her stereo and moved her hairbrush back to her dresser. "Besides, he's known me since I was a child—it'd be too awkward, for both of us."

Lin was glad that Mina kept her wits around Cole and his sea lion-kin down by the Wharf. "Have you seen your mother?"

Mina shook her head. "She called before and said she was grocery shopping."

Lin turned to go. "Well, tell your mother when she gets home that I went to a meeting. She normally would want to go with me for something like this, or maybe talk me out of going, but I don't want to worry her."

"What if we call her?" Mina asked, folding her arms.

"Alas, I must have left my phone behind at work," he said easily.

"But she has her phone, so we could call her from here," Mina suggested.

"I don't want to bother her," he reiterated, more firmly.

"That means you've already made up your mind. Should I go with you, then?" she asked. "If *ma-ma* wouldn't want you to go alone, maybe you shouldn't."

80

"Your mother worries too much, Min-Min," he said, pivoting on his heel and starting down the hall. "I'm not leaving town, and this is someone I know." *Sort of.*

"Is it someone *I* would know?" she called after him, as a way of inquiring whether he was meeting with someone dangerous or otherworldly, or both.

"I don't think so. You travel in different circles." Lin looked over his shoulder at Mina lingering in her bedroom doorway, with a concerned frown on her face that reminded him so much of her mother. "Fine, you can come along, but you need to change your clothes, and wear a dress."

"A dress? Why?"

"Because I said so, Min-Min." He chuckled at Mina's arched eyebrow. "Do you want to come with me, or not?"

"If Adam was going with you, you wouldn't tell him to wear a dress," she said acidly.

Lin looked stoic, but he found Mina's indignation heartening, as it meant that his daughter's fire and ferocity were returning. "That is true, but I also wouldn't have offered Adam the opportunity to come along. I'm leaving in two minutes, with or without you."

Chapter 5

1870, Fujian Province, China

Jin Mudan awoke to the sound of a loud wind blowing against her sensitive ears. A loud, hot and humid wind, which was unexpected in the cold winter weather. She picked up her head without uncurling her tail and stayed very still, trying not to startle the gigantic bovine snuffling her fur. Slowly, she shifted her gaze and was astonished at how massive the creature was.

It was larger than any yak or water buffalo that she had ever seen, plus it boasted a set of thick, ram-like horns and heavy, matted black pelt that added to its formidable silhouette. It curled up its lip as it snorted through its flared nostrils, and Jin Mudan caught a glimpse of pointed teeth and tusks, the smallest of which was longer than her snout.

She had stumbled into the lair of a *lin*—a chimerical, elemental nature spirit—and she immediately bowed her head in respect to the creature. Whereas she was decades old, *lin* were as old as the lands they guarded and stewarded, possibly centuries or millennia old.

Why are you in my lair, little huli jing*?* it addressed her telepathically, in a deep rumbling voice.

Jin Mudan recalled her desperation that had driven her into the unfamiliar den. *I was being chased. I'm sorry, I didn't realize I had trespassed into your home.*

The humans have erected new fences and laid more traps, and I had nowhere else to go.

You cannot stay, it said gruffly, turning around more smoothly in the snug, foliage-lined space than Jin Mudan would have expected, given its considerable girth and height. *I live alone.*

I understand, she answered with trepidation, but she was wary of going back outside. She had sought shelter there because she had been stalked and chased by a pack of male foxes. They were usually solitary creatures, but sensing her proximity, they had banded together to track her through the woods…

Well? Why are you still here?

If the males are still outside, they will probably kill me if I won't mate with them.

That's not my concern, if your standards are too high.

That's not our way. I'm not old enough to breed, she confessed, her voice like a whimper. *I can't explain that to natural foxes, any more than I can speak to humans. They shouldn't even be drawn to me—their behavior is irrational and abnormal.*

The humans shrink our territory and range every year, so resources are limited for all of us, the *lin* said. *Most creatures instinctively know that they must adapt and compete more aggressively in order to survive.* The gargantuan beast turned its dark eyes to her. *I'm sorry that you are harassed, but I don't foster juveniles, no matter how winsome. You'll find a way to get your point across, somehow, or you do not deserve to live as* huli jing.

It was harsh, but it was true. Her kind hadn't survived since before the age of man by being meek or slow, either in mind or body. She uncurled and shook her coat vigorously, to steel herself to venture out into the cold. As she approached the entrance, she felt the gaze of the *lin* tracking her.

83

She had scampered a good distance from the *lin*'s lair before she heard the excited barks and whines of the male foxes that had caught her scent. She was forty winters old, not quite an adult *huli jing*, but she apparently looked and smelled enough like a grown vixen to draw them from miles around.

She was eventually trapped near an outcropping, with no clear path for escape, with several males enclosing her slowly and cautiously. While they all were vulpine outwardly, she was as different from them as she was from the humans who hunted them all, and she struggled for a way to explain the futility of their efforts.

As the first male darted at her, testing her receptiveness, she instinctively let out a defensive yelp, but the sound that came from her throat sounded almost human. The unexpected voice surprised the males into keeping their distance, at least for a few seconds. She tried to make another noise, and this one actually sounded like "*ting!*"—the human command to stop or stay. The word itself meant nothing to the foxes, but the human-like sound spooked them, and they scattered.

Jin Mudan knew that she wouldn't be left alone for long, but she had a new problem now.

"I heard the voice coming from here," shouted an actual human voice, an adult male calling to others of his kind. "Who's there? Show yourself!"

"Don't shoot! It's just me," replied a man's quavering voice through the thicket. "I thought I heard a leopard and got startled, that's all."

From her hidden vantage, she saw a man in rags hobble past, and at first she thought that he was injured, then realized that he was actually lame-footed.

"You idiot!" rebuked the first man, dressed in the stiff uniform of the Baron's men. "You scared off the foxes, too. They were all clustered and ready for culling. You imbecile!"

"My deepest apologies, sir!" the ragged man cried, bowing deeply despite his physical challenges. Despite the shabbiness of his clothes and superficial grooming, he didn't have the same sour, cloying human stench on him that permeated the other men. He smelled like their surroundings: open air, pasture, bamboo and stone pine, mixed with the animal dander of countless species.

"Just…go away before you scare away all the game!" bellowed the hunter. "We'll go this way," he directed the others. "Don't cross our path again, or you may find yourself mistaken for the Baron's wild boar," he warned the cripple.

"Worthless fool would be a waste of a bullet," muttered one of the other hunters, as the group filed off to chase their real quarry.

The ragged man watched the group move off before he hobbled back to where Jin Mudan had coiled into a ball to hide amid the tall browned grass. He crouched nearby but not directly next to her position. *Are you hurt, little* huli jing?

Jin Mudan untucked her muzzle, recognizing his voice in her head. It was the *lin* whose lair she had inadvertently invaded, now in human form. *I'm not hurt. Once the area is clear, I will go*, she said. *Thank you for helping me, but I'm afraid you've exposed yourself unnecessarily.*

He scratched at the grass and plucked some dandelion greens that he wiped off and nibbled. *Being so unsightly to humans, I'm avoided and overlooked in this form, so I'm safer than you are.*

I have years to go before I can change form and be safe, Jin Mudan said, *if I survive that long.*

The *lin* laughed. *You have a great deal to learn about humans, if you think you'll be safer in their form. Your pretty face and body will always be coveted and prized, regardless of your nature and guise.*

85

Nevertheless, we all have to learn how to live among them, she said, ignoring his casual compliment, as she got to her feet and surveyed the land stretched out before them. *The humans say this land is eight parts mountain, one part water, and one part farmland—and they are taking it all, leaving little for the likes of us.*

Our kind need to adapt, as the humans do, that is all, he said, lowering himself to the snow-dusted grass beside her, with an effort. *We will survive the age of humans, just as we have for millennia.*

This is different, Jin Mudan said. *The humans live in societies to combine their resources and skills, and they no longer fear or respect the old traditions, but you and I are solitary by nature.*

The *lin* looked at her for a moment. *Perhaps we can be stronger together, as well.*

For lin *like you, maybe, but not for me*, she said, recalling how the other foxes stalked her. Absently, she dug free a couple of lichen clumps hidden under snow, that she nudged towards him; she didn't eat them, but she knew they were a delicacy amongst browsing herbivores, especially in winter.

He grinned wryly, and the unguarded smile made his pock-marked face less dour. *You saw the horns and tusks of my natural form—they're not merely decorative amongst my kind, and I've had to use them several times over the centuries to maintain my solitude.* He picked up the mushrooms with an appreciative nod. *You have a good nose for foraging. I could provide shelter and protection, if you need a den to overwinter.*

It was an unexpected and extraordinary offer, given his earlier surliness. *That's very generous of you.*

He rose to his uneven feet with an effort and started back towards his den. *Are you a good mouser?*

She nodded. *I've been surviving on rats and voles for most of the season.*

Well, they infuriate me, as they keep stealing my food and soiling my bedding, he said gruffly. *I cannot catch them in either my human or natural guises, so if you can keep the vermin away, you can stay until you find something better.*

She felt a chilly breeze race along her tail and back, reminding her of how warm and secure it had been in the *lin*'s den. *Just for the rest of the winter,* she said, scurrying after him.

Naturally, he smiled. *I'd be amazed if you don't flee my company before the plum trees start to bud.*

1881

Jin Mudan watched the twenty-year-old young man run past with his friends. She had known young Bo for over fifteen years, ever since he was a small child, and he was growing into a handsome young adult. He was fine-looking but arrogant and selfish, modeling his egocentric behavior more after the foreigner Baron who held the title to the lands, rather than his own father, the Baron's game warden, who still respected the land that provided for their family and its natural spirits and forces. He had even adopted a European name, to fit it better with his more fashionable friends.

"Isaac, it's your yellow fox again. Call to her," said one of other youths. Even the language the boys used was the tongue of their invader lords, not the dialect of their fathers. "See if she'll come out."

"She won't come anymore," young Bo said, meeting her eyes across the field. "Not after you tried to shoot at her last time. She's not as forgiving or as obedient as a dog."

"Ah, who needs her, then?" one of the other boys laughed. "Hey, look, it's Lao-Má, trying to catch a fish."

Jin Mudan followed at a safe distance, watching the boys approach the stream where the beggar had cast his line. The locals called him "Lao-Mázi" or just "Lao-Má," for his crooked, worn figure and pock-marked face. Despite multiple attempts by the Baron to evict Lao-Mázi from the area, the hermit managed to elude capture and return after every failed attempt, until the Baron stopped dedicating any resources to the effort and let the vagrant stay, as long as he remained at the periphery of the property and didn't attempt to poach.

"Don't fall in, Lao-Má," said Bo with feigned concern, practicing his Chinese with the hermit. "You might foul the water and poison Baron's fishing stock."

The beggar smiled patiently and nodded without comment, refusing to let the boys goad him.

"Do you cook your fish, or eat it raw like animals do?" teased one of Bo's friends.

"That's if he even catches any," Bo laughed. "With him hobbling around in the water, he'll be lucky not to scare them off. I guess worms can be as tasty as fish, if one is hungry enough."

Jin Mudan was disappointed and upset by Bo's mean-spirited joking, saddened that he had fallen under the influence of such disrespectful and cruel companions. He had been a bright and sweet boy when she first knew him, until he was charmed and seduced by the trappings of the colonialists' lifestyle. He even dressed and smelled like the Baron his family served. While she was initially gladdened that he was accepted readily by his European counterparts, she saw him drifting away from the old ways, following instead the exploitative practices of the newcomers.

She followed Bo and his companions until they parted ways, and she continued to see him safely towards his home. Once they were in an isolated patch, away from others, she took her human form and pulled her found robe from its hidden nook in a stand of trees, donning the dusty garment hurriedly, as she called to him. After months of finally being able to take a human shape, her human voice still sounded stilted and alien to her own ears.

"What do you want?" he asked her stiffly.

"We haven't spoken in a long time," she said, wrapping her robe tightly around herself to stave off the sudden chill from losing her coat of fur.

"We have nothing to say to each other," he said. "We have nothing in common. My friends would more likely put you in a cage to display for others, than talk to you."

She kept pace easily with him. "Do you feel the same way, Bo—"

"My name is 'Isaac' now!" he said sharply, turning to her. "And there is nothing for you here! You need to go."

His words cut and confused her. "This is my home. Where would I go?"

"I don't care! But you can't stay here." There was a panicked shrillness to his voice, and he sounded once more like the little boy who had befriended her and spared her life.

She heard and smelled the approaching horses before Bo noticed them, and she smelled the sour sweat and cloying cologne of the human riders long before she and Bo were met by the Baron, his daughter and their guards. Jin Mudan fought her instinct to flee from horses and hunters, knowing that she was safer in her human form, at least marginally.

"Master Bo, who is this lovely creature?" the Baron asked, almost derisively, as he looked at her soil-stained robe.

"A visiting cousin, sir," Bo covered. "My Lady," he said, greeting the Baron's daughter with a bow.

The Baron's daughter had her father's strong jaw, sharp green eyes and vividly orange-red hair, and she looked at Jin Mudan's robe critically. "Father, that looks like my silk wrap, that was stolen from my laundry line! She's a sneaky little thief!"

"Is that true, young lady?" the Baron asked mildly. "Did you steal my daughter's clothes?"

Jin Mudan was silent and rigid, unable to bring herself to answer or show any deference to the Englishman who occupied and controlled the lands that used to belong to others. She had found the scrap of silk snagged in brambles, far from the Baron's estate, probably carried by the mountain breezes.

The Baron leaned forward and repeated his question in the local Chinese dialect. When she still did not answer, he turned to Bo. "Does your cousin speak at all?"

Bo hesitated, flashing her a worried look. "Ah, she does, but she's shy."

"We'll sort this out at the house," the Baron said, his voice deceptively good-natured and calm. "If she is a thief, I'm sure she can provide something for recompense," he grinned, with a predatory gleam. "Bring her," he ordered one of his guards, who rode forward.

Bo pulled her back, out of the guard's reach. "You need to leave, before you cause more trouble."

"Is there a problem, Isaac?" the Baron frowned.

"No, sir, it's just a simple misunderstanding. Whatever the cost of the robe, it can be taken from my pay," Bo offered, shoving her away, towards the stream, the way they had come. "Go!"

She ran clumsily on bare human feet, but she knew she would be in greater danger if she changed back into her fox form, so she struggled to stay ahead of the horses and heard them about to overtake her, when she suddenly heard a deafening bear-like roar, and the startled whinnies of her pursuers' rearing mounts.

"What the hell is that!" shouted one of the Baron's guards, as she looked across the field at the chimeric beast charging towards them, scattering the horses. Jin Mudan recognized the curled horns of a ram, the heavy mane and the dagger-sharp tusks of her erstwhile *lin* protector.

She hadn't seen the *lin* in his natural form in some time, as he attracted less attention in his crippled human form as Lao-Mázi, but he was never far when she was in danger. He barreled past the horses, ignoring her and Bo to stampede towards the Baron and his daughter, with the Baron's men in pursuit with their rifles drawn. The Baron's daughter screeched in terror and rode back towards the house first, while the Baron raised his telescopic rifle scope to his eye and took careful aim at the beast rushing at him.

"The Baron's going to kill him!" she cried, as Bo tried to keep her from running after the creature.

"Better that monster than us!" Bo said, grabbing her arm. "The Baron is an experienced marksman, and once he kills that thing, he'll turn his attention back to you. I told you: there's nothing for you here. Please, go!"

She looked at her old playmate and companion, the boy who had once pleaded for her life, who now wanted her gone. "What about you?"

"I will be fine, but not with you here, *huli jing*!" he snapped.

And that was the root of it: her nature denied her a place in his human world, and he didn't want or need her in it.

She jumped at the sound of the rifle shot and the pained bellow of the chimeric *lin* that had saved her from the Baron. Feeling duty as well as kinship with the creature, she turned towards the gunshot, now joined by a second and third, from the Baron's guards.

"You're running towards the gunfire, you fool!" Bo scolded, clutching her sleeve.

"I am joining my kind," she said, unwrapping her robe and slipping free of the silk, as she reverted to her vulpine form and raced towards the hunt.

"There she is! The golden fox!" the Baron called. "Fifty pounds to the man who captures her!"

She knew she didn't stand much of a chance in the open grass, so she ran towards the horses instead of fleeing, taking a risk that the hunters wouldn't shoot near each other or their mounts. She had no defense against the humans' rifles, but she knew a thing or two about how to spook horses, so she ran underneath the beasts, nimbly avoiding their powerful hooves and legs while nipping and scratching at their tender skin.

With their mounts rearing, panicked and tangled together, the riders struggled to regain control and forgot about the hunt, with the Baron bellowing at them that their quarry was escaping. Keeping the horses between herself and the Baron's sight, she was able to gain some distance, and she fled alongside her lumbering monstrous companion.

"This is not over!" the Baron hollered. "I will hunt you for the rest of my days, until I have your pelts hanging from my wall!"

Jin Mudan followed the *lin* into a dense stand of bamboo, and she noticed that he followed a specific path that was wide enough to accommodate its girth. She smelled the *lin*'s dander amid the lush, verdant bamboo scent, but she also smelled blood.

Do you need to rest?

Soon, he said shortly. *Once I am back at my den.*

His tone was almost chastising, rightly so. She had taken a great risk in showing herself openly, even though her reasoning had been borne out of care and concern for her human friend. That had been *her* reason, however, not his. *Why did you show yourself? If the Baron hadn't been distracted, you would be dead.*

I'm not that easy to kill, the *lin* said haughtily, *and I certainly would not let myself be taken down by human weapons.*

You exposed yourself to save me, she realized. *You didn't have to do that.*

Really? You would be dead, or captured, if I hadn't given them another target, he snipped. *You are young and naïve, and you put too much hope in the goodness of humans. Your young man, Bo or Isaac... he will never choose you over one of his own kind.*

I know that, now, she said sadly. *I was foolish to try to rekindle our friendship.*

You can have human friends, but don't expect too much from them. Their minds don't work the same as ours. The *lin* stopped, looked back the way they had come, and lay down heavily on a worn patch of brush. *We are at a safe distance now, so you can go without fear. I will rest here for a while.*

Jin Mudan sat and smelled fresh blood coming from his wounds. *You need care.*

Later. My body is stronger in this form, so I will stay like this until I've recovered a little, he said. *The bullets are too small and inconveniently placed, so removal will have to wait until my human form can stand being riddled with holes.*

His voice was steady, but he was clearly tired and in pain. She didn't want him suffering longer than necessary, especially as he had sustained his injuries for her sake, so she offered: *I'll pull them for you.*

You have nimble claws, but not enough to pull bullets from flesh, he said.

Stay still, she said, as she transformed into her human form. The shifting of her senses and the rapid change of her body were jarring, especially after she had already switched twice within hours, and she shivered with a gasp, as she returned to her human shape.

93

The *lin* lowered his head and turned to show her his injured flank. He had been struck by two of the shots that the Baron had fired, once in the side and once closer to his neck. Pulling aside his thick tufts of hair and hide, she followed the trail of drying blood to the wounds and struggled to grasp the metal chunks without worsening his injuries.

You don't need to be gentle with me, he said. *The more quickly you do it, the easier it will be for both of us.*

Gritting her teeth, Jin Mudan dug her fingertips into his torn flesh and locked her fingers onto the tacky, blood-stained bullet. With an effort, she yanked it free, and before she waited for the *lin*'s reaction, she repeated the process with the second bullet. Only when both metal slugs were extracted did she release her breath and relax her jaw.

"Just the two?" she asked, smoothing the fur over the wounds.

Yes, thank you, he said. He peered at her with a large black eye. *I've never seen you in your human form this close. It's very beautiful.*

Jin Mudan smoothed down her dusty black hair with her clean hand, self-consciously. "I must be lacking in some way, otherwise…" She was about to admit that if she had been more human, Bo wouldn't have rejected her so decidedly. She had spent countless hours observing him and his friends, and their interactions with girls in the Baron's household and the nearby villages, trying to learn the nuances of their courtship rituals. Always from a distance, unless she managed to find Bo alone, which happened less frequently, as he matured…

False modesty does not become you, he said. *You are not human, but you know about* huli jing*, so you know your allure. You will always be desired and pursued, whatever form you take, but your admirers may not always be to your taste.*

94

She scowled and changed back into her fox form, curling into a ball on the grass. *Then, it is a curse, and I will never have peace.*

The universe does not give us more than we can endure, he said. *But you don't need to endure your 'curse' alone. If you ever need a place to hide from your predators and suitors, you are welcome to den with me, to come and go as you wish.*

Jin Mudan listened and looked for some clue that he had some ulterior motive for his invitation, but the *lin* had merely lay down on his side and closed his eyes.

It is an open offer, little huli, *for whenever you need it*, he said, with his eyes still closed. *I have little to give you, to repay you for your aid, but I will share what I can.* He cracked his eye open briefly. *We spirits must help one another, if we are to survive the age of man.*

Chapter 6

Present Day

As Mina took her father's hand to climb out of the cab, she fought the temptation to tug at the hem of her mid-thigh skirt or draw together the gaping décolletage of her plunging neckline. She also kept her hands away from the glittering gold lariat chain that dangled between her breasts, as any fidgeting would only draw more attention to her cleavage. *It's my own damn fault, isn't it.*

When Lin had told her what part of town they were visiting, Mina had decided to wear something that would fit better with their disreputable, decadent destination, so she picked out a slinky black party dress that her father had always hated.

When she had initially bought it as a young teen, her father had threatened to slash it to ribbons if she dared to wear it out of the house, so it had languished forgotten at the back of her closet. Now, Mina's father still despised the dress, but more for the way it objectified her and drew the stares and hushed whistles and comments of men they passed.

"You could've let me wear it when I was still a teenager, when I had less to show off," Mina whispered, tucking herself closer to her father. He wasn't particularly tall or physically powerful, but she always felt safe in his presence, despite sharing her mother's deeply-rooted concern that he was the one who needed protection and guarding.

Lin covered her hand with his, as they bypassed the regular guest queue and approached the nightclub door directly. "You still would've gotten unwanted attention, but from pedophiles rather than lechers, and you wouldn't have had the skills and awareness that you have now." He whispered aside to her, "I loathe how many here see you as just a piece of meat, as little more than a decoration."

"Imagine how weird it is for me, seeing these girls younger than me, checking you out like a snack," Mina muttered. Impartially, she was aware that her father was a handsome, charming man: well-mannered, well-dressed, with perfect hair and cheekbones, for as long as she could remember. But he was still her dad, and it felt uncomfortable seeing him objectified and sexualized by strangers. At her father's grin, she fought the urge to slap his arm. "I think I know why Mom doesn't let you come to these places alone."

"Your mother draws a great deal of attention, too, when she accompanies me," Lin said, turning his attention to the security detail, a trio of unsmiling Asian men in black suits and black sunglasses. "I'm expected," he said tersely, and the guards let them in wordlessly, with one of them gesturing for Mina and Lin to walk ahead of him.

"You didn't say you were visiting one of the *tongs*," Mina murmured under her breath, noting the inordinate number of serious-looking, black-suited figures throughout the establishment, both on the main floor and posted on the balcony level. There were a few women, too, heavily made up and skimpily dressed, some of them looking bruised and wasted, and far too young to be customers.

"These are gangsters and thugs, a far cry from the *tongs* of tradition," he replied grimly. "This is very different from how things used to be run. A hundred years ago, no one like young Fang would've had the audacity to summon me like this."

Mina and Lin were led to a private upstairs room, lit with a curious mix of stained-glass lamps and neon accents along the walls. Fang, a young man with slicked black hair, an inordinate number of rings on his fingers and a garish gold cross pendant at his neck, lounged in a leather armchair behind a desk, looking over the two of them. Min took a quick scan of the personnel in the room: two guards behind her, two posted at the door, and four more seated at a table against the far wall, watching the proceedings closely. Subtly, she slipped her lariat from around her neck and coiled it loosely around her wrist to keep it handy.

"Xing Lin…and guest. You got my message, then?"

"Yes, and out of respect for the relationship between your late grandfather and me, I chose to give my reply in person: I reject your offer, and you will refrain from issuing threats or calling me again."

The young man laughed brashly, and a ripple of chuckles carried through the room. "Is that so, old man? Is that why you've been calling my mother, to ask her to tell me to leave you alone? What kind of man involves a woman in business?"

"I don't engage in the types of business you run," Lin said evenly, taking a seat across the desk from the gang leader. "I used to bounce your mother on my lap when she was an infant, so I called her as a courtesy, to warn her that there would be repercussions if you continued on this path."

"You made my mother very upset," Fang growled. "She still worships the old gods and follows the superstitions of the old world."

"I know you claim a different faith," Lin said, gesturing to the young man's cross. "That doesn't concern me, but your disregard for your mother's pleas does. She's your elder, and she understands much better than you do, that I don't make empty promises."

"Neither do I, so you're smart not to ignore me," Fang sneered. "I want the arrangement that you had with my grandfather."

Lin shook his head. "Your grandfather was benevolent with his power, unlike you, and he earned the protection I provided. He never threatened me or my family."

"I'm not negotiating with you, old man," Fang scowled. "I intend to get what I want, by whatever means necessary."

Mina was aware of the thug looming behind her, but she was surprised by the audacity of the goon to actually grab her arm and pull her away from Lin's side. "Hey!" she shouted.

For her outburst, Mina received a slap across the face. As the thugs snickered at the rebuke, she saw the murderous glint in her father's eyes, and she gave him a subtle shake of the head to let him know that she was fine. She had suffered worse.

"Your new bitch there needs to learn some manners," Fang grinned. "Maybe you're too *soft* on her, eh? Maybe she needs someone younger to keep her on her toes…or on her back or her knees?" he guffawed.

Oh, you fucking asshole, you are so dead. Mina gritted her teeth, not even needing to look in her father's direction. "Hey, shithead, you should apologize to him, while you can still talk."

Mina could barely keep her father in view, as she had her own hands full. Feeling the guard at her elbow reaching for her again, she slammed her pointed heel down through his shoe and into his foot, distracting him long enough to grab his gun hand. She didn't try to wrestle the gun from him, but redirected it, so that when he fired, the shots killed the guard on her other side.

She took advantage of the shooter's momentary shock at killing his cohort, to knock his gun from his hand and wrap her gold wire lariat around his throat like a garrote, tightening her grip until he slid limply to the floor. With the two guards down, she looked over to her father, but Lin had everything under his control.

Lounging in the guest chair, Lin watched the chaos he had unleashed in the room: the gangsters beat each other bloody with their bare fists, resorting to biting one another when their hands were beaten raw, screaming with pain but unable to stop, driven by a frenzied, uncontrolled bloodlust. The two guards at the door joined in the gory fracas, as well. Their unseasoned, arrogant young leader was rooted to his seat and watching the brawl, his sanguine fascination quickly replaced by horror as he realized that Lin had no intention of stopping the brutality.

It was always morbidly interesting to witness the "ah-ha" moment when someone realized that they had grossly underestimated her father, but Mina had only ever experienced it in a corporate setting, never during a scene of such stomach-turning carnage. In this situation, Mina's priority was to watch the door to ensure that her father concluded his business undisturbed. At the sound of running footsteps approaching, Mina retrieved her gold lariat and took one of the guards' guns, just in case.

"Okay, you've made your point, old man!" Fang shouted finally. "You're free of the deal. You can go!"

Lin swiveled in his seat playfully. "That's the worst apology I've heard in a long time. You've disgraced your family and your grandfather's *tong*." He tilted his head to give Mina a reassuring smile, then looked back at their host, as two of the berserker foot soldiers fell together, either unconscious or dead. "And you've disrespected her, which is the most unforgivable offense of all."

"Her?" the young man shrieked, pointing at Mina. "Who the fuck is she? Some crazy bitch—"

100

Those were the last words that Fang was ever heard to speak, as he was compelled by an unseen force to pinch his own tongue with his left hand, as his right hand fumbled around and seized on a pair of scissors from his desk drawer. Even as he screeched in terror, knowing that he was being led to sever his own tongue, he was unable to fight against the directive.

Mina stood away from the locked door, putting her back to her father's seat, in case anyone entered firing. She flinched a little at the awful, gurgling sound of Fang's agonized screaming at his self-inflicted mutilation, then his choking on his own blood, but she was more focused on the flood of black suits streaming through the door.

She stood stock still as the half-dozen thugs flowed around her and her father, with the last of them closing the door quietly, and proceeded to join in the bloody clash, in some cases, finishing off their fallen compatriots, while their bloodied, maimed leader could only sit and watch helplessly.

"You can leave the gun on the table," Lin suggested to Mina, passing her a handkerchief. "We don't need it."

Mina wiped down the gun and set it on the desk, where it was ignored by the gangsters, most of them holstering their own guns. Lin rose to his feet and pushed in his chair, leaning over briefly to whisper something in his defeated foe's ear that left the younger man sobbing. Lin took back the handkerchief from Mina and wiped a couple of blood droplets from her cheek before offering his arm. "Come along, dear. My business is finished."

Mina held her father's arm for the duration of the silent walk from the meeting room and through the empty upstairs corridor. In the rest of the club, aside from the dearth of black-suited thugs, the patrons and party-goers were entirely unaware of the carnage in the executive office upstairs. There was a single gunshot, which sounded like just another sound effect over the

101

driving, bass-heavy club music, as Mina and Lin continued down the stairs and out the club door. She was relieved but not entirely surprised that they were unaccosted, to the point that none of the remaining black-suited guards crossing their path even seemed to notice her or her father—or if they did, they didn't want to draw their attention by making eye contact.

"Was this your intention this afternoon, *ba-ba*?" Mina asked quietly, once they were several doors down from the end of the velvet rope.

"Death is usually not my first choice, Min-Min," he said, "but sometimes, reminders of the old ways are necessary to keep things in order. Fang's grandfather would've never let him rise to that level of power, if he were alive." He flagged down a cab easily once they rounded the corner, and held the door open for Mina, listening briefly to the sound of approaching police sirens. Climbing into the back row next to her, Lin gave the cabbie the address of the park around the corner from their house and settled back into the seat.

"These thugs don't even realize who you are, do they?" she whispered, too quietly for the cabbie to overhear.

"Even the ones that do, don't necessarily care, if they worship other gods and idols. Generations ago, my kind commanded more respect, as heralds and delegates for our masters, but over time, the reverence for the old ways has eroded, and reasons for the old alliances have been forgotten," he sighed. "Sometimes, I miss the tribes and chieftains that used to make sacrifices to seek my favor against their enemies," he said, wiping at his jacket sleeve with his handkerchief. "They were simple, but honorable."

"What kind of sacrifices?" Mina asked warily.

"The blood and pluck of slaughtered animals, originally," he said. "My worshippers eventually took a clue from my bovine form and offered grain and fruit, instead."

Mina recalled her mother's descriptions of her father's natural form: his thick, bony brow and horns, his heavy, massive pelt and sharp boar-like tusks. "How does an herbivorous *lin* become a spirit of warfare and bloodlust?"

Lin chuckled. "Ever see large herd males competing for breeding rights during a rut, or protecting their families? There's plenty of bloodshed and mauling involved."

"Humans haven't evolved all that differently, they just don't have horns or tusks," Mina said. She hadn't fired a gun in a long time, and the gangster's heavy handgun had felt bulky and unwieldy in her hand, but she knew she wouldn't have hesitated to shoot, in defense of her father. Just as she hadn't hesitated to take down Ashu'ral to protect her brother. "Would things have unfolded otherwise, if Mom was here instead of me?"

"Perhaps, but your mother wields a different kind of power," Lin said. "You did well; I'm proud that you're more than a pretty face," he said, pinching her chin.

"I think a pretty face would be more trouble than it's worth, around some of these people," she said, recalling the women in the club, who were probably prostitutes, now that she thought about it. She had been so focused on watching her father's back that she hadn't even considered their fate. "Those girls…"

"We have to let the police sort it out," he said, as a patrol car zipped past their cab, its lights flashing and sirens wailing.

"When we were leaving the room, what did you say to him? To Fang."

"I told him that if he wanted to die, he would have to take his own life," Lin said. "That I would not be the one to put him down."

103

Mina thought of the Fang's traumatized, mutilated state, contrasted with his swaggering, boastful arrogance just moments before her father's involvement. "He might have survived the injury."

"The physical injury, but not the shame," Lin said. "When word reached his family of what happened here, he would have lost face and been cast out for his ineptitude and conduct, and that would have been worse than a quick death." He smiled grimly. "I guess some of the old ways have endured, after all."

Mina felt a buzz in her pocket, signaling an incoming call. She tried to ignore it, keeping her eyes on her father, but Lin just patted her hand.

"Duty calls, Min-Min," he said.

She pulled the phone and was relieved and astonished to see the caller's name. "It's from Cindy, my friend in New York."

"The fae," Lin nodded solemnly. "Then you should take the call."

"Are you sure? I can let it go to voicemail—"

"I think you'll want to talk to your friend directly," he said, looking out the window. "It's time you got caught up."

"Okay." Mina gave her father a final, wary glance and answered the phone, holding it to her ear. "Hi, Cindy. What's up?"

Adam had just come back to the house, after picking up a gift for Xani and taking a long walk around the neighborhood, passing the picturesque Painted Ladies and skirting the lively Castro along his route, as he usually did when he visited San Francisco. Instinctively, he kicked off his shoes in a rush to get to his parents' home phone, summoned by its ringing, despite not knowing whether he should answer it. He picked up the receiver when he saw his father's office number appear on the caller ID display.

"*Wéi*?" Adam answered in Chinese. "Dad?"

"Hi, Adam," greeted Yumi Taira's silky voice. "Mister Xing left his phone behind when he left for the day, so I was wondering if you'd like me to bring it by on my way home."

Adam listened for signs that his parents were home, but he seemed to be alone in the house. The sky was still bright outside, and he noticed that it wasn't quite five o'clock yet. "Sure, my dad should be home soon. I'll be here, if he's not."

"Great," Yumi replied. "I'll be leaving in a few minutes."

Adam darted upstairs to rinse off, changing out of his stifling "office clothes" and into a t-shirt and jeans that he had packed from New York. He was tickled that his mom had unpacked everything from his under-bed storage bin, while he was out, leaving his other clothes all freshly ironed and hanging in his closet.

He had just zipped up his jeans when he heard the chime of the front door. "Mom? Dad? Mina?" he called, just in case he had missed anyone's return, and was met with silence. "Shit."

Instinctively touching his father's white jade pendant hanging from around his neck, for confidence and luck, he took a deep breath, as he recognized Yumi's slender silhouette through the frosted glass of the front door. He opened the door with a welcoming nod. "Hi, Yumi."

Yumi feigned surprise at seeing him, which afforded her the opportunity to react with a cute, coquettish gasp and giggle. "Hi, Adam! Are your parents home yet?"

Adam had a déjà vu moment, of Yumi standing in the same spot, more than ten years earlier, asking him the same exact question. He was barely twenty years old, then, and he had no idea how old she was, but she looked as exquisite and lovely now as she had, then.

"No, but they shouldn't be much longer," Adam said, leaving the door ajar as a hint to Yumi to keep her visit brief. "I don't want to hold you up, so I can take the phone."

Yumi closed the front door with a quiet click and set down her bag on the side table. "I don't mind waiting," she said. "We haven't really had a chance to catch up since you got back. How long has it been? Five years since we saw each other last?"

"I guess, something like that," Adam said, trying to hold his ground, knowing that if he retreated, she would follow him, just like the last time she caught him alone at home, years ago. "You haven't aged a day since we first met."

She smiled shyly, but the humility didn't quite reach her dark, fathomless eyes. "You've changed," she said, stroking her fingers down the front of his shirt. "You're not a boy anymore," she said, hooking her finger onto his belt loop to tug him closer. When he dug in his heels, she took a wider step towards him. "You've learned how to kiss."

In a replay of her greeting when he and Mina arrived at the airport the night before, Yumi curled her slender hand around his neck and pulled him in for a deep, breathtaking kiss. He responded automatically to her sweet, playful lips and tongue on his, but just as he had done the night before, he came to his senses and stepped back brusquely.

"I'm sorry, I have a girlfriend," he said, trying to hold her arms back.

"I know. That just makes this more fun," she laughed, somehow slipping through Adam's hands to mold herself against him, pressing his backside against his mother's antique apothecary sideboard. "Come on, Adam. Once more, for old times' sake."

Her kiss transported him to his callow youth, when he had felt infallible and superhuman, in part because he had managed to catch Yumi's eye. She seemed almost perfect—beautiful, smart and ambitious—and inexplicably, she had wanted him.

It was the last attribute that had opened his eyes, ultimately; to Yumi, he was a means to an end, a way for her to earn favor with his parents, and she was not the type to act without a contingency plan in place. Previously, Adam had discovered that he was one of several prospects that she had explored, in one sense or another, and that bruise to his ego had been enough to end their involvement. He focused on his past realization to find the new resolve to push her away.

"I can tell you still want me," she said, undoing the top buttons of her blouse, revealing a green jade and gold pendant in the shape of a fox. "Your girlfriend's not here, is she? So, what's the harm? If you were mine, I'd never let you out of my sight."

"That's why we would never be a good fit," Adam said, shaking his head. The shine of the green jade was reminding him of Xani's eyes. *Xani trusts me.*

"You never complained about the way we fit before," she smiled. "I can respect your loyalty, so if you want to keep your conscience clear, you can just close your eyes," she said, reaching for his jeans again. "And pretend that I'm her."

Adam sidestepped her. "Yumi, you don't have to do this, and I don't want to be a part of your schemes."

"Schemes!" she laughed. "I've already landed where I want to be, in my career. I just want us to enjoy each other's company, while you're in town." She sighed and started rebuttoning her shirt, shaking her head. "Okay, you win. It's a shame—I was looking forward to seeing what you'd picked up since our last time."

It was a deliberate taunt on her part, and the sight of Yumi inches away, with her partially-undone shirt providing a tantalizing peek at her pink satin demi bra, was certainly enough to give him pause, but Adam was safe from her powers of enticement.

"Sorry, you'll just have to use your imagination." He held out his hand. "I'll take my dad's phone, please."

Yumi straightened her skirt and blouse with a sigh and retrieved Lin's phone from her bag. As she passed it to Adam, she held onto it to draw his eyes to her.

"My offer stands, so if you change your mind while you're in town, let me know." She stood on her toes and kissed him again, scratching her fingernail down the teeth of his jeans zipper. "Anytime."

The front door opened unexpectedly, and Lin Xing stepped into the foyer. He smiled bemusedly at meeting Adam and Yumi at the door and seemed aware that he had just interrupted a private moment.

"Dad," Adam greeted, subtly checking the hem of his t-shirt and his jeans zipper.

"Mister Xing," Yumi said, picking up her bag. "I was just leaving. I came to drop off your phone."

"Thank you for going out of your way, Miss Taira," Lin said, swapping his shoes for house slippers by the door. "We won't keep you any longer, then. Have a good night."

As Yumi let herself out, and Lin went to the kitchen, Adam pretended to check his hair in the mirror over the sideboard, sinking heavily against the furniture as soon as he was alone. He felt as though he had just come off a head-spinning roller coaster.

"Adam?" Lin called from the kitchen. "Are you alright?"

"Yeah," Adam said, following his father's voice to the kitchen.

"'Yeah'?" Lin said mockingly, plucking his phone out of Adam's hand. "You look like you could use a drink."

"Do you have something stronger than water or tea?" Adam asked.

"I'll check," Lin chuckled. "Yumi can be a little forward. Is your girlfriend in New York more reserved?"

Adam smiled sheepishly, recalling Xani's enthusiasm. "She's actually very expressive, but she wouldn't be as bold with someone she hasn't seen in years." As soon as he said it, he doubted the truth of his own statement, but he couldn't exactly explain why.

"Mm-hm," Lin said, dubiously. "Well, certain women are more persistent than others, so if you're serious about keeping your distance from Yumi, you should ensure that you are never alone with her. Your jade can only help you so much," he said, gesturing to the carved white pendant hanging from Adam's neck.

"I shouldn't be using the jade's protection as a crutch," Adam said, feeling his warmth reflected back by the jade against his skin. "My thoughts and actions are my own responsibility."

"Yes, they are," Lin smiled, pulling out a half-filled glass bottle from behind a pantry panel. "There are limits to the jade's power, after all. Did your mother explain to you about its effect?"

"No, but it seemed to shield me from harm and influences, at least a little bit, and reverse the injuries I sustain," Adam guessed.

Lin sighed. "You know, your mother loves you, but I think sometimes that she loves you too much, and she keeps too much from you in order to protect you." He looked at the pendant again, but shook his head when Adam moved to take it off. "Don't do that, not until I explain."

Adam looked at the characters on the pendant, trying his best to discern the ornate etchings in the milky white jade, but he could make out one or two of the archaic, seal-type Chinese characters, *bǎo* and *hù*, which

109

used together usually meant "protection," or "to safeguard."

"The jade preserved what existed inside you, at the moment you put it on," Lin said, passing Adam one of the glasses he had poured of straight bourbon. "In I.T. terms, it's like a full backup. Everything that happens afterwards is like a shell, which sloughs off the second you remove the jade."

"The backup gets restored," Adam said.

"Correct. That includes your memories, your experiences… Everything that happened to you from the time your mother put it around your neck, would be undone," he said, snapping his fingers, "in an instant."

Adam gripped the jade tightly. "You're saying that everything that I experienced this last weekend can be forgotten and reset—if I take the jade off, I go back to how I was in the airport before I returned to New York? My brain becomes whole again?" He recalled his mother slipping it over his neck in the terminal at Logan airport, hearing her assurance that it would protect him—he had no idea that this was what she had meant.

"And you would lose your memories of what you experienced since the jade was yours," Lin said, clinking his glass with Adam's, and he took a seat at one of the counter stools. "Whatever conversations and interactions you had in New York when you returned from Boston would be forgotten, but your brain and your body would be whole again. Whatever damage this demon did to you would be reversed."

It should have been an easy decision, but Adam was torn. He had a chance, literally in the palm of his hand, to regain what he had lost, at the cost of losing the memories of one of the most harrowing weekends of his life. He would forget the horror and dread of facing Ashu'ral, the sensation of the spike boring into his brain, his bleak helplessness of seeing Jonah plunge to his death, and Mina's heartrending anguish and her

110

gruesome show of rage against the demon who had caused their pain.

But he would also forget the time spent with Galen and his young family in New York, and Jonah's sacrifice, as well as Xani's steadfast love, her declaration to stay with him even if it meant that he would never recall their time together the way she had. It felt like a betrayal to them, to disregard what others had suffered for him.

Adam let go of the jade and took a small sip of the bourbon, taking a seat at the counter next to his father. "Jonah's death should be remembered, and Mina shouldn't have to remember it alone. I could write down or record what I recall, and remind myself after the restoration, but it wouldn't be the same, would it?"

Lin shook his head. "No, it would be like reading a story, no matter how detailed you try to be."

"You've tried it?" Adam realized.

"I've tried more methods than you could imagine," Lin said. "I've been in your place more times than I can recall, literally, and the choice is never easy. As you get older, it gets harder to let go of the little moments that mark your life."

Adam sighed. "I want to keep all the memories, as terrible as they are."

"Remember, whatever physical damage you've suffered—"

"They're a small price to pay, compared to what others have lost and sacrificed," Adam said. "Anyway, the injuries are temporary, aren't they? Something happened to me long before I ever wore your jade, that speeds my healing. I should be dead, several times over, from everything I've endured these past few months."

Lin took a drink from his glass. "You'll have to ask your mother about that."

"What do I do with this thing, in the meantime?" Adam asked, pointing to the pendant.

Lin set his glass on the kitchen counter and looked at the jade. "You want to stay as you are?"

"I need to move forward in my life, not backwards," Adam said. "Whatever is lost, is lost."

Lin faced him. "You're wiser than I was at your age. It always felt easier to revert back to old ways than to adapt to the new." He rested his fingertips on the carved characters of the pendant and whispered under his breath.

The words weren't in any Chinese dialect that Adam had ever heard his parents speak, or any other language that Adam recognized, but the sounds were mellifluous and natural on Lin's tongue, and Adam wondered if he would ever learn their meaning someday. In the meantime, Adam felt a soothing warmth pass from the jade into his body, seeping through his head and joints, before returning to the pendant.

"It is done," Lin said. "Your jade has let go of its memory of your old self, so you can take it off now, or keep it on, and it will continue to protect you from harm."

Adam got to his feet. "Your jade, you mean."

Lin returned to his feet. "No, it belongs to you, now. I have no need for such a thing, not any longer."

The men returned to the foyer when they heard the front door open, and Selina breezed in with a grocery tote bag, filled to the top with produce and a fresh loaf of sourdough. Adam automatically moved to help her take the bag to the kitchen, just as he used to when he was a child.

"Dungeness crabs were on sale, and a fresh batch of tofu was just brought out, so I had to pick some up," Selina said, more to Lin than to Adam.

"And greens?" Lin asked.

"The *gai lan* was cheaper but looked a little wilted, so I got some baby *yu choi* instead."

It was one of those ordinary, routine exchanges that Adam and Mina had witnessed countless times during their childhood, and his mother's frugality was a holdover from their parents' years of practiced parsimony. Adam always liked hearing his parents talk like a normal human couple, and it comforted him to know, that no matter what other turmoil had entered his life, his parents were still the same.

"Isn't Mina home?" Selina asked, looking around. "She was here when I called home earlier."

"She came out with me to run an errand," Lin said. "She took a phone call on the way home and said she'll be back soon."

"I see," Selina said, putting stashing a pack of dried rice noodles into a pantry cabinet. "Adam, leave out the ginger and scallions. I'll need them for the blood cake soup; it's restorative, and you look a little drained."

"Thanks, *ma-ma*," Adam said, avoiding looking in Lin's direction, but catching his father's knowing grin and raised brow, that reminded him of his recent close encounter with Yumi.

"Rough day for both of you?" Selina remarked, taking the two empty bourbon glasses from the counter to the sink, then waved Lin over. As he stepped closer, she tore off a corner from a paper towel, wet it under the sink and wiped his temple clean of some brown flecks. "Should I bother asking whose blood that was?"

"Could be from any number of people, my love," Lin said diffidently. "But not Mina—she's fine."

Okay, not exactly like a normal human couple, Adam corrected himself. With his dapper father fawning over his raven-haired mother, as they conversed casually about bloodstains, they reminded him momentarily of Gomez and Morticia Addams.

The front door opened, and Adam heard the hard *clop* of Mina's heels against the foyer tiles, before she

113

appeared in the doorway to the kitchen, with an unreadable, stony expression.

Mina noticed both of their parents in the kitchen but looked at Adam directly. "I need to talk to you, in private."

Mina looked over Adam's shoulder to ensure that neither of their parents had followed him out of the kitchen. She doubted that anything she had heard from Cindy would be a surprise to them, but Adam deserved to hear the news in a private setting, as she had.

"What the hell are you wearing?" Adam muttered, following her to the living room.

Mina had almost forgotten how revealing her dress was, open from the neck to the sternum, and equally exposed in the back. "Cut me some slack, okay? I just had to watch Dad drive some stupid asshole to cut out his own tongue."

"Shit!" Adam exclaimed.

Mina waved it aside. "That's not even the most fucked-up part of today," she said. "I just got off the phone with Cindy. What do you want first: the good news, the bad news, or the weird news?"

"Cindy? News from New York?" Adam guided Mina to a seat on the sofa and sat next to her. "Let's get the bad news over with first."

"Okay," Mina said, taking a grounding breath. "Millie Krantz passed away this morning. She was in her apartment, and it seems that she died peacefully in her sleep."

"I'm sorry, *mei-mei*." Adam touched her hand briefly, but Mina barely felt the glancing touch, as her head was still spinning from the other news. "Do you need to go back to New York?"

Mina shook her head. "Her family's been notified, and Morgan's taking care of getting them into the

114

apartment for anything they need. There's nothing more for me to do there."

Adam nodded. "So, that's the bad news."

"So," Mina said, taking another breath, "the good news is: Jonah's alive." She smiled at the wide-eyed astonishment on Adam's face, as it perfectly reflected the amazement she felt at hearing the news from Cindy. "He's been alive for a few days now, apparently, but everybody wanted to make sure he was actually himself before telling me—us."

"And not a zombie, or some other undead thing? Who's 'everybody'?" Adam asked cautiously.

Mina chuckled dryly. "You haven't gotten any calls from Xani or Morgan, right?" she asked rhetorically, then nodded her head towards the kitchen. "I mean *everybody* knows."

"Mom and Dad knew?" Adam asked, appalled. "And they didn't say anything, either."

"They were being cautious, I get it," Mina said, understanding their parents' perspective, now that she had had a moment to reflect on the overall situation. "And there's good reason for it. Because I haven't even told you the weird news yet. I call it 'weird' because I can't tell whether it's good or bad."

Adam shook his head tiredly. "Fuck it, just spill it."

"Cindy says Jonah is the reason that Millie Krantz is dead." It felt strange to even say the words, but having heard the whole story from Cindy, it made perfect sense.

"That doesn't make any sense," Adam said. "How is he the reason for Millie dying? Was it an accident, or was he possessed or something?"

Mina shook her head. "Jonah's been made a reaper, and Millie was his assignment."

"Reaper, as in 'Grim Reaper'?"

"It's not always grim," Mina said, laying her head on the cushioned sofa back. "Death can be a liberation, and reapers help facilitate the passage between worlds.

115

Millie told me a couple of weeks ago that she had cancer, and it had metastasized; she was living in constant pain, with no idea of how long she had left, but she was emotionally and physically exhausted. I didn't want to add to her worries, financially, so I told her not to even bother with the rent anymore, and I would cover her utilities."

"I had no idea," Adam said quietly. "That's why you said you weren't sure whether the news was good or bad. What does your gut tell you?"

Mina sat up. "Jonah's kind and fair, so if he had a say in how to do his job, he would've made it easy for her. He would be merciful and compassionate, to anyone who needs it. But I'm afraid not all of his assignments will go as smoothly; not everyone wants to go when it's their time."

"Well, I guess we'll figure it out together when we get back to New York."

"Oh, that's the last thing Cindy told me," Mina said, recalling the end of the call. "Jonah's on his way here, to San Francisco."

Chapter 7

"A penny for your thoughts?" Lin prompted, coming next to Selina to lower the flame under the furiously-boiling pot of water, bringing the water down to a simmer.

"The children have been in the other room for a while," she remarked, turning to the freezer where she had left the live Dungeness crabs to chill.

"You know they're discussing Jonah," he said. "It's going to take a few minutes for them to go over what Mina's fae friend told her."

"I'm guessing it was Cindy, her fae friend who used to be a boy?" Selina asked, quickly lowering the twine-bound crabs into the water head-first to kill them quickly before they awoke. In her younger years, she would've eaten the crabs alive and whole, but the children didn't share her natural constitution and pragmatic palate, so she made an effort to cook humanely. "How much does Mina's friend know?"

"Bullfinch says she's smart, discreet and well-connected, despite her youth," Lin said. "He brings his prospective clients to the Red Lotus when he wants a second opinion about their veracity and intentions, so he trusts her," he said, chewing a shred of raw young ginger from Selina's *mise en place* plate of aromatics and vegetables.

Selina sighed, as she washed the crab brine from her hands. "Mina trusts her, too, so I suppose we have no choice but to follow suit."

"They're adults, with their own wisdom to impart," he said, nuzzling her ear as he embraced her from behind, with her hands still soapy under the faucet. "Their independence is good, isn't it? Isn't that the goal of raising children?"

"Soon, our children won't need us." Selina turned off the faucet but stayed in her husband's embrace, feeling his powerful energy through their contact despite the gentleness of his arms.

"Perhaps, but *I* will always need you, beloved wife."

"You're getting sentimental, husband," she chided gently. "But it's kind of you to say."

As a *lin* of the old world, he had been worshipped and exulted by warlords, chieftains and warriors, and in his current guise, he could still incite savagery and murderous rage in a roomful of strangers with the merest whispered suggestion. Yet, he never failed to protect her and see to her every need, and was always present and nurturing to her and later, to their children. Over years, he had made himself indispensable to her, and in turn, she had grown to love and care for him, too.

It wasn't her style to ever voice such maudlin, greeting-card romanticisms as he did, but she did kiss his cheek, on impulse. "Get out of my kitchen. I have to finish cooking dinner."

"I'm not hungry," he said, reluctant to leave her. "Adam wanted to get Mission burritos for lunch."

Selina laughed. "You won't be hungry till morning, then, but the rest of us still need to eat."

She caught a shimmer of glowing white out of the corner of her eye and turned, with Lin's hands still on her waist. "Dawa?"

The silver-white lion-dog bounded to their side with a wide, natural grin across his broad, hairy muzzle. The *ruishi*'s fur shimmered with its own white light, except where the shadows and folds of his fur reflected azure, like the snowcaps of its Himalayan home, as he bounced back and forth.

"It is good to see you again, too, old friend," she said, but noticed that his serpentine tail didn't sway with its usual banner-like zeal. "It's odd that Dawa would come all this way from New York," she remarked to Lin.

"You've brought news for us," Lin realized, releasing Selina to stroke the velvety white tufts behind Dawa's ears. The spectral dog seemed to relax a little, but was still anxious. "Not about the children, obviously."

The *ruishi* whined and howled, finally lowered his head to the floor at their feet, almost in apology. Dawa expressed himself more in images and emotions than in words and sentences, but Selina and Lin understood him perfectly.

Still, what Dawa told them made little sense to her. *Jonah killed Millie Krantz?*

"Jonah's not violent. I know you saw it happen, but it doesn't sound right," Selina frowned. "Why would he do such a thing?" she asked, more to herself than to Dawa, then noticed Lin's silence. "What do you know about this?"

Adam and Mina appeared in the kitchen doorway. "Yeah, Dad," said Adam, "what do you know?"

Jonah looked at the business card he had palmed, and back up at the unlikely façade of the tailor shop where he had been sent. With its dingy windows and peeling paint and signage, the shop had the faded, weathered look of a child's plastic pretend castle that had once been loved and well-cared for, but eventually neglected and left to languish in a backyard over too many winters.

A pile of discarded cardboard and fabric refuse littered the corner of the storefront, adding to the dilapidated atmosphere of the isolated stretch of Pine Street. That section of Pine passed through a well-traveled part of town, but Jonah found saw no one else on the street for several blocks in both directions. His flight had gotten in late, but it was still hours till midnight, so the isolation felt eerie.

Luc-Isaac Fournier. On the card, only the initials "L. F." had appeared with the address, but now prominently printed in faded gilding on the shop window, the most intact lettering spelled out: *Luc I. F...er.*

"Ah, shit," Jonah muttered. *No escaping the devil, if he's hell-bent on keeping tabs.*

A snorting grumble sounded from amidst the cardboard and fabric pile, and a shambling, grizzled figure rolled out onto the sidewalk. He rose unsteadily to his feet and looked cross-eyed at Jonah. "Do you have an appointment," he growled.

"No, I don't," Jonah said, "but—"

"Shop's closed," the figure mumbled, shuffling back towards his cardboard hovel.

"I just wanted to see what I was getting into before I scheduled time," he finished, noting the accumulation of leaves and old newspapers around the door. "Not exactly what I expected."

"Well, what did you expect, hmm?" the vagrant chuckled with a phlegmy rattle.

Something more reputable, less seedy...cleaner. "Something busier," Jonah said at last. He noticed the crumpled wrappers and foil littering the cardboard shelter and remembered that he had an unopened granola bar and water bottle in his bag from the plane. "Hey, are you hungry? Do you want this?"

The vagrant crept back out cautiously. "You're not going to poison me, are you?"

If I was, I wouldn't say so, Jonah fought the urge to reply. "No, the stuff is unopened and weighing down my bag," he said, holding out the food and bottle.

As the man snatched the offerings from his hand and scrambled back to his corrugated home, Jonah straightened the strap of his messenger bag over his shoulder and took out his phone to call the number on the card. Sure enough, the distant metallic ring of a phone bell sounded from inside the darkened shop, and Jonah prepared himself to leave a message, however, the ringing stopped, and a woman's voice replied: "Fournier."

Caught by surprise, Jonah took a second or two to reply, "Hello, yes, I'm looking to set up an appointment?" He looked around and noticed that the vagrant had vanished, along with his makeshift shelter, as well as the granola bar and water bottle.

"Yes, you must be Mister Gideon. We've been expecting you," the woman replied warmly. "When would you like to come in?"

Jonah looked at the darkened, dingy shop windows and doors. "I'm in the neighborhood, actually, but…"

"Are you interested or available to come in this evening?" she offered.

"I wasn't sure if you were open tonight." *Or ever.* Jonah looked up and down the block, which was still devoid of other pedestrian traffic, then turned back to face the shop, and found it transformed: signage freshly painted, glass windows and door sparkling clean, entrance clear of garbage, and lights glowing brightly from inside. *What the hell?*

"Of course, we serve our clients at all hours, sir," she replied. "'If you're close by, we can see you at nine this evening?"

"Sure," Jonah said, glancing at his phone. Half an hour to kill.

"Earlier, perhaps, Mister Gideon?" she asked laughingly. "Are you very close by?"

"You could say that," he replied.

"Is that you darkening our doorstep?" she asked playfully. The gauzy curtain on the door pulled back, and a pretty, doe-eyed young woman peered out at him with a smile, phone receiver pressed against her ear. "You're welcome to come in, take a seat and have some tea, while you wait."

The phone disconnected, and the curtain on the door fell closed. The front door opened, with the quaint sound of a jingling bell sounding overhead, but there was no sign of the young woman who had answered the phone. As Jonah tucked his phone back into his pocket and stepped inside the brightly-lit shop, he saw her at the register counter, preparing a tray with a fine china tea set and a small dish of shortbread. She was slender and impeccably groomed, with her dark hair pulled into a low ponytail, and her tailored ivory suit still crisp and unwrinkled.

"Please have a seat, Mister Gideon," she greeted, and her voice had a subtle French accent that hadn't come across over the phone. She gestured to a clawfoot armchair near the counter display of various men's accessories: cufflinks, suspenders and the like. "How do you take your tea, sir?"

"I'm fine, actually," he said. "I'm sorry, I can only drink green tea, and not very much of it."

"I am aware," she said mildly, setting the silver tray on a side table next to him. "This is decaffeinated matcha green tea, and perfectly safe for you, unless you prefer water?"

"This will be fine, thank you." Jonah took the cup to be polite, but the tea was pleasantly warm and bracing on his palate: slightly buttery, with a leafy finish, like a butterscotch rolled in grass clippings.

122

"Mister Gideon," called a man's voice from the back room, before he appeared in the doorway to the back room. A middle-aged gentleman in a fitted tweed waistcoat, round gold-rimmed spectacles and a full gray beard stepped out.

"Mister Fournier?" Jonah replied, setting his tea aside.

The older gentleman smiled sheepishly. "No, I'm simply one of his many servants. My name is Metzger, and I will be seeing to your needs today. If you would come with me, please," he said, brushing aside the drape obscuring the back room.

One of his servants, Jonah mused, as he followed the man into the back room, with a cluttered work table strewn with patterns and swatches. He tried to place Metzger's face or voice but could only hear a tinge of a German accent. "Have we met before?" he asked, setting his bag down in a nearby chair.

"Have we?" Metzger said, setting out an assortment of fabric samples on a table. "You're not the first reaper I've outfitted, but you are the first American I've dressed in many years."

Metzger turned and crossed his lean arms, as he looked Jonah over from head to toe. "Is this your usual attire? Not a critique, just a question."

Jonah looked down at the t-shirt, hoodie, jeans and sneakers that represented most of what remained of his wardrobe. "Yes."

"I see," Metzger said, pushing up the bridge of his spectacles. "Your clothes are comfortable, loose, worn but clean and well-kept." He looked askance at Jonah's grooming. "You prefer not to draw attention to yourself, but you know your own worth, and you don't neglect your self-care."

"Am I getting a makeover of some sort?" Jonah quipped.

"Not unless you want one," Metzger replied lightly, stepping around Jonah to view him from different angles. "Please remove your sweatshirt," he said, noting how Jonah removed the garment. "You respect your clothes—that's good, it means you shouldn't need to come back to us anytime in the foreseeable future. Straight, even posture, not even a discernible slouch or asymmetry—what a pleasure this will be, for a change."

Jonah stood still, as Metzger starting measuring him with a fabric tape measure. "How long will the process take?"

"It varies, depending on the customer, but for you, Mister Gideon, I should have your suit ready within an hour or two," Metzger said, pulling the tape measure across the span of Jonah's shoulders. "You're not the fussy or ruffly type."

"No, definitely not," Jonah said. "Only two hours, really?"

"Well, what did you expect, hmm?" Metzger said laughingly. "We service a very exclusive, very demanding clientele, so we don't keep anyone waiting longer than absolutely necessary."

Jonah honed in on the first part of Metzger's comment: *what did you expect?* For the first time, he noticed the half-eaten granola bar and nearly-emptied water bottle on the corner of Metzger's work table, that were the same Northeast-brand snacks that he had given away to the vagrant outside the shop. "By any chance, were you the man who spoke to me earlier, outside?"

Metzger looked at Jonah over the edge of his spectacles. "You're a good human being, Mister Gideon. Not many people would've spoken to me outside, or offered food and drink, humble as it was. I think I will add a few extras to your order; I don't think my masters will mind."

After a few more measurements, Metzger said to Jonah: "I have everything I need for now, if you'd like to get a drink or have a seat outside. Sarah can attend to you while you wait." He craned his head to call to the front of the shop: "Sarah!"

The shop assistant appeared in the doorway. "Yes, Mister Metzger?"

"See that Mister Gideon has everything he wants," Metzger said, and Jonah shot him a sideways glance at his deliberate intonation, but the young woman merely nodded with a smile.

"Of course," she said. "This way, please?"

As Jonah picked up his bag and followed Sarah back to the front, he reached into his sweatshirt pocket and pulled out his phone to check the time, with the notecard stuck against it, detailing his second assignment. He hesitated in looking at the card, as he recalled the details of his next reaping: a young Chinese-American man, twenty-five, located in the Chinatown area, scheduled for termination by...

Except that the details had changed. Jonah sank into a chair and read the new set of instructions, now indicating a middle-aged white man with a Union Street address in Russian Hill listed as his residence.

"Is everything alright, Mister Gideon?" Sarah asked, bringing Jonah a fresh cup of green tea.

"My assignment changed somehow," he said, then shook his head, pocketing the card. He didn't want to say too much, especially to a relative stranger.

"It happens occasionally," Sarah nodded. "If the subject has already passed, through other methods or means, the reaper is redirected to the next assignment, and the cards are updated automatically. It's an efficient system, isn't it?"

Jonah took a sip of the tea, surprised by how casually she referenced the process. "How long have you worked here, for Fournier?"

She smiled, smoothing the lapel of her ivory suit. "More years than I can count, but not always in this

125

location. Mister Metzger is an artist, but like most true artists, he is mercurial and disorganized, so Mister Fournier wants to keep him under supervision."

Jonah looked around the neat, elegant decor, wondering briefly if his imagination was getting carried away. Maybe it really was just a coincidence the tailor was named Luc-Isaac Fournier, and the shop wasn't some front for one of Lucifer's clandestine businesses. As soon as he set down his teacup, Sarah refilled the cup, leaning over with a flirtatious smile.

"Is there anything else I can get for you, or do for you, Mister Gideon?"

"No, thank you," he said. "I'm good."

"Where are you staying tonight?" she asked, glancing at Jonah's sparse luggage. "In case we have to have some items delivered to you?"

"I don't know yet," he said reluctantly, noting Sarah's curious eyebrow twitch. "If there's anything else, I'll come pick it up."

"If you need a place to stay, I live close by," she offered.

"Thanks, but I'll be fine," he said automatically. Jonah was suddenly reminded of Bullfinch's question to him earlier, at the Lotus, when Jonah asked about overnight accommodations: *Are you presuming that you won't be invited to stay with anyone?* In the back of his head, Jonah had hoped to see Mina again by now, but he had known that he would have to straighten out his own business first, to avoid pulling her into his brand new shit—

"You're thinking of someone," Sarah said, returning to the counter. "A wife, or a girlfriend?"

"My fiancée, apparently," he said, recalling Cindy's update that Mina still wore his mother's ruby ring. "We had to separate before she officially agreed to marry me."

126

"She's a lucky girl," Sarah smiled. "Does she know that you're a reaper?"

Jonah chuckled dryly. "Before today, *I* didn't know I'd been made into a reaper," he said. "Mina Gideon is nothing if not resourceful, so she may be aware of my situation, but it's complicated." He had stopped compulsively checking his phone once he boarded the plane back in New York, reasoning that he was torturing himself waiting for Mina's call or text, when he wasn't even sure that she knew he was alive.

"Mina…Gideon?" Sarah asked. "*The* Mina Gideon? I didn't realize that her last name was yours."

"She was once married to my cousin," Jonah clarified, surprised by Sarah's recognition. "You know the name?"

"The Xing family is well-established and well-connected here, so her name and reputation are known, within the right circles," Sarah said. "I wonder if Metzger is aware of your importance."

Jonah shook his head. "I don't want preferential treatment, really." The whole arrangement of being outfitted by a tailor with connections to Lucifer was unnerving enough, without dropping Mina's name into the mix.

"It's not really your decision, Mister Gideon," Sarah said lightly, heading to the back room. "Your fiancée's family is protected, for good reason, so those protections must extend to you. Please excuse me for a moment."

For the minute or so that he was alone in the front room, Jonah texted Aciré and Bullfinch to ask for hotel recommendations, forgetting briefly that it was nearly one o'clock in the morning on the East Coast. To his surprise, Aciré replied promptly with a hotel name, address and reservation number.

Chuckling, Jonah texted: *WTF AH? Past bedtime for you?*

Aciré texted back: *Having late night snack with a friend. Polpettes from North End. Learned my lesson, getting my own order next time.*

Jonah's mouth watered. Italian meatballs sounded scrumptious, and he was reminded that he hadn't eaten since he left New York, and he had already given away his complimentary plane snack. *Does hotel have 24-hr room service?*

Of course. Staying in SF after all?

Assignment updated on me. New target, but still SF.

Aciré and Jonah exchanged a few more texts before Sarah returned to the front. "Is everything alright, Mister Gideon?"

Jonah nodded and pocketed his phone. "Aciré Hart says hello."

Sarah flashed Jonah a sly simper. "She owes me a visit, the little tart. What color is her hair, nowadays?"

"Mostly burgundy, as of a couple of days ago," Jonah said, getting to his feet as Metzger appeared by the doorway. "That was quick."

Metzger nodded, pushing up the bridge of his wire-rimmed spectacles a smidge. "As promised, Mister Gideon, we don't like to keep clients waiting longer than absolutely necessary. In light of the revelation regarding your ties," he said, flashing a glance at Sarah, "it is especially important that we have you properly outfitted, as soon as possible. Please come with me, and we'll get you on your way promptly."

Adam followed the quiet music and the dim light in the hallway to Mina's room, feeling just as restless as she had been during the family conversations before and during dinner. Their father had been honest and open, once it was apparent that there was no longer a need for secrecy. It was common knowledge now: Jonah was alive, in San Francisco, with his own to-do list given to him by his divine supervisors. While Mina was eager to see Jonah again, she also wanted him to have the opportunity to handle his obligations, so that when she saw him next, she could be assured that she had his attention to herself.

Adam knocked quietly on Mina's door but didn't wait for her to answer before he turned the knob. She was sitting cross-legged on the middle of her bed, playing solitaire and singing along to Duran Duran, and for a moment, he recalled seeing her in that same position, listening to the same music, over fifteen years earlier. It was her default for burning off energy mindlessly, a kind of pre-meditation for whenever she was too wound up to actually get to a more productive, meditative state.

Dawa was curled up behind Mina like a glowing white body pillow, his cloud-like fur fluffing in time to his deep, silent snores.

"It's one of those nights?" Adam asked. The spirit lion-dog lifted his head and flicked his tail briefly to acknowledge Adam, but stayed in his cozy spot in the middle of Mina's bed.

"Still a little wired." Mina gathered her cards into a pile. "Funny how I can recall every word to songs I haven't heard in ages, but the first time I heard Dad talking someone into taking a life is a blur."

"It's probably for the best," he said, coming into the room. "I still hear snippets from the Smiths and Leonard Cohen in my head from time to time, but I also remember hearing Dad ordering a hitman to shoot himself in the head."

Mina looked up with a wry smile. "Remember when we were kids, we would listen to our friends complain about how mean and scary their parents were?"

Adam laughed, nodding to Dawa. "I remember not being to tell anyone about our magic dog." He gestured to the cards. "Up for a game of bullshit?"

She looked at him. "With a single deck?" she asked warily.

He shrugged. "With Fujian rules, it should be a quick game."

She collected the cards, shuffled them and split them into two equal piles. "Why are you still awake?" she asked. "You should be sleeping, letting Mom's elixirs do their work to patch up your brain."

"I can't help wondering if certain memories are gone for a reason," he said, arranging the cards in his hand and wondering how they had managed to balance twenty-six cards in their tiny palms when they were children. "That certain aspects of me should be excised, for the greater good, or my own good. One ace," he declared, throwing down a card face down.

"You can't miss what you don't remember ever having," Mina said. "One ace," she said, tossing a card to cover his. "What's with this second-guessing, *ge-ge*?"

"I was just amazed, listening to everyone tonight, casually talking about what happened in Fang's club, like it was a regular day at an office job. You and I haven't even discussed what happened in Ashu'ral's lair."

"What's there to discuss?" Mina said. "I wanted Ashu'ral punished, and Lucifer was fine about it, so I took him down. It wasn't anything that I haven't done before, and it probably won't be the last time. Play a card."

Mina's voice and posture were forced, and Adam knew that Mina was bothered, on some level. "It was the way you went about it. You were cruel, and you're never cruel. Dad has that tendency, but not you." He picked a card from his hand. "One seven."

"I didn't enjoy it, if that's what concerns you," Mina said. "I was pissed and took out my anger on Ashu'ral, but there was still a purpose and order to it. He had to be made into an example of what happens to demons who try to prey on us, but I did save the worst breakages for after he was already catatonic," she said, as a way of justification. "One seven," she followed with a card.

"Bullshit," he called her bluff, flipping over her card to show the six of clubs, as he had the other three sevens already in hand. "You took your time, long enough for a roomful of witnesses to see what you did. One six."

Mina picked up her rejected card, along with the others underneath it, and covered Adam's play. "Yes, we needed an audience, so that word gets around about the consequences of messing with our family." She flashed Adam a look. "Dad taught us that: potential enemies and friends should always be forewarned that our family comes first."

They played back and forth without further comment, except to call their cards or call each other's bluffs. Dawa watched the game for a while, before he leapt off the bed and passed through the wall, towards their parents' bedroom.

Adam emptied his hand to a single card, that he put down. "One king," he said, expecting her to flip it over.

Instead, Mina nodded and put down four random cards from her hand on top of his. "Four queens."

It was her way of ending the game. They were down to their final cards, with most of the deck discarded in a pile between them, but he knew that she had bluffed, because the last card he had played was the queen of spades.

"You can call me on it," she said, palming her remaining cards. "You know I'm lying."

"Why did you cover my card?" he asked. "You know how to count, so you knew I was lying, too."

Mina collected all the cards and stacked them neatly. "Do you remember, when we played as kids, you would deliberately throw a game from time to time because otherwise, I'd start crying?"

Adam shook his head. "I remember playing cards with you, but not letting you win."

"You didn't lose often, but I always knew when you did it on purpose, because you'd be laughing," Mina said. "It was nice to know that you thought my feelings were more important than your winning."

Adam shrugged. "I wanted you to know how guys are supposed to treat you."

"Yeah, I guess that lesson didn't stick, otherwise I would've avoided Malcolm," she muttered, getting up from the bed to turn off her stereo.

"What *did* happen with Malcolm?" he asked. His memories about Malcolm were still spotty, but he remembered when his best friend and baby sister had fallen in love, their subsequent whirlwind courtship and marriage, all over in less than a year. Mina and Malcolm never spoke ill of each other, and Malcolm clearly still cared about Mina, but she was clear on her stance that there could never be a reconciliation.

"Shit, you forgot that, too." Mina shook her head. "Well, fuck it, I'm not repeating myself."

"You told me already?"

"Yes, and last time, you looked like a kicked puppy, or like someone told you there's no Santa Claus," she said.

"Okay, I won't make you rehash it now, but did Mom and Dad know?" he asked. "Did Jonah?"

"Jonah found out around the time you did. I told Mom back when Malcolm and I were still together, but I don't think she told Dad until we had already split. Otherwise, I probably would've been a widow instead of a divorcée," she said dryly.

"That bad?" Adam frowned.

"Drop it," she replied sharply. "It's over, and there's nothing to be done about it. Can we just…call it a night, please? It's been a long day, and I think I need another shower. I'm not sure I got all the blood out of my hair."

132

Chapter 8

1888, Fujian Province, China

On one cool autumn morning, Jin Mudan timed the opening of her chamber door with that of her husband, and she greeted him with a warm smile, as she always did. He was her oldest and dearest friend, but she was unable to muster any romantic feeling for him, and in turn, he never asked for more affection that she offered.

After crossing paths and denning together from time to time over several years, they had become bosom companions, and eventually, the *lin* offered Jin Mudan the security of an actual house. With the growing presence of humans in their territory, he spent more time in his human shape than in his natural spirit form, so he resigned himself to building and living in a house like humans did. If she agreed to stay with him, then he would build extra rooms for her comfort. It was unseemly for unwed and unrelated humans to live together, and she was tired of having to avoid the attentions of human males as a single, unprotected maiden, so Jin Mudan agreed to the formality of a marriage arrangement.

After almost three years of living as "Lao-Mázi"'s wife, she still enjoyed and appreciated how safe and serene she felt within the walls of the house her husband had built, not too far from where they had first met, years earlier. Despite the limitations of his human form, her *lin* protector had constructed a sturdy, capacious home that provided all the space and comforts she required in her human form. Just being able to leave her room without having to watch the shadows for danger or look over her shoulder was a simple but welcome privilege, after years of living in the wilderness, alone.

They were married, from an official perspective, but they were still spirits of the natural world: he was still *lin*, and she was still *huli jing*. To the human world, he was still "Lao-Mázi"—the old pock-marked outcast—but between the two of them, he allowed her to call him "Xing," one of his many names from antiquity.

The disparity of their physical appearances, and rarity of their appearances together in public, caused their neighbors to speculate about the nature of their relationship, what they provided to each other, and who had the better end of the bargain; he was scarred and crippled but a talented craftsman and builder, and she was sweet and beautiful but had no family or independent means to provide her stability.

"I started the kitchen fire already, I hope you don't mind," she said, walking next to him, as he left his chamber. "It was a cold night, and I thought you would want some tea to warm you up this morning."

"That was very kind, thank you," he said, shuffling his feet with an effort, despite her deliberately slowed pace to accommodate him. "Did you see the extra package of sugar that the spice merchant gave to me last evening? He asks about you very often, when his mother isn't looking."

Jin Mudan smiled. "That was generous of him, but I should return it. It's too expensive for him to simply give away on a whim."

"Then you would have to speak with him, and that is precisely what he wants," he said.

"It cannot be helped," she said. "But I will come back to you, as I always do."

"Someday, if you choose not to, I only ask that you tell me first," he said, his eyes downcast.

"I won't stray," she said, touching his arm. It was a strong, muscular arm, that compensated for his withering leg. "You may hear rumors and whispers, but trust that I will never leave your side, unless you force me to."

"That is overly gracious," he said. "You are still young and lovely, and you should have the opportunity to raise a family."

She simpered at the irony of being called young and beautiful, when she was decades old and had the natural form of a sickly-colored fox. "That is a human aspiration, and not for the likes of us, husband. Besides," she said lightly, "your size would kill me if we attempted to mate. Could we even have a child?"

"We could, if we were in our human forms," he said, then followed quickly: "No, forget that."

"If you want a child," she said solemnly, "it would be my duty to bear one for you."

He glanced aside at her and laughed. "What a face you made when you said that! No, sweet little wife, I would never force you to carry an heir for me. I have lived for eons without a child, and I see no need to burden you with one, especially if it's as unsightly as I am. I would rather let our neighbors continue assuming my impotence."

She helped him step over the threshold into the kitchen and led him to the bench to sit near the fire before she went to prepare his tea. Despite the power of his spirit form and the feebleness of his human one, Lin spent most of his time hiding behind his homely veneer. Then again, their home was too compact and tidy to accommodate the immense dimensions of Lin's ungulate spirit form…so why had he chosen to build his home that way, and how had he done it by himself?

"What is going through that wily *huli* mind?" he cajoled.

135

"Why did you build your house like this: too small to fit your true form?"

"What better way to keep us safe, than to remain disguised among the humans?" he said. "We will always be hunted by them, to be slaves or trophies, but I want this place to be a sanctuary for you, where you have nothing to fear."

"Not even from you," she realized, setting down his warmed cup before she poured his tea.

"Never from me, Jin Mudan," he said gently. "When you agreed to become my wife, I swore that I would never raise my hand to you. After a lifetime of strife, you have provided me peace, and that is something that I would die to protect."

1890

Jin Mudan was in the habit of listening for the sound of her husband's opening chamber door before she ventured from her room each morning to start her day. She often awoke in the middle of the night and spent long, quiet hours listening to the songs of crickets and cicadas before returning again to bed to await the dawn.

This morning was different, after the peculiar events of the night before. She had been stirred from sleep by a clear and melodious birdsong, but when she had arisen to find the source of the mysterious melody, she had encountered a strange man in the courtyard, wearing Xing's clothes and acting as though he lived there. It was his skillful whistling that had roused her with its uncanny avian mimicry.

Her exchange with the handsome stranger had been contentious and heated, as she had refused to respond to his flirtatious tone and had eventually scratched him across the cheek. He had brought it upon himself, as he had continued to insult and disparage Xing's meekness and humble looks, even after she had demanded that he stop. She had finally struck him, when he mocked her habitual frigidity: *Benefiting from your husband's charity for five years, couldn't you even tolerate lying in your marital bed for one night, bearing his touch for just a few hours?*

Once she had cooled her temper, she had broken off an aloe vera leaf from one of the courtyard planters to treat the stranger's injury. She was embarrassed about her angry outburst, as it would've reflected badly on Xing's ability to keep a docile and accommodating wife, but the stranger had seemed amused and impressed by her outrage in defense of her husband. He had even tried to convince her that he was her husband, just healed and transformed into a different guise, but he had given up the ruse when she rejected the possibility outright.

Soon after, he had left the house of his own accord and assured Jin Mudan that he meant her and her husband no harm, even referring to Xing by name. He expressed his admiration for her unshakable devotion and left without further comment.

Now, in the clear, sober light of morning, the evening seemed like a strange dream. The house and courtyard seemed the same as it had been hours earlier. She even recognized Xing's distinctive shuffle while struggling to his feet, and the creak of his wicker and bamboo furniture under his uneven weight. Her husband had returned, much to her delight and relief, and she went to meet him at his chamber door.

He was already outside his door, and he looked different to her. His disheveled, mop-like hair fell more smoothly across his eyes, and his posture was straighter than usual. With a sheepish smile, he played with the aloe leaf that she had picked the evening before, dabbing a couple of last drops of the juice onto the scabs marring his cheek, exactly where she had scratched the stranger.

"Xing, your cheek," she said, reaching for him.

He avoided her hand and dropped the spent leaf into the aloe vera planter. "If anyone asks, I will say that you defended yourself against my unwelcome advances. No one would doubt such a reason, or blame you for spurning me."

"I don't understand," she said, quickening her step to keep up with him, as he strolled to the kitchen with an easy, graceful gait. Looking at him out of her corner of her eye, she saw that the pock marks and old scars on his face were a mask over smoother, more handsome features. She screamed and stopped short. "What is this! Who are you?"

"You're impossible to please, little *huli jing*," he muttered. "I tried to show you my true human face, and you called me a liar. I try to give you the face you know and trust, and still, you shun me. Perhaps I should give up pretending to be human, and rebuild this house to accommodate my spirit form, after all."

She steeled herself to see him by the bright light of morning. "Show me your true human form again. Let me see you in daylight."

He nodded and held his hands out to his sides to allow her an unobstructed view. He let his illusions fall away like a curtain, and she saw his human form. He was one of the most beautiful humans she had ever seen, either man or woman, with thick, shiny black hair, smooth golden skin, dark and curious eyes, and a rosy smile naturally curved into a smile. His legs were whole, and his stance was straight and steady.

"Why did you hide this form of yourself?" she asked.

"It wasn't my intention; I only returned to this form last night. As I was trying to explain last evening, the gods healed and restored me, perhaps as a reward for trying to live as a good man, or for attempting to be a good husband to you these past few years. Who can say?" He lowered his eyes. "I confess: I toyed with you

138

to test your reaction to this new shape, so you were right to admonish me. But you would not waver, and you looked at me last night with such suspicion and revulsion that I wanted to give your husband back to you."

"You would go on pretending to be crippled and scarred, for my sake?"

He shrugged. "It's never mattered to me how I'm seen outside of these walls, but within my own home, I expect your acceptance, even if it is coupled with pity. If I must wear a mask for your comfort, then it's a small price."

He seemed sincere, but that did little to set her mind at ease. It unnerved her to see him in another guise, and she focused her attention on preparing their morning tea. "If this is your human face, what does my comfort matter to you? As a man, you can find affection elsewhere, and even bring home a second wife to please you, if you want."

"That's not what I want," he said sternly. "I chose you for a wife, and you accepted me as your husband, despite my homeliness. You've only ever given me your true self, and I don't have to question your feelings or meanings—I could never find another like you." Her continued coolness seemed to confound him. "Would you really prefer the crippled version of me?"

"You called yourself homely, but I never did," she said. "You were never plain or ugly to me, in any of your forms. I have no preference, either, but it'll take time to adjust to this new shape of yours. I will do my best, but if you bring home another to satisfy your needs, I'll understand."

"I wouldn't disrespect you like that," he said solemnly, holding his hand out to her. "Come. I am still the man you married, my sweet girl."

She held out his cup of tea to him and felt his familiar warmth beneath his old callouses, as his fingers brushed against hers. "You've always been a good man, so why did the gods choose to change you now?"

"I've always strived to be good to you, little *huli*, but I wasn't always a benevolent spirit," he said, taking a small sip. "For thousands of years, I grew my power by challenging the gods, and exploiting the vices of men, to drive them to kill and enslave one another. In time, as I saw the ugliness that I exposed in others emerging in me, I renounced my old ways and changed my guise to live on the fringes. I've tried to live peacefully in the centuries since then, with mixed results," he shrugged. "The gods let me keep my humble figure, until last night, and now I can't change back to it without using a mask."

"Does this mean the gods have finally forgiven you for your past sins?" she asked, taking her own cup in hand.

"This is almost a more poetic punishment for me," he laughed, setting down his tea. "They restored the human form that I had enjoyed for so long, to show me its worthlessness for keeping what matters to me now. This is a test for us, to see whether I have changed my ways sufficiently to deserve your devotion, and for you to decide whether you wish to stay, knowing my history."

"Why should the gods care about our marriage? I am a small, insignificant fox spirit, a tiny part of your extensive lifetime of experiences."

"Because you are not insignificant to me," he smiled. "I'll take whatever form you prefer, even keep the mask on, if it makes you happier."

"I don't want illusions or secrets between us, so stay as you are, and I'll get used to it. There is enough artifice in our lives, that we should be honest with each other." She kept her hold on her tea cup and held it close, despite its searing heat. It seemed easier to use the burning ceramic cup as a prop, to keep him at a distance. He was more handsome with his new face, but he was a stranger to her.

"In the interest of honesty, then, dear wife," he said wryly, "tell me why you've never kissed me, in all the years that we've been together."

"You've never tried to kiss me, either," she returned. "You have your rights, as my husband."

"Because you've never wanted me," he said, stepping towards her. "I have your devotion, but not your desire."

"I can't give you what I don't have," she said, finally setting down her scalding tea.

"You felt it, once," he said, swiftly taking her hands in his. "Before you became my wife, you used to watch the humans from a distance. You liked Isaac and followed him sometimes, and you would become jealous when he smiled or flirted with another girl. That was clear and unabashed desire that you felt."

Jin Mudan reddened with embarrassment at recalling her youthful folly. "I was silly and irrational."

"Says the female who would rather burn her fingers than touch her husband who cherishes her," he chuckled, pressing his cool lips to her smarting fingertips. "Silly as it was, wasn't it also exhilarating and glorious to have that fire in your core, to feel that sweet madness overwhelming your sense of reason?"

"It was stupid and futile," she said, recalling the pain of being ignored and ultimately, being spurned.

"It's inescapable," he said, laying her scalded fingertips against the cooler skin of his cheek. "For others, anyway. Maybe you have somehow mastered the ability to banish desire from your emotions, but if that's true, you're missing out on one of the best parts of mortal life," he said laughingly.

He dropped her hands and returned to his tea. "Of course, it could also just be me. You're still young and don't need to be saddled with a relic like me. If you find

141

another who reawakens your senses, then be honest with me, and go with my blessings."

Closing her eyes, sensing his warmth and calm energy, she realized her feelings towards him hadn't changed, regardless of his appearance. He was still her *lin*, her Xing, endlessly selfless and patient, who put her feelings and needs before his own. "You would give me up, if I asked you to?"

"With reservations," he said, sipping his tea, as he finally took a seat at the kitchen table. "But if you can't be happy here, your presence would just be a constant reminder of my failure as a husband."

"You've always been generous with me, so any failure or lack would be mine, not yours." She circled around the back of his seat and touched the tight, knotted muscles in his neck and shoulders. Xing always had a strong back and shoulders, owed to the physically taxing nature of his labor, and the feel of the hard contours of his musculature reminded her that this was still her husband. Instinctively, she deepened her strokes to soothe and relieve the tension in his muscles, as she sometimes did after his more arduous days. It was easier to touch him without having to look at his new face.

"If you were to leave me, I would miss your touch," he said quietly, relaxing under her hands.

"I won't leave you," she vowed, continuing her massage. Administering the therapeutic touch relaxed her, as much as it soothed him, as she knew he would never misconstrue her attention or force any additional touching without her consent. "I know my good fortune, and if the gods were trying to test my loyalty, they have failed."

He laughed and cupped his hands over hers. "For now, perhaps, but the gods and spirits of the universe are always watching for the next opportunity to try us." He leaned his head to feel the back of her hand on his healing cheek. "We will puzzle through the next trial, when it comes, but for today, we are safe."

Chapter 9

Present Day

Jonah picked up his head from the cloud-white pillow, untangling himself from the layers of pristinely crisp bedsheets, as he spied his discarded clothes at the foot of his king-sized bed and on the back of the armchair next to his picture window.

From his oversized bed, he also spotted the laden, bagged hangers he had tossed carelessly over his messenger bag, as he recalled staggering into his hotel room around midnight—almost three o'clock in the morning back in New York and Boston. He had been famished, but he was more exhausted than he was hungry, and he could ignore his hunger more easily than he could delay his need to sleep. He had washed his face and brushed his teeth in the dark before stripping off his stale clothes and tumbling into bed.

He glanced at the alarm clock and confirmed on his charging phone that it was almost six o'clock, but his body was still on East Coast time, so he felt as though he had overslept, nearly to the point of feeling a headache coming on. The thought of "sleeping in" any longer almost made him nauseous, so he tossed the covers aside and went to shower and shave.

By the time Jonah finished his regimen, he had planned out his day, with the hope that *maybe* he would have time after the completion of his assignment to contact Mina. Maybe it was better to call Adam first, to test the waters and warm up before talking to Mina.

Fucking coward, he berated himself. *If you can't even have a conversation with Mina, you have no business marrying her. You're on her parents' home turf now, so straighten up!*

Slipping his new clothes over his refreshed, bare skin, he did feel like a new man. The thin fabric of his cream-white dress shirt slid on weightlessly, as did the dark charcoal jacket and trousers. Metzger had tailored everything to fit exactly and had laughed when Jonah had commented about how the unforgiving cut would show every extra pound he gained. Metzger had reiterated that it was *his* suit, and that it was more forgiving than Jonah realized—whatever the hell *that* meant.

Even the soft underlayers felt weightless and invisible, as though he wasn't wearing anything at all. As Jonah looked at himself in the mirror, he admitted that the new wardrobe imparted a kind of gravitas and structure that he had been missing with his old clothes. Especially with his overgrown scruff trimmed to a stubble and cleaned up along his jawline, he didn't look like a grad student living in his parents' basement anymore. He looked and felt like a grown-ass man.

He brushed his fingers through his overgrown black hair, some of which covered his ears now and seemed to show a few more strands of silver since he last looked. A trip to the barber would have to wait until after he finished his assignment.

As he collected his wallet, his room key, his phone and the notecard with his assignment details, Jonah answered the unexpected ring of the room phone without a thought. "Yes?"

A bright, sunny young man's voice chirped: "Good morning, Mister Gideon. Your 6:30 wake-up call, as requested?"

145

"Okay, thanks." Jonah vaguely remembered accepting the offer during check-in for a wake-up call, but the entire exchange, as well as the late-night walk from Fournier's to the hotel, was a blurry recollection. It didn't matter, anyway, since he was wide awake already. He tucked away his wallet and room key but checked his phone.

He had a text message from Aciré, alerting him that he would likely be contacted by Mina's parents, or one of their local contacts. A second message came from Cindy, stating cryptically that she had "told Mina everything."

Upon opening the door to his suite, Jonah momentarily forgot about his messages, as he stared down at the morning paper on his doorstep. There, alongside one of the front-page headlines, was a headshot of Austin Fang, the young Chinese-American whose soul Jonah had been sent to San Francisco to reap.

The name, age and photograph exactly matched the details that had appeared on Jonah's card before they changed during his appointment at Fournier's. The news article reported an "incident" at a nightclub where Fang was headquartered as the suspected leader of a local gang, and the sudden deaths of Fang and his henchmen were being investigated as an incident of probable gang violence.

I guess that explains why my services were no longer required for this one, Jonah remarked, adding his mostly-untouched newspaper to the neat stack in the hotel lobby, as he exited the elevator. He crossed the spacious, gilded lobby with a fresh eye, appreciating the bright, sumptuous environs better, now that he was better rested.

While he still had a free moment, he called Cindy to get a better understanding of her message.

"Good morning, handsome," she greeted. "How's San Francisco?"

"Not sure yet. So far, I've only seen it after dark," he replied. "You talked to Mina yesterday?"

"Yes, and she was happy to hear that you're alive, but I also had to tell her about Millie passing away, and your role in it," she said. "Maybe I was overstepping on that last part, but Mina has to find out sooner or later that you're a reaper."

"No, that's fine," Jonah said, a little relieved. "I wasn't sure how I would broach that topic with her, so you did me a favor."

"I also told her that you were heading to California," Cindy said. "Again, maybe I was premature in telling her, since you didn't expressly tell me that you planned to see her, but San Francisco's not a big city, so I didn't want her to faint dead away if she saw you on the street." She added, a little hesitantly: "Plus, her parents have gotten a briefing from their advisors about your situation and whereabouts, so she deserves to know what I know."

Jonah looked over to the concierge desk, where an elegant woman in a slender, blue sheath dress, carrying a designer handbag, was speaking with the lobby clerk. Her sleek black hair reminded him of Selina Xing's neat style, except that this woman's hair was longer, like a black silk veil. Before he could look away, the woman turned and stared directly at him.

"One last thing," Cindy said. "Mina and Adam's parents may want a private word with you, so you may be contacted."

"So I've heard," Jonah said, as the beautiful young Asian woman came directly towards him. "Thanks for the warning, Cin."

"Is everything okay there? You sound a little distracted."

"Kind of early to tell," Jonah said. "I'll talk to you later."

As he disconnected with Cindy, he studied the woman out of the corner of his eye. She was stunning: flawless skin and hair, dark almond eyes and trim hourglass figure. She was almost mannequin-like in her perfection, which made Jonah think of Mina's unpretentious, messy, uninhibited spontaneity, by contrast.

"Mister Gideon?" the young woman greeted.

"I am, for now," he said evenly.

"My name is Yumi Taira, and I work for the Xing family," she said, pulling a folded, wax-sealed note card from her handbag. "I have a message from Selina Xing," she said, passing the unmarked note to Jonah with both hands.

"Thank you," Jonah said, accepting the note with both hands and a nod, the way it had been presented, and he noticed that the young woman stood expectantly. "Is Missus Xing waiting for an immediate reply?"

"If you have one ready, certainly," she replied with an enigmatic smile.

Jonah opened the wax seal and scanned the note quickly. It was perfunctory but polite, written in a compact cursive style that Jonah recognized from Selina's condolence card message to his aunt and uncle for his cousin Malcolm's funeral.

Jonah refolded the note and mentally restructured his schedule for the day; Selina Xing was one of the last people on earth that he wanted to keep waiting on him, and he was more willing to suffer the ire of devils and angels than risk displeasing Mina's mother.

"Please let Missus Xing know that I am honored and humbled, and I accept."

Selina sipped her tea, musing about the early years of her marriage to the one known nowadays as "Lin Xing." She still called him "Xing" sometimes, in private, but most days, she didn't need to call him by name at all. If he was nearby, he seemed to just know when she wanted his attention or presence.

They had made their home half a world away from where they had started, but still, some days it felt as though they hadn't gone far enough. She still felt watched, and she sometimes looked over her shoulder for the one that she knew still hunted them. Lately, she had felt the presence of their own enemy more distinctly, and she hoped that Adam and Mina would be safely away, back to New York, before the inevitable confrontation.

She and Lin loved their children, but the family was always more exposed when they were all together. Now that Mina and Adam were older, with their own lives and their own allies and enemies, it was more difficult to keep them shielded.

If Lin had only spoken with Selina before going to confront Fang, she would've advised him against taking Mina. As Mina's father, he was given to extreme measures to protect her, risking his own exposure in the process. Even Mina had only an inkling of what Lin had planned for Malcolm's punishment when he learned of their son-in-law's abusive tendencies, before Selina convinced Lin to trust their daughter's ability and wisdom. In the end, Lin had feigned ignorance of the matter, to let Mina free herself of the situation, but Lin swore never to be so passive again regarding their children's welfare.

Selina stayed apprised and actively engaged in Adam and Mina's lives, as well, but she was more subtle in her involvements and machinations. It made for fewer confrontations like as the pre-dinner discussion that Mina and Adam initiated the night before with their father. Despite their outward consternation about his secrecy and ruthlessness, their children understood their father's logic and intentions, even if they didn't agree with them, and by the time that dinner was ready, the tensions had eased.

Still, Selina preferred to avoid heated discussions with her children, especially with Mina. She still recalled holding Mina as a fussy baby, pacing the nursery in the middle of the night to soothe her back to sleep, for the first year of Mina's infancy. As Mina grew older, she became less vocal about her discomforts and concerns, and Selina took extra care to preserve the connection and open communication they had established, as it was a kind of trust that she never had with her own mother.

Selina looked down at her phone and saw Yumi Taira's number appear. "*Moshi-Moshi*," she greeted.

"*Ohayou gozaimasu*," Yumi replied, more formally, and Selina pictured her bowing on her end of the line. "The message has been delivered and accepted, *Xing-sama*."

"Thank you," Selina said, relieved that Yumi was able to contact Jonah so soon; Bullfinch had relayed the information about Jonah's hotel in an overnight text, but didn't have much information to share about Jonah's agenda for the day. "What were your impressions of Mister Gideon?"

"He is very handsome," Yumi answered readily. "He was respectful and polite. I didn't test him, as he doesn't seem to be the opportunistic type and showed no interest in me. He was unassuming, but he is an attractive man."

Selina smiled, pleased that Mina's instincts in choosing Jonah were validated by Yumi's discerning eye. Selina would need to make the final determination in person, but so far, Jonah seemed unaltered by his recent life changes, at least superficially. "And the other task?"

"Until half an hour before noon, your schedule for this morning has been leaked, as you requested," Yumi said, more hesitantly. "Since I've taken the day off, I would still feel better accompanying you—"

"I will be fine by myself," Selina said tersely. "It is more important to me that your skills and time are used to protect my family, so I am not distracted with worrying about them. Is that clear?"

"*Hai, Xing-sama,*" Yumi replied. "I understand."

"I trust you to keep your focus," Selina said. "Mina gets easily distracted and sidetracked, nowadays more than usual."

"I will," Yumi said solemnly. "I will defend them with honor, to my last breath."

Spoken like a true samurai, Selina noted. Despite her relative youth, Yumi embodied the stalwart devotion of the warriors descended from the venerated Taira clan, and Selina had mentored her through her transition to adulthood without any expectation of servitude, but Yumi had pledged herself to serve the family, unconditionally.

"Text me around noon with a status, Yumi," Selina directed. "You shouldn't need me before then." It was a more polite way of saying: *don't disturb me until noon*.

"*Hai,*" Yumi replied. "Good luck, Ma'am."

"Thank you," Selina said and disconnected, as Lin came to the kitchen. She nudged a mug of green tea towards him, as she did most mornings. "I left a list for Mina for what we need to prepare for Adam today," she said. "And Yumi confirmed a meeting for me at noon, with Jonah Gideon."

"You've had a busy morning, my love," Lin said, sipping his tea. "It's not even half past seven."

"I needed to act quickly, before Jonah is pulled too deeply into his duties," Selina said. "And before Mina has an opportunity to see him in person; her judgment may be clouded, and she may overlook aspects of him that she shouldn't."

151

"Bullfinch and Hart have both signed off on him," Lin reminded. "As well as Mina's fae friend."

"And you? " Selina asked.

Lin raised his eyebrow. "I haven't seen Jonah in years, and you saw him just last week. It's hardly a fair comparison."

Selina smiled, recalling Lin's disclosure to the children of what he knew, from the circumstances of Jonah's resurrection to what had unfolded to lead him to the deathbed of Mina's elderly tenant. "And yet you spoke about him with a civil tongue, despite not knowing him."

"He gave his life for our son, and postponed his afterlife for our daughter. That is all I need to know about his character." He took another sip of his tea and mumbled, "Plus, I think I stole his target by accident."

Selina set down her cup. "You *what*?"

"By accident," Lin repeated. "I think Fang was supposed to be his. Bullfinch texted me this morning that Jonah's assignment details updated, which means that his assigned soul was already claimed."

"That could be a coincidence," Selina said.

Lin shook his head. "When Mina and I went to see Fang yesterday, I saw the dark halo around him, so I could tell that he was marked by Lucifer and his ilk. I thought about leaving him alone, and letting the devils take him, but I couldn't let Fang's behavior towards Mina go unanswered," he sniffed. "Bullfinch texted me last night that the devil knew of my intervention, but he will overlook it, given our mutual courtesy. I think Lucifer's amused, actually, that Fang ended up being a suicide; the soul is all but his, now."

"You know Lucifer watches Mina closely," Selina cautioned. "He's always been protective of her."

"Yes, my love," Lin smiled. "It's one of the reasons that Lucifer and I tolerate one another so well."

"He's still a devil, and not to be trusted," she warned.

"And I'm still the same *lin* you took for a husband," he said earnestly. "I keep this form for you, and to help keep our children safe, but I'm still pledged to the old gods and my brethren of our ancestral home. If I let a conniving devil like Lucifer get the upper hand on me, I would become a laughingstock for the next century."

Adam fought the laughter bubbling in his throat at Mina's antics in the kitchen, as she was making eggs for the two of them. His baby sister zipped back and forth with a hunk of sourdough toast in her mouth, looking like an overcaffeinated chipmunk sporting a black ponytail extension.

They had the run of the house, as their parents had already left for their morning obligations: their father to the office, and their mother to the local soup kitchen for her weekly volunteer visit. Their mother had texted them as a form of wake-up call, and to let them know that her schedule would keep her out for most of the day, but they could text her after noon if there was anything urgent.

Mina looked refreshed and alert, given how little sleep they both had after their late-night card game. At the moment, she looked at him and mumbled through her toast, gesturing at the melting butter in the pan.

"Just two, thanks," he said, slicing extra pieces of bread from the crusty, tangy loaf of sourdough, as he dialed Xani's number and put his phone on speaker.

Xani answered on the third ring, with a whispered: "Hello? Adam?"

"Why are we whispering?" he replied in a mock hush, hearing what sounded like choral music in the background.

"I'm in church. Hold on, let me head back to the narthex," she replied, as the choir and music became quieter, but still discernible. "I was lighting candles and saying a rosary for you and your family."

"Thanks, Xani," Adam smiled. He wasn't a believer like she was, but he appreciated her genuine concern and sentiment. "Is everything okay at home?"

"Yeah," she answered, without much enthusiasm. "It's quiet without you guys, and we're still dealing with Millie's passing." She paused. "Cindy told Mina everything, right?"

Mina nodded, as she gently stirred the eggs in the pan to a custardy consistency, per Adam's preference.

"She's here, and I have you on speaker. I guess I should've mentioned that first," Adam said.

"We're all sorry about the secrecy around Jonah's return," Xani said. "He's harder to read, and Cindy still thinks there's something else at work with him, but…well, you'll probably know when you see him, better than we can. How are you guys doing?"

Adam answered, as Mina focused on turning his eggs onto a plate for him. "I'm okay. My brain feels a little more intact, with our parents' help. They seem to know what they're doing," he said. "Our mom made blood cake soup for us," he said, then looked at Mina's grimace and laughed. "Okay, mostly for me."

"That sounds…" Xani said. "It must be tastier than it sounds."

"It's *exactly* like it sounds," Mina called out. "Little cubes of coagulated blood, they have a weird squeaky texture against your teeth, and it tastes like when you swallow a clot after a bloody nose. Thankfully, Mom uses a load of ginger, garlic and scallions in the broth to mute the flavor."

At Xani's disgusted noise through the phone, Adam laughed. Hopefully, if their relationship continued to progress, Selina wouldn't decide to make blood cake for dinner, otherwise Xani would feel obligated to try it, despite her own aversion.

"Whatever it takes to get better, I guess," Xani said. "Are you coming back soon?"

Adam exchanged an uncertain glance with Mina. "That's the plan. We don't have a date yet."

"That's okay," Xani said brightly. "I just miss you, that's all."

During a brief lull, Adam heard the church choir harmonizing the melody for the hymn "Hosea," and while he couldn't discern the words over the music, Adam recalled the sentiment and refrain of the song, of the faithful Hosea pleading to his adulterous Gomer to "come back to me." It was considered a symbolic hymn, with Hosea representing God, and Gomer an analog for His wayward worshippers, but Adam couldn't help hearing something of Xani's own voice in the lyrics, entreating him to return.

"I miss you, too," Adam said quietly, picturing Xani's beguiling jade-green eyes and smile in his head. "I'll be home, as soon as I can."

Jonah visited the address listed for his assignment, observing it from across the street, and blending easily into the affluent, fashionable crowd that lived in the Russian Hill neighborhood. Several minutes ticked by without any activity or sign of occupancy coming from the building, and Jonah was considering a return visit, after his noon meeting with Selina, when he finally saw his target emerge from the building.

Jonah was struck immediately by the man's shifty, stern bearing, as he kept his head low while darting his eyes around furtively. He was slender with short graying hair, and he looked like any of the middle-aged, white-collar professionals that filled the streets at morning rush hour, except that he eschewed the typical designer tie and suit for more comfortable jeans and a sports jacket, and carried a large black duffle bag instead of a briefcase or laptop bag.

Following his target from half a block away, Jonah expected him to hop a bus or hail a cab, but ended up trailing him on foot eastward to Washington Square, across from Saints Peter and Paul Church, where the peaceful, quiet stillness and wide-open doors indicated that its daily 9AM Mass service had long since concluded, and that the church was open to visitors and tourists.

To avoid losing his target in the park crowd, Jonah gradually closed the distance between them, but his proximity revealed his position, and the man looked at him directly, before he ducked between two of the buildings across the street from the park. Any chance of surprise gone, Jonah followed him into the alley anyway, preparing himself for a confrontation.

What Jonah was not prepared for, was a gut shot that struck him squarely in the liver, and he reeled back for a second, clutching his side instinctively. It took a couple of additional seconds for Jonah to realize that he wasn't bleeding into his hand, and he heard a muttered "What the fuck" from the other end of the alley.

Jonah straightened and felt another bullet slap into his shoulder, a blow that should have broken his clavicle, but Jonah glanced over and saw the bullet embedded in the smooth fabric of his suit jacket like a decorative stud. He lifted his hand from his side and noticed the first slug flattened against the crisp cream-white fabric of his shirt.

"Who the fuck are you? Why are you following me?" the man demanded.

"William Grant," Jonah called, picking the slugs off his clothing like bits of lint, feeling only a little soreness from the gun shots. He took a deep breath, to make sure he was as intact as he felt. "My name is Jonah Gideon, and I've been sent for you. I'm here for your soul."

Instead of scoffing at Jonah's claim, or futilely firing his gun again in defiance or panic, Grant calmly lowered his gun and squared his shoulders. "You're a reaper, like me?"

Jonah recognized the expert tailoring on Grant's jacket for the first time, and noticed the open duffle at his feet, filled with an assortment of firearms weapons and accessories. "I'm a reaper, but not quite like you."

Grant followed Jonah's line of sight and chuckled. "Oh, you're one of *those*. I suppose I'm lucky that a reaper like you was assigned to me, instead of someone more like myself." He uncocked his gun and dropped it back into the duffle, letting it clatter noisily against the other weapons. "You're wearing a Metzger suit, though, so our keepers must expect you to be shot at."

Jonah had expected more of a fight, given that Grant seemed healthy and strong. He remained on his guard, in case his target tried to get the upper hand or slip away, but Grant seemed impassive. even resigned.

"Let's get this over with, then," Grant said. "I'm sure you have other things you'd rather do."

"You're not going to argue or fight me on this?" Jonah asked, taking a tentative step closer.

Grant stooped briefly to zip the duffle bag closed, then stood with his hands held out to his sides, with a peaceful, placid expression. "There's no point in trying to cheat or outrun the likes of us, Mister Gideon. When it's time, it's time. You would find me again, eventually, and I'm tired of running."

Jonah wasn't expecting so little resistance, Grant's initial greeting notwithstanding. "Do you need a moment, to make your peace or say any final prayers?"

"No, I was ready to leave this world long ago, and I've been looking forward to this day for a long time." Grant reached into his pocket and pulled out a blank ivory-hued note card, similar to what Jonah carried to detail his assignments. Grant seemed bemused, turning the card around in his hand, then sighed with relief. "It's blank."

"Was that your last assignment?" Jonah asked, standing at an arm's distance from William Grant.

"It was, but I guess it's been reassigned, since I've been released," he said, holding the dog-eared card out to Jonah. "It's a shame, I was actually looking forward to taking out the bastard, but it's out of my hands, now. Maybe you can give this back to our keepers for me, when you see them next."

Jonah took the notecard and tucked it in his jacket pocket without looking. "Sure."

"Hey, do you want equipment? I won't need it, where I'm going," Grant asked, tapping the duffle with his foot. "I have some cash in my wallet, too, that I have no use for."

"I'll pass on the hardware, thanks." Jonah glanced at the bag and wondered if he would ever need to be as heavily armed as Grant. "I don't need your money, but I can drop it in the church donation box for you."

"Why not? One last charitable act," Grant smiled, holding out a wad of bills.

As the money changed hands, Grant stepped towards the wall and leaned heavily against it, sinking down to sit with his back propped against the painted brick.

Jonah shoved the bills in his jacket pocket with Grant's card and crouched down, reaching out to catch him, in case he started to topple. "Shit, I'm sorry," he said. "I didn't realize it would happen so fast. I don't want you to die in an alley."

Grant laughed weakly. "Kid, I just tried to shoot you a minute ago and would've been fine watching you bleed out. Why do you care how I spend my last minutes?"

"Maybe because I see my future in you. I'm just starting out my sentence, while you're at the end of yours." He offered his hand to Grant.

"Relax, we don't all end this way," Grant said, looking at Jonah's hand. "Just like we don't all start out the same way. I pledged my soul, as I lay dying, because I wanted vengeance against the man who murdered my family and shot me. I didn't realize that I'd spend forty years paying off the devil's favor." He took Jonah's hand, finally, and seemed grateful for the contact.

"Did you ever get your vengeance?" Jonah asked.

"He was assigned to me, eventually," he said, "but I had taken so many other lives by that point, that his death had no meaning for me anymore. I barely recalled his face. I was tired of reaping, and I just wanted to rest."

Grant closed his eyes, and his features stiffened and paled, almost instantaneously. The flesh that had once housed William Grant's soul now looked dull and flat, like a wax figure. Jonah felt a flutter of energy pass from Grant's hand into his, before the energy started dissipating into the air.

Thanks for coming, kid, and I'm sorry I tried to kill you. Good luck.

"You, too," Jonah said, spotting a cloudiness out of the corner of his eye. Grant's pale, ephemeral shape nodded and passed into the brick wall next to Jonah, and the energy dwindled and faded.

At the sounds of bicycle bells and children playing in the park across the street, Jonah was reminded that he was in a public alley with a dead man and should probably leave before he was spotted.

He exited the alleyway quickly and darted across the street, to cut through Washington Square Park to deposit Grant's final donation to Saints Peter and Paul Church. As he pulled out his phone to check the time, he was surprised that his assignment card was gone from the pocket. "Let me guess," he muttered to himself, as he reached into his jacket pocket and found Grant's card.

The dog-eared card had been blank when it changed hands, but now, Jonah saw the details written clearly. In reaping Grant's soul, he had inherited the other reaper's last assignment.

His next target was still in San Francisco, with a current location not too far from where he presently was, which Jonah had guessed from Grant's location. The target's date of birth was curious, as it listed "1810" as the year, and there were few other details apart from name, sex, hair and eye color, but Jonah would have to leave his research for later.

At the sound of a muffled cough from one of the shrines inside the church, Jonah remembered that he was in a sacred space, and why he was there. Stepping to the side, out of the path of other visitors, he pulled William Grant's wad of cash from his pocket and crammed the dead man's bills into the church's donation box by the door. Jonah didn't stop to count the money, but glancing at the denominations, it seemed like a few hundred dollars.

Jonah ignored the gawking stares of the people nearby and exited the church with a hasty, automatic sign of the cross. The time had somehow gotten away from him, and now he had less than half an hour to make it across town to keep his noon appointment with Selina Xing.

Mina glanced at her parents' kitchen calendar and was surprised that it was after eleven on Wednesday, already. She and Adam had arrived from New York late Monday night, but the last day and a half had gone by quickly, between catching up with old acquaintances and spending time with their parents. Now, the siblings were sharing a cup of tea in the kitchen, looking at the

160

calendar together and deliberating on when they wanted to head back.

She had checked her phone messages and hadn't heard anything urgent or pressing that required her to rush back to New York, while Adam had a reminder to call back Stanislav Sobol at Global Pacific to either counter or reject the job offer that their father had brokered, but he could do that from California.

"Friday morning?" Adam suggested. "That gives us about two days to finish up here."

"Saturday?" Mina countered. "Or, do you want to get back to Xani sooner?"

"A day won't make much of a difference," he said. "I'd rather make sure that I'm fixed up, as much as I can be. It wouldn't be fair to her, for me to go back still broken and glitchy."

Mina could understand Adam's perspective, but she also knew how Xani thought. "She doesn't expect perfection. If she did, she wouldn't have settled for you."

"You're hilarious," he deadpanned.

"She'd rather have glitchy you than not at all, is all I'm saying. You can think about it while I'm out," she said, checking her jeans pocket to make sure she still had her mother's list.

"Where are you going?" he asked.

"Mom wants me to go down to Grant Avenue to pick up some ingredients from an apothecary. I think she's planning on making you some tea tonight."

Adam shuddered. "Earthworm or starfish on the list?"

"Maybe," she said coyly, as the doorbell chimed. "That would be Yumi. Mom wants her to come with me," she said, noting Adam's agitated twitch. "You got your chastity belt on?"

"Funny. You're on a roll today," Adam glowered, taking a sip of his tea.

161

"You're just cranky because you have a headache, *ge-ge*," she teased, slapping his arm gently as she passed by him on the way to the foyer. "Take a couple of pills, and go back to sleep. Your eyes are still blood-shot."

Yumi bowed her head with a small smile to greet Mina at the door. Effortlessly pretty, Yumi wore faded, pencil-slim jeans and a light, pearl-pink sweater that matched her manicured nails exactly. "Good morning. Your mother asked me to accompany you on your errands today, to make sure you don't get sidetracked?" Yumi asked uncertainly. "Her words, not mine."

"That sounds like my mom," Mina nodded. Knowing that Yumi had was probably twice her age—at least old enough to be able to switch between fox and human forms—yet still showing her such deference, was a little discomfiting. She reminded herself of her mother's assurance the morning before, that she had no reason to resent or envy Yumi's presence. "I appreciate it. You probably know where my mom shops, better than I do."

"I have some ideas," Yumi said diffidently. "Oh, there's a chance of showers this afternoon, if you want to bring an umbrella," she suggested.

Mina laughed. "Now, I know my mom didn't say that. She knows I haven't used one in years."

Yumi sighed. "Of course, you don't wear makeup. It must be liberating not to need them."

"I'm just lazy. I don't have the discipline to look as beautiful as you do, day after day," Mina shrugged, grabbing her denim jacket off the coat rack. "Hey, text me if you go out!" she shouted to Adam in the kitchen, before she shut the door behind herself and skipped down the step after Yumi.

"I didn't realize Adam was still home. Is he avoiding me?" she asked, sounding disappointed. "I've offended him with my forwardness."

"Not offended," Mina half-smiled. "However, he's trying to be a good boyfriend, and unfortunately, a picture of the two of you at the airport the other night was sent to Xani."

Yumi looked at her askance but kept pace. "If that happened, it wasn't by my design, but I'm sorry if she was hurt or disrespected. I presume that she is a friend of yours?"

"She was my friend before she and Adam became involved," Mina said. "I know you're loyal to my parents, and you wouldn't do anything that would dishonor or betray them, but Adam isn't the type to take liberties, no matter how tempted he is."

Yumi smiled. "He is an honorable and faithful man, much like your father."

Mina gave her a sideways glance. "Did you try to…"

"I tried to seduce your father, once, and I failed, miserably," she said without chagrin. "I would've been a fool not to try—he's a powerful, charismatic and handsome *lin*," Yumi said, shooting a glance around to ensure that no one was following or listening. "But for all their might and otherworldly nature, your parents are deeply devoted to each other, and in all the years I've known them, I've never known either of them to stray."

Mina was relieved and pleased to hear a third-party confirmation of her parents' mutual fidelity. "My mother didn't send you away, even after your attempt to steal my father?"

Yumi shook her head, playing absently with the jade fox pendant that dangled around her neck. "I was young and stupid, then, still getting used to my human form and learning my preferences and limitations, so your mother knew I wasn't any real threat, especially when I offered myself to her, too."

Mina joined Yumi in her laughter. "Now, I think I'm insulted that you haven't tried anything yet with me."

"I'd considered it, but I've since met your Jonah Gideon," Yumi simpered. "If he's your type, I don't think I have anything to offer that you would like better."

"You spoke to Jonah? Here, in San Francisco?" Mina slowed in her step, as they turned east onto Broadway towards the Pacific Heights area. The streets teemed with all types of spirits from across all denominations and eras, and Mina was careful not to make eye contact or draw unwanted attention from anything malicious or violent.

Yumi nodded, pausing in her step to let a pale, white-robed phantom with long, stringy black hair cross in front of them, moving south towards Japantown. "Briefly, by your mother's directive."

Before Mina could ask for details, the ghost pivoted sharply and peered at the women from beneath the fall of its black hair, speaking rapidly in shallow whispers. Yumi bowed solemnly and whispered a brief reply to the spirit, who seemed satisfied with her response and bowed in turn, floating on the air to resume her path.

"My Edo dialect is a little rusty," Mina said, staring after the willowy, delicate-looking *yurei*. "What did she want?"

"Her elderly husband is near death, so she's waiting to greet him when he passes, but she would like a blessing for him first, to ease his suffering," Yumi said. "I promised her that I would stop at the Shinto shrine and make an offering on her behalf before the next new moon."

"But you don't know her, personally," Mina said, guessing by the polite, perfunctory exchange.

Yumi shook her head. "You must have similar experiences, of *yurei* and *yokai* coming to you for help.

With your sensitivity to other realms, you can notice them all around you, can't you?"

"New Yorkers learn to tune out things and people coming into our personal space," Mina said, recalling the density of the Manhattan crowds, especially during the rush hours. "Word seems to get around about how to contact me, so I don't get approached randomly on the street very often."

"It's difficult for me to say 'no' to a soul in need," Yumi said. "I recall feeling that kind of despair before your mother became my mentor and guardian."

"Setting boundaries is less about empathy, and more about not spreading yourself too thinly," Mina said gently. "I would do my clients a disservice, or worsen their situations, if my attention was diverted or split. I know that's not exactly the same as the relationship between you and my parents, but…"

Yumi shook her head with a smile. "Your parents were beyond generous with me, and I'll be forever indebted to them for their charity, but your mother was always very clear about her expectations and rules for me. As *kitsune…huli jing*, a hierarchy must be respected for harmony to follow."

"Yeah, that sounds like my mom," Mina said lightly, checking her mother's to-do list for the number of the Chinatown address. "You're not obliged to stay with us, if you find another opportunity."

"True, but fealty aside, I'm content in your parents' service," Yumi said, turning at the corner to lead the way without Mina telling her the address. "They are fair, discreet and honorable, and they've instilled those values in you and Adam."

"We have responsibilities to each other, and to the people around us," Mina said. "Any carelessness by one of us would threaten us all."

165

"That sounds like your mother *and* father," Yumi remarked, stopping in front of an herbal medicine shop's open storefront.

Even before she caught up with Yumi in front of the store, Mina caught the pungent, heady aromas of various animal and plant materials. Across the width of the shop, and as deep as she could see, bins, jars and bags displayed and teemed with all types of organic components, many marked only by a scrawl of Chinese script.

Yumi gestured for Mina to enter the shop first. "This is your mother's usual shop, where she gets most of her dried ingredients."

Mina looked up at the red and gold signage above the awning to confirm the name and street address. "Okay, let's go get some dried earthworms."

Chapter 10

Xani warmed her hands on her cup of Irish coffee before she took a sip, peering over the top of her laptop at the pre-rush hour and post-matinee customers starting to file into the Red Lotus. Some of them were there for a quick bite and drink before heading home after a day in the city, while others were just arriving for the start of their evenings on the town.

Cindy was as captivating and charming with the patrons as always, but Xani noticed a slight dimness in her dark eyes that she only recognized from the years they spent together as roommates and partners. Xani had an idea about the reason for Cindy's melancholy and waved her over.

Cindy came from around the counter and leaned against Xani's banquette. "You need something, sweetie?"

"Take a break, Cin," Xani said, patting the seat next to her. "You've been on your feet since I arrived, and Micah says you barely eaten anything today."

Cindy slid into the booth with a shrug. "I just haven't been hungry."

"Did Morgan talk to you?" Xani asked. "He's been out on calls for most of the day and dodging me at the office, too."

Cindy shook her head. "Morgan texted me that he wants to talk, after closing. That's not good, is it?"

Xani squeezed Cindy's hand. "He's been running around a lot, between work and helping Millie's daughter and granddaughter move her things out." In fact, for the past couple of days, Morgan was spending more of his free hours at Millie's apartment than he had at home, but Cindy didn't need to hear that.

"I know the signs, Xani," Cindy said. "I used to be the cheating type, myself, remember?"

"You don't know for sure that he's cheating. Give him a chance to explain himself," Xani said, setting aside her memories of Cindy's past infidelities. "Morgan loves you."

"Yeah, but I never stopped loving you, either, honey," Cindy said wistfully, reminding Xani of their deep connection, even during their most tumultuous times. "Sometimes, love isn't enough reason to stay in a relationship, no matter how hard we try."

Xani hated hearing her own words repeated back to her, and she tried to convince herself that the situation was different: she had broken off their relationship because she no longer felt the same passion that she once shared with Cyril McManus. Cyril had cheated on her, which caused Xani to withdraw, and the cycle repeated until they were both miserable. Once Cyril made the decision to transition, Xani knew it was time to go. That wasn't the same as the relationship between Morgan and Cindy; at least, it didn't have to be.

"It sounds like you're already expecting the worst," Xani said.

"It wouldn't be the worst," Cindy said, nudging Xani's coffee cup towards her, to remind her to drink it before it got cold. "Morgan's a good guy, and I'd like to think that I helped him find his mojo. I'll be fine—I've been dumped before, and I'd rather be alone than keep him from being happy with someone else."

"You deserve to be happy, too," Xani said.

"I don't have to be in a relationship to be happy," Cindy smiled. "I still have family and friends who love and support me." She glanced at Xani. "But if you feel like you have to take Morgan's side, I'll be okay with that, too."

"Fuck, no," Xani said shortly. "If he's really an asshole, I'll call him on it. Being my brother doesn't give him the right to mistreat you."

"It'll be fine," Cindy assured, giving Xani's hand a last squeeze before she slipped out from the booth. "If it doesn't work out, it's not meant to be, and your mother will be relieved, again," she said cheekily.

As Cindy returned to her usual station behind the bar, Xani received an incoming call on her phone. While the number was unidentified, she recognized it as the source of the photograph of Adam in a liplock with the mystery woman at the San Francisco airport from two nights ago. Without hesitation, Xani answered and held the phone to her ear.

"Who is this?"

There was just a second's pause before a gentle man's voice answered, "Someone who cares about you."

It wasn't a voice that Xani recognized, but she wasn't creeped out or put off by it. In fact, she found the voice calming and uplifting, in a surprising way. "It's hard for me to believe or trust someone that I can't see face-to-face."

The man laughed softly. "Yet, that is the basis of your faith, isn't it?"

Xani heard something like an echo of the man's voice in her ears, and she looked around the lounge.

"To your right, Miss Crain," the voice directed, and Xani looked back at the bar, where Cindy was serving a lime-garnished sparkling water to a figure with long dark hair and a tan suit, who was speaking on a phone. The man turned to face Xani directly and bowed his head. "May I join you?"

169

Xani nodded and disconnected, and she watched as the man approached her booth with drink in hand, pulling a chair up to the table to join her, despite the generous dimensions of the red velvet banquettes. He looked vaguely familiar to her, like a face from a dream.

"Why did you send me the photo? How did you even get it?" she asked, before the man even took his seat.

"You deserved to see it, as a woman who values honesty and transparency," he said, taking a sip of his drink before setting it on the table. "As for how I obtained it, well, everything is visible to the All-seeing Lord. A photograph is a frippery to the Almighty."

Xani caught a glint of gold shining on the man's jacket lapel, from a pin with a shofar motif. "I remember you now. You're Gabriel, the herald." She had always thought that she would be awed or inspired, or hear a celestial choir whenever visited by an angel, but she actually felt quite grounded, as though she were admiring any other earthly marvel, like a rainbow or a sunrise.

"At your service, Miss Crain," Gabriel said with a nod. "It is good to see you again."

"Really?" Xani said dubiously, recalling that Gabriel visited Cindy, Mina, Jonah and others with more regularity. "There's nothing special about me."

"On the contrary, you are blessed by your devotion," he said. "Surrounded by your companions, you've nevertheless remained unwavering in your faith. Even now, you believe that your lover is faithful to you, despite the distance between you and the enticements that tempt him."

Xani closed her laptop to give her full attention to Gabriel. "You haven't told me anything that I don't already know."

"What do you want to know, Miss Crain?"

If you could talk to God, what would you ask…
"What does God want with me?"

170

"Your continued piety," he said. "In your times of need and uncertainty, you must trust that you will not be abandoned, and grace will be yours."

That sounded eerily ominous. "I'm not going to be asked to sacrifice my life for someone, am I?" she asked half-jokingly, recalling Jonah's recent trial. "I'm not sure I would have the guts for that.

He smiled, and it was an engaging, genuine grin. "Mister Gideon's skillset and circumstances are rather unique, so his trial needed to be a rigorous one." Gabriel finished his drink and rose from his seat.

"That's it?" Xani asked. "That's all you have to say?"

Gabriel bowed his head. "That's all you need to know, for now. Additional words would only serve to confuse and complicate the matter, and you have enough on your mind." He returned the chair to the other table and handed Cindy back his empty glass before turning back to Xani. "Have a good day, Miss Crain."

Xani shot a questioning look at Cindy. "Is he always like that?"

"You'll get used to Gabe," Cindy laughed. "He's getting to be a regular, here. I think he's starting to like slumming with us mortals."

Six minutes before noon, Jonah stood across the street and looked through the window of the restaurant where he was scheduled to meet with Selina Xing. It was a bustling Chinese establishment specializing in dim sum, judging by the metal pushcarts that crammed between the crowded round tables, and Selina managed to be seated at an ideal table: near the kitchen, for first pick of the freshest dishes, but out of the direct path of the carts, to avoid being jostled.

Jonah was cautious and indirect with his approach, sensing that there were watchful, suspicious eyes on him, but he was also aware of how alien he must have appeared, as a bearded, blue-eyed white man lurking on a street where every storefront was labeled in Chinese characters. Sensing that he was being watched by more than just the local residents, he took a last glance around, while he was still far enough to avoid Selina Xing's detection, or at least, he thought.

Jonah felt his phone buzzing in his pocket and glanced at the unfamiliar number that appeared. Looking back up towards Selina through the window, he met her enigmatic smile and subtle wave, and saw her phone pressed against her ear under her fall of black hair.

He answered Selina's call, and heard her voice: "You're early."

"And somehow, you're even earlier," he returned.

"I like to know my surroundings before going into a meeting," she said, and gestured to the chair next to her with a subtle flick of her finger. "Would you like to join me now, or do you want to wait another five minutes?"

"I'll be with you in a moment, if that's alright," he said, noticing the different servers and patrons at the nearby tables, as well as strangers on the street outside. "I'm sorry, but I may be a couple of minutes late."

"Of course," she said. "Take your time." She disconnected and returned to her cup of tea, avoiding any glances in his direction.

Jonah liked and respected Selina, and for that reason, he wanted to ensure that their meeting would go as smoothly as possible, free of interruptions and distractions, as much as such a thing was possible in a crowded dim sum restaurant during the midday lunch hour. As soon as he had seen to the last of the details, to the extent that he could, he rushed inside and made his way to his seat next to Selina.

"My apologies for keeping you waiting, Missus Xing," he said contritely, taking his seat and nodding a terse greeting to the strangers sharing the round table with them.

"You're forgiven, as you had arrived on time, technically," she said. She watched, as Jonah unwrapped his chopsticks and rinsed his plate and cup with a splash of scalding tea and wiped them clean with his napkin, as he learned to do when he was young. "Not your first dim sum," she noted, filling his empty cup from the teapot.

"No, Ma'am," he said, knocking on the table to show his respect to his hostess. "Thank you for the invitation, and making the time to meet with me."

"I'm trying to be a responsible mother," she said. "Some events have transpired since we last talked, and it appears that you may be family, soon, so I thought we should catch up."

"You wanted to be sure that I'm still the same man you knew," he read from her words, taking a sip of the hot tea, speckled with tiny flower petals, tasting mildly sweet on his tongue.

"Do you like the tea?" she asked. "It's chrysanthemum, with some dried wolfberries added," she said. "Goji berries, by another name. I wanted to pick something that is safe for you to drink."

"Thank you, that was very considerate," he said, "but isn't chrysanthemum rumored to be an aphrodisiac?"

"Anything can be, in the right company, but I trust your self-control," she said unsmilingly, then flagged down one of the dim sum carts and ordered an assortment of delicate-looking dumplings and a dish of braised chicken feet. "I'll advise you on anything that can make you ill, so don't be shy about helping yourself. From what I've heard of your new responsibilities, you'll need to stay in top condition."

"Actually, I don't think I've eaten since I left New York," he said with chagrin, plucking one of the tender, spiced chicken feet from the serving saucer, while Selina sipped her tea and silently judged his aptitude for using chopsticks with slippery food.

"Well, that won't do," she frowned, setting a couple of translucent-skinned dumplings on his dish with a deft hand. "You didn't have any excess weight to spare, to start."

Jonah laughed softly at her maternal tone. "And here I was worried that my tailor would need to let out my suit before long."

"Probably not that one, if you have the same tailor as my husband, on Pine Street," Selina said knowingly, glancing at the suit's needlework and close cut. "Lin has a similar suit, which looks like it fits like a second skin, but he says it feels like wearing pajamas."

"It's my new reaper uniform," Jonah said lightly. He didn't see the point of dancing around the topic of what he was, as it was understood that Bullfinch had kept Selina and Lin Xing apprised of the situation. He picked up the chicken foot, glistening and jiggling with sauce and dissolved collagen, and felt the savory morsel fall apart in his mouth, the tiny bones slipping loose easily. His canine instinct nudged him to eat the whole thing, bones and all, but in public, and especially in present company, he refrained and plucked the bones from between his lips with his chopsticks.

"How is your job going?" she asked casually. "Is it what you expected?"

"My employers didn't give me much guidance, so I wasn't sure what to expect," he said. "I don't have any special powers or weapons, so they either don't expect me to need them, or they don't expect me to last very long."

Selina refilled his teacup and nodded when he knocked on the table again. "When you were in the demon's lair, the angel came to speak with me. He wanted to assure me that my children would be fine, but he also mentioned that you would be undergoing a trial."

174

"He didn't mention that what happened was a test," Jonah frowned, picking up one of the dumplings.

"Why would it matter, after the fact? You met their expectations, clearly, or you wouldn't be here," Selina said. "It's an encouraging sign that your divine watchers have chosen to invest in you. It means that they intend a greater purpose for you."

"The greater the heights, the harder the fall," Jonah said. "But I guess we all have our trials—I shouldn't complain."

"Only if you think the test was unfair." Selina glanced down at her phone at an incoming text and attached photograph, and she actually giggled. As she picked up her phone, Jonah took the moment to refill her teacup. "Thank you, Jonah."

It occurred to him then: "Is this meeting a test for me, too?"

Selina raised her brow. "If Mina were your daughter, what would you do, in my place?"

"Exactly the same," he admitted. "I'd want to see for myself that she wasn't making a mistake." It was a parent's instinct to want to analyze and scrutinize the people in their children's lives, and given Mina's past, Selina was right to be cautious.

To Jonah's surprise, Selina passed him her phone, which showed Mina taking a delicate bite of a pink-tinged *manju*, a Japanese rice dough snack, this one filled with fresh strawberry. Jonah only knew the name because of the accompanying text: *Stopped in Japantown for manjus. Almost done with errands.* Jonah fought the temptation to zoom in, to see Mina's face in more detail, and instead passed Selina's phone back to her.

"Have your feelings for my daughter changed?" Selina asked quietly, turning her phone face-down. "If they have, I wouldn't blame you for it. You've gone through a profound change, practically a metamorphosis."

"I still can't see living my life without her," he answered. "I can't say for certain that she's the only reason that I returned, but she's certainly the main reason that I would stay."

"And apart from your feelings, what do you have to offer?" she asked impassively.

"I would support her, in whatever she way she needs me. She would never have cause to doubt my love or my loyalty."

"You've described the qualities of a devoted pet," she said, then raised her hand. "Let me clarify: what do you envision for *your* future, apart from spending it with Mina?"

Shit, what does she want to hear? About his career path, his finances? There was a moment of awkward silence, as Selina looked at him stonily, and he blurted: "'I don't want to sell anything, buy anything, or process anything as a career.'"

At her continued blankness, he said, "Sorry, 80's John Cusack movie quote."

She nodded. "I know. *Say Anything* from 1989. I only remember the year because it was a date night movie with my husband. Speaking of whom, if you dare show up in the middle of the night to serenade Mina with a boombox, he will make you eat it."

She spoke with such straight-faced solemnity that Jonah struggled with trying to read whether she was actually serious. "That's okay. I don't even own a boombox."

"About that," she sighed. "You've been forced into asceticism, I understand. I'm sorry about the loss of your home. I know what it means to lose most of your worldly possessions by no fault of your own."

"Thank you."

"So, this isn't about financial security. I know you've been compensated by Garrison Brothers, so you could provide for Mina, if she ever needed it, but so could Malcolm. And Lloyd Dobler quote aside, you haven't said anything that your cousin didn't already promise, when he asked for our blessing."

Jonah followed Selina in picking another dumpling from one of the steamers and realized belatedly that the bright green filling he had mistaken for spinach through its translucent rice skin was chopped garlic chive, which was potentially toxic to him. He steeled himself for the possibility of becoming ill, hopefully after lunch and in private, rather than being openly rude to Mina's mother.

As he aimed his chopsticks for it, Selina snatched it from his plate and set it on her own.

"I hope you weren't going to deliberately poison yourself, just to impress me," Selina said, taking a bite of the dumpling herself.

"Maybe," he said flippantly, disguising his relief. "Would it have worked?"

"I'd rather attend your wedding than your funeral," she said, pushing the dishes towards Jonah with the morsels that were safe for him to eat. "But I can see that you are different from Malcolm. He wouldn't have risked his own well-being for the sake of being polite."

Jonah marveled at the assortment of dishes at their corner of the table, as he had barely noticed Selina ordering from the dim sum carts that zipped past them. He wondered how much Selina understood about his nature, when he was still figuring out his newly-remade body for himself.

Selina sipped her tea. "It wasn't my intent to interrogate you, or to discourage you from continuing your relationship with Mina, but merely to know you a little better. You have my number now, if you ever need to talk. In the meantime, you should eat, while you have the opportunity."

Jonah refilled Selina's cup before he finished what was on his plate. "I have to ask: are you planning on

177

having a similar discussion with Xani Crain, or am I getting special treatment?"

"If Xani ever proposes to Adam, I will certainly have to have a chat with her," Selina said lightly. "But it's true that my questions for Miss Crain would be a little different, simply because Adam and Mina are different."

Jonah peered over the edge of his teacup at the police car that was slowly rolling down the street, and the passersby outside who quickly scattered, and his subtle glance did not go unnoticed by Selina. As the patrol car came to a stop in front of the restaurant, she straightened in her seat.

"I wonder why the police are here," she whispered.

Jonah shrugged. "Maybe someone reported seeing suspicious-looking white men in dark clothes, brandishing guns in Chinatown?"

She looked aside at him. "Did you have something to do with this?"

"I *am* a suspicious-looking white man," he joked, finishing his tea, "but I don't carry a gun."

Despite the breeziness of his voice, he was trying to downplay the threat that he felt, the prickling at his nape whenever he sensed the presence of those dark-garbed, military-looking men, more so when they seemed to be observing him earlier, in the street. Jonah understood a little better why William Grant had shot him before he had introduced himself, as Grant had probably encountered these mercenary types before.

Selina leaned on the table with her arms crossed, relaxing as the police car continued on its way. "Thank you, Jonah, but I can deal with them, myself. I try not to involve the police in my private concerns."

Jonah blinked. "Those guys are after you? Why? I thought they were following me," he said, adding, "for whatever reason."

Selina smiled knowingly, as she flagged down one of the waiters with their order card to calculate the bill. "I don't think these men understand the threat you pose, or your unique skillset, otherwise, you *would* be as hunted as me."

He wondered about the reason that anyone would go after Selina, aside from a sizeable ransom as the wife of one of the wealthiest businessmen in San Francisco. Given her additional connections to the divine forces, however, only a desperate or insane person could possibly think that any violence towards Selina would go unanswered and unavenged. Then, there was her own otherworldly nature, as a pure-blooded *huli jing*, in the form of a beautiful, elegant Chinese woman at the dawn of her middle years.

Selina shot a look at Jonah, as she finished double-checking the tally, and as he made an earnest attempt to take the bill from her. "I'll cover it," she said.

"No, please, let me."

"I invited you, so it's my treat."

"Perhaps we can split the check?"

"We don't do that, in our culture," she explained.

"Well, in *my* culture, a gentleman always pays, if he is able, even if the lady invites."

Selina seemed amused by his fight. "You would argue with me—your fiancée's mother?"

"I don't think I could call you my mother-in-law, if I couldn't be myself around you," Jonah said, snatching the bill from her hand when her grip loosened. "That may mean doing things that go against your wishes, on occasion, if I believe I'm right."

"You're persistent, I'll give you that," she said imperiously, rising from her chair before he could offer a hand.

"Yes, Ma'am," he grinned unapologetically, pulling enough cash from his wallet to cover lunch and slipping a ten-dollar bill under the teapot for a generous tip.

"Mina wouldn't be wearing my mother's ring, otherwise."

Selina watched Jonah dart across the street and disappear around the corner. He was getting back "on the clock," she suspected, and from his stoic, unsmiling demeanor, as they parted ways, his current assignment was either very unpleasant or very challenging. It could also be his concern for her, as his dismay when she disclosed her familiarity with the hunters couldn't be more evident. He had verbally acknowledged her assurance that she would be safe, but Selina laughed at the cynical, skeptical glower of his ice-blue eyes.

She felt better with some distance between herself and Jonah, as any recognized association with her could only endanger him. Just as she had asked Yumi to tease details of her morning schedule, as tantalizing breadcrumbs to ensure that her enemies' focus remained on her, and not directed towards her family, Selina wanted to make sure that Jonah stayed out of harm's way.

Or, at least the harm meant for me, she amended. She had been honest with Jonah: the formidable combination of his shapeshifter traits and reaper instincts made him just the sort of ultimate game sought by the man who still pursued her, across continents and over a century later. As she continued to elude her enemies, she didn't want Jonah targeted as the consolation prize.

As the drizzle began, Selina hailed a cab to head home, to get started on the elixir that she planned to prepare for Adam, to finish his treatment. He was better than he had been when he arrived on Monday night, but he still experienced moments of aphasia and loss of concentration, and it pained Selina to see his visible frustration at his own absentmindedness. The more quickly she could restore her son, the better.

As she exited the cab, Selina was aware of the men, dressed in black and sporting matching buzz cuts, emerging from a black SUV parked in front of the house. She saw no point in delaying or vacillating her approach towards the stairs, as she was obviously being followed and observed, and there were protections around her home to ensure that no one would have access without invitation.

As one of the men moved to intercept her, while the other stayed with the car, the front door flung open, and Mina loomed in the doorway, her slender form dwarfed by the grand, oversized entrance. "Take another step towards her, and I will make you regret it," she growled. "Back off!"

"What are you—" Adam joined Mina at the door. "Oh, it's you," he scowled.

Before Selina could ask how her children knew the man, he took a step back with his hands raised. "I told you I couldn't leave until I spoke to your mother," he said evenly. "I'm under orders from my lord to deliver a message, only to Selina Xing."

"That's what he said before," Mina said, crossing her arms. "He arrived a few minutes before you."

"What is your message?" Selina asked, ascending the steps to pass her bag to Mina.

The man slowly reached into his inner jacket pocket to pull out a tablet device, which he passed to Selina, to show her an image, angling the tablet directly so that only she could view it.

Selina took a sharp breath, relieved that her children didn't have to see the closeup of Yumi's bruised and cut face, but Adam and Mina saw her dismay through her stoic countenance.

The man said, solemnly, "If you need additional proof that the image is real, you can swipe to the next photo."

181

The second photograph was an image of the gold and jade fox pendant that Selina had given to Yumi years ago, when the young *kitsune* had entered her service, next to a torn fingernail, bloodied and bearing the pearlescent pink polish that Yumi favored.

Selina passed the tablet back, seething silently. She had expected her children to be targeted, but not Yumi, and for that, she was furious at her own oversight. "What does your master want?"

"The Baron requests your company," the man said, tucking the tablet back in his jacket pocket. "We'll drive you there, but only you, Missus Xing," he said, looking pointedly at Adam and Mina. "If we catch you following us, we're under orders to shoot her."

"That's bullshit!" Adam snapped. "Without knowing where you're taking her…"

Selina took each of her children's hands in hers and gave them her best reassuring smile. "Listen to me: we all have our responsibilities, and this is mine. Stay in the sanctum, where I know you'll be safe." She turned to Mina. "Start the brew for your brother, while everything is at its full potency. Watch over your sister," she said to Adam. "And, *don't* tell your father about this."

As Mina and Adam opened their mouths to protest, Selina reminded: "You know how your father gets."

"With good reason," Adam muttered.

Selina smiled, more sardonically. "It will be fine, children. The Baron and I just have some unfinished business to resolve. Isn't that so?" she asked her old foe's emissary.

"Last time, it was a pearly pink fingernail. If you delay, the next time, it may be her finger," he said humorlessly.

Selina nodded and followed the man down the steps, to the car, turning at the sound of Mina's voice.

"Be careful, *ma-ma*," she called.

"Of course, Min-Min," she answered breezily. "How would your father get along without me?"

Mina leaned against the closed front door, fighting back tears, as she gripped her mother's handbag in her balled fist. "This is so fucked up! How did we just those shitheads take her like that?"

"We didn't let it happen. Mom left willingly with them, because of whatever was in the pictures… Did you see?"

Mina shook her head, heading towards the kitchen. "The guy mentioned a fingernail." She dropped her mother's bag on the counter and sagged against the cool granite. "Shit! 'Pearly pink'—I think they grabbed Yumi. When we parted ways at the corner, she seemed distracted, but she shrugged it off and just told me she'd text me later."

"That wasn't too long ago," Adam said.

"I'm calling her. She'll forgive me, if I'm being paranoid," Mina said, pulling out her phone as she grabbed one of her mother's saucepans to fill it halfway with water.

"What are you doing?" Adam asked, watching as Mina unpacked an assortment of dried and fresh ingredients onto the counter, while she dialed Yumi's number from her contact list and turned on her phone's speaker.

"Mom wants me to start your earthworm tea, so I'm going to be useful until I find a more productive way to spend my time." Her brow knitted, as the phone continued to ring and finally go to voicemail. "Hey, call me when you get a chance," Mina said brusquely and disconnected.

"Mom said 'Baron,'" Adam said, opening some of the packages for Mina. "Do you know who she's talking about?"

"Mom and Dad used to mention something about a Baron, when we were younger, and before we moved to New York," Mina said, placing the ingredients carefully into the saucepan before she turned on the flame. The way her mother had taught her, Mina knew to wait for the water to come to a low simmer, never to boiling, for the best steep.

"That's right, I'd forgotten about that," Adam said. "They had taught us not to stray from their sides when we were out, or 'the Baron would get you.' Shit, I thought it was just a bogey-man to get us to not wander off or talk to strangers."

"Well, it would've been nice to know that the motherfucker was real," Mina muttered, watching the water shimmy and steam. "But I guess Mom and Dad didn't want us growing up being afraid that someone was really out to get us. "

"Why is the Baron showing himself now, do you think?" Adam found the lid for the saucepan and covered the pot. "Has it really taken this long for him to find Mom and Dad, or was he waiting for something?"

"Dad would probably know, but we promised not to tell him," Mina said glumly, observing Adam's revolted glare at the handful of rubbery, freshly-dried earthworms that she had bought earlier. "Relax, they're scrupulously washed, and their tracts are entirely flushed before they're flash-dried."

"What are the worms for?" Adam asked, turning his head at a buzzing coming from Selina's purse.

"Nerve regeneration, among other things," Mina said, adding the dried ingredients to the pot, as she turned off the flame and covered it securely. She turned around, as Adam pulled their mother's phone from her bag. "Who is it?"

Adam's eyes widened with surprise, as he answered and held the phone to his ear. "Hello?"

184

Mina set her arms akimbo. A "hello" meant the caller was a native English speaker. "Who is it?" she repeated.

"Yes. How did you get Mom's number?" Adam asked the caller, after a brief pause, swatting Mina's hand away, as she reached for the phone. "Yeah, she wasn't given much of a choice about how she left. Where are you? Let us—"

Adam's attempted offer of help was rejected, apparently, as he rolled his eyes in a gesture of frustration. "Well, fuck that. You can't do this alone. Yumi's also being held somewhere, probably close. Yes." He glanced at Mina. "She might be a little banged up, but hopefully, she's okay." She nodded, and he answered, "Thank you."

The pieces clicked in Mina's head from what she heard from Adam's side of the conversation. "It's Jonah, isn't it."

Adam nodded, as the lower tones of Jonah's voice filtered through the phone speaker. "I wish you'd just tell us where you are." Adam paused briefly. "Yeah, whatever. Just be careful, okay?"

He disconnected and set the phone on the counter. "Jonah says 'hi.'"

"It would've been nice to talk to him," Mina said sourly, lifting the edge of the cover to check the steeping brew.

"He wasn't in the best spot to chat, judging from his whispering. And he doesn't need the distraction, given that he's actually outside the Baron's house. He called Mom's number because he saw her being brought inside by a small army, and he wanted to check that it was really her."

"Did Jonah happen to mention why he was there?" Mina asked quietly, as she took one of her mother's cooking chopsticks to gently stir the steaming mixture, aromatic with herbs and spices.

185

"No, he didn't," Adam said. "You don't think he's working with the Baron, do you?"

"If Jonah's a reaper, then he's probably there for a soul," Mina said grimly. "We just don't know whose soul he's there to collect. Yumi's probably hurt, and Mom's a prisoner, but we don't know how strong the Baron is—they're all candidates."

"I didn't even consider that," Adam said, dismayed. "Jonah says the house is the Nob Hill area, but he wouldn't get more specific than that, so finding it would be tough."

Mina strained the tea into a waiting mug, and passed the concoction to Adam. "Drink your earthworm tea, then we'll figure something out." Mina suppressed a grin at Adam's initial grimace, which softened to a resigned frown, as he took the first sip. "A pinch of ground *reishi* mushroom balances it out a little and boosts your immunity. Drink up."

Mina covered the pot again and moved it from the hot burner. "Hopefully, Jonah knows to get to Yumi first."

"You think she could be hurt that badly?" Adam scowled.

"On the contrary," Mina said, "I think Yumi's captors probably underestimated how tough she really is. You know Mom asked her to be my bodyguard today, right? If Mom's in trouble, and I can't be there myself, I couldn't pick a better backup for Jonah than Yumi Taira."

Chapter 11

1895, Fujian Province, China

Xing trembled with rage, watching the inferno engulf the house that he had constructed, the home and sanctuary that he had provided for himself and his wife. He had sworn to always keep her safe, and the structure he had built was falling to charred pieces, seemingly mocking him for his hubris and inadequacy.

He felt Jin Mudan curl her arm around his midriff for warmth and comfort, and he wrapped his arm around her instinctively, tucking the quilt around her shoulders. A few minutes longer, and it would've been too late to escape the flames and crumbling rubble, or they would have been flushed directly into the path of the Baron and his men.

Xing was furious with himself for underestimating their enemy. Even if Jin Mudan had not expected the Baron to track them to the bucolic farmlands where they had made their home, Xing should have known the treachery and doggedness of evil men. He had grown too comfortable and content, and he had endangered his love with his laxness. For now, the most he could do was to get her away from the ruins of their home, and for that, he led her towards the woods, eventually to find shelter in the hills or down by the river bank.

He whipped around at the sound of an approaching horse. "You!"

Isaac looked down from the saddle at both of them, and he looked haggard…and old. "Why are you still in the area? The Baron's men are going house to house to find you." He didn't just look old; his voice was gravelly with age, and his face was lined and sallow.

"And he sent you to search the hills for us?" Jin Mudan asked coolly.

"I never thought he would do something like destroy your home," Isaac said, clearly aghast at the scope of the devastation behind them.

"And if you'd known beforehand, would you have warned us?" she asked.

Xing caught the change in the Isaac's focus and his hesitation, as his gaze flashed to him and back to Jin Mudan. "You think my wife is worth saving, but not me. Isn't that so?"

Isaac squared his shoulders. "All of her suffering is because of you. Without you, the Baron would have no reason to go to such extremes to protect his subjects' livestock—"

"How can you still serve the Baron?" Jin Mudan cried. "You know that we've never taken a single head from the village's flocks. Your Baron wants to see me in a cage, or hanging as a pelt in his trophy room. If not for my husband, I would already be dead!"

She cut short her tirade, and they lowered themselves to the grass at the sound of more horses.

"You found them! Excellent work, Mister Bo," praised the Baron, readying his rifle. Despite the years that had passed since their last encounter, the nobleman looked strong and vigorous, even stronger and healthier than some of his younger men, including Isaac.

"I thought you wanted them captured, sir?" Isaac asked, eyeing his lord's rifle.

"The fox, to be sure, but the beast would be just as impressive dead as alive," the Baron said, cocking his rifle. "It's not as satisfying to shoot it in human form, but

188

its carcass will revert to its demonic form, and no one will know the difference. Weaken him, men, but leave his head for me."

Jin Mudan growled in outrage and shielded Xing with her body.

He kissed her forehead. "Be brave, my love. When they raise their guns to shoot, run for the bamboo stands—the horses will be unable to follow through the shoots and undergrowth."

"I won't leave you," she swore. "We can both run."

"We are fast, but we can't outrun bullets," he said in jest. "Go, my love, and live for both of us."

She locked her arms around his neck, unwilling to release him. "There is no life for me, if you are gone from it."

"What dialect are they even speaking?" the Baron muttered. "Well, I'd rather have her alive, but her fur will still make a lovely muffler for Catherine."

Unable to peel away his wife's surprisingly strong hands, Xing turned around to give the Baron and his men his back, intending to spare her the direct barrage, but he heard Isaac's stern, tired voice: "They will go free, or the first bullet will be for you."

Xing and Jin Mudan looked over to see Isaac's rifle raised and pointed at the Baron's head. The entourage were just as stunned by Isaac's demand, and they looked at their lord uncertainly.

"You are making a mistake, Mister Bo, to treat these creatures like your friends," the Baron said. "They may wear human faces, but they are certainly not human."

"They may not be human, but they deserve to be treated with dignity," Isaac said. "Give the order."

With his jaw visibly clenched, the Baron lowered his rifle, and his men followed suit. "I will be sporting, and let you reach the edge of the clearing before we give chase," he said, relaxing his jaw with an effort. "That is more than fair."

Xing gave a terse nod of thanks and changed into his fast and powerful *lin* form, tearing his thin garments in the process and taking advantage of his ungulate hooves and powerful haunches to get an initial boost of speed. He felt Jin Mudan change, as well, and she clambered up his mane and held on by her claws through her half-shed clothes, digging into his thick hide to stay mounted on his broad back. Once he knew that she was secured, he broke into a full gallop, only turning his head briefly at the sound of distant gunfire to confirm that Jin Mudan hadn't been hit.

Once they reached the heavy brush at the edge of the clearing, Xing avoided the brambles and sought to get them deeper into the woods, but Jin Mudan jumped down to look back the way they can come.

She was whimpering, trying to stifle the pain in her voice, and he followed the direction of her gaze, to the sight of the Baron overseeing the transfer of Isaac's limp, bloody corpse from the grass to the back of his horse, while the Baron handed Isaac's rifle to one of the other men.

Her ears were pinned, her golden fur stiff and raised along her spine, and her teeth bared in a grimace, as one of the other hunters draped a saddle blanket over Isaac, less for the dead man's dignity than to spare the others from having to glimpse his lifeless, staring eyes.

Xing changed back into human form to move more easily through the dense foliage. "We have to keep moving, or Isaac would have died for nothing." Already, some of the Baron's men had started towards their position, denying them a real head start.

Jin Mudan perked her ears and relaxed her muzzle, and he knew she had regained her composure, at least for the moment. She coiled her body around and swept along his bare legs, as she led the way into the woods, her golden coat and tail like a beacon for him to follow.

Once they were deep enough in the woods, far and well-hidden enough to elude the Baron's men, they waited until their pursuers gave up their hunt. Xing found a small patch of tall grass that was large enough to accommodate his natural form but still sheltered by tree cover, where they could rest for a moment.

As they bided their time, waiting for nightfall, they were visited by a mother and son from the nearby village, who brought them some spare clothes, food and drink. The villagers silently set the provisions on a low boulder and departed quickly with a low, respectful bow, affording them their privacy.

Jin Mudan changed into her human form and slipped into the tunic and skirt she had been gifted. "That was very kind of them. How did they know we were here?"

Xing changed into his human form to make use of the shirt and trousers that were left for him. "I saved the boy's father from wolves last year, so they know me, in both my forms, and they no doubt saw the fire from their farm," he said, smiling at his wife's modesty in averting her eyes, as he dressed.

Once she spied that he was clothed, Jin Mudan broke off a piece of sweet, white *mantou* bread and passed the rest to him. "Where do we go now?"

"As long as the Baron knows we're alive, he will stalk us," he said. "We could stay and fight, but we have more to lose. These aren't the Baron's lands or people to protect, so he would burn and destroy all of this without remorse," he said, looking towards the village from where the family had come.

Jin Mudan took a sip from the gourd bottle that had accompanied the bread. "What if we left this behind, went south?" she asked.

"Hong Kong and Shanghai are controlled by the British, so the southern regions are not as open and welcoming to our kind as they used to be," he said.

"Eastward to the coast?" she suggested.

He shook his head. "Nippon has a solid hold on Taiwan, now that the Guangxu Emperor has shown that he cannot rule well, without the Empress Dowagers to guide him. Now that Taiwan is ceded, I fear the Fujian coast will not remain safe much longer."

"We could leave the continent altogether," she said. "A new land, across the ocean, and a new start for us."

Xing hadn't traveled by boat in centuries, and never across the sea, and the idea of leaving his land behind filled him with a deep trepidation, but the hope and determination shining in her eyes erased his doubts. "I would follow wherever you wish to go. When do you want to leave?"

1896, San Francisco

Jessup Bullfinch looked up from his second-hand pine desk at a knock on the door. "Yes, Miss Hart?"

Annie Hart stood in the doorway of the drab office, a flash of vivid color like a fuchsia bloom, and smoothed the bows on her calico bodice. The bright hues of her evening dress complemented her dusky complexion and the highlights of her dark, reddish-brown curls. Her makeup was already done to get ready for her evening work shift at the saloon, but Bullfinch didn't mind her taking off a little early, if she needed to. He and Annie had known each other for ages, from when he was known as "Josiah," and she was named "Aimee." They had changed and remade themselves so often over the years that the names hardly mattered anymore—he was always "Mister Bullfinch," and she was always "Miss Hart."

Soon, it would be time to reinvent their identities again, to avoid arousing suspicion with their abnormally long careers and lives, by establishing a paper trail for when they needed to pass down their business. He was considering the name "Jacob," while she was thinking something exotic and unique, like "Aciré," to rhyme with "Desiree," but maybe that was too exotic, and she could wait another few decades for that.

"Mister Lin is here," she said, her ruby-tinted lips curved into a full smile. "He looks young."

"They usually are," Bullfinch said. "Send him in."

The man entered with a crushed, narrow-brimmed woolen hat in hand. "Mister Jessup Bullfinch?"

Bullfinch visually assessed the man who had arrived for their appointment. Chinese, at a guess, clean-shaven, as most of his ethnicity were, with a sack-cloth suit as neat, clean and unwrinkled as he was.

"Yes, and you are Mister Lin…?" he prompted for a full name.

"Just Lin," the man said, taking Bullfinch's hand. "Thank you for agreeing to see me."

Bullfinch nodded, impressed by the young man's fluency and easy manners. "I'm not sure if I'll be able to help, but I thought I should hear you out."

"It is more than the other attorneys in town will do," Lin said, "so thank you."

"Well, unlike them, I care more about being fair than being rich, and I like a challenge," he said. "I'm sure you're aware that immigration from your country has been sharply curtailed in most regions around here. You're brave to even show your face on the streets in daylight."

"I am aware, Mister Bullfinch, so you understand my desperation. I need an exception, not only for myself, but also for my wife."

"If she is your legal wife, then that should be an easy addition, comparatively, and would even help your case. It would be more challenging if you were unwed, as people around here have a strange notion of morality and are suspicious of the intentions of foreigners," Bullfinch said.

"I have heard that you can make arrangements to document me as a 'paper son'."

It was a new term for a new procedure—a loophole, really—and Bullfinch was surprised at Mister Lin's familiarity with it. "Well, yes, I have some documents that can be amended to give you the identity of a native-born Chinese," Bullfinch said. "Usually, the papers are needed before you would even be allowed to set foot on American soil, so how did you even get here without them?"

"I found my way," he said evasively, "but I would prefer not to have to repeat the journey again, so I would like to stay, and bring my wife here, legally. For both, I'll need documents."

"That's fair," Bullfinch said. "How did you even hear about this, and about me?"

"I make it a point to learn about the laws and politics of my new environments," the young man said, "and those most qualified, able and willing to help me."

Lin's entire demeanor suggested a more sophisticated individual than he appeared, who was more worldly and experienced than his seeming youth suggested.

"Mister Lin, not to be indelicate, but I need to be aware of any outstanding warrants or legal trouble. My reputation necessitates caution, and I can't be associated with criminal elements."

"I'm not guilty of any crime, Mister Bullfinch, apart from the color of my skin and shape of my eyes."

"I see. Why are you seeking a life here, then, knowing how you'll be treated?"

"This place still offers more than I can ever have at home," Lin said. "I can make it worth your trouble." He reached into his pocket and pulled out a short stack of gold coins, and Jacob gawked at the unexpected show of wealth.

"Name your price, Mister Bullfinch, but I seek to have my wife and me safely and legally on these shores, as soon as possible. Ideally, by the end of the month."

Bullfinch raised his eyebrows at the aggressive deadline. "I'll try my best, but I won't know the price until the process is underway, in case of complications. Also, there may be other parties to pay to turn a blind eye…"

He saw Lin's determined scowl and knew that none of that mattered to him. "Never mind. We'll settle up the charges later. What did you say your occupation or skills were?"

"I didn't," Lin said. "Does it matter?"

"Well, the officials who review your documents and those of your wife will want to know what demonstrable skills and talents you have to contribute, to ensure that you won't be begging, soliciting or creeping in and out of opium dens."

"I understand. I was a farmer back home, but I built my own house, and have stoneworking experience, and my wife is a skilled seamstress, midwife and cook."

Bullfinch picked up one of the heavy gold coins, noting the unique printing around a profile image of Lady Liberty on one side. "You claim to have a humble background, yet somehow, you got hold of Confederate gold coins from the opposite end of the country, and you speak English very well for a recent arrival."

"I lived near the estate of an English expatriate back in China, so I learned from interacting with them," Lin shrugged. "As for the gold, I was playing cards the other night, with some men from Georgia, and I was luckier than they were. I didn't ask the other players about their money. Is it legal tender?"

"It is. After all, gold is gold." Bullfinch opened his ledger and pulled out a stack of forms. "Let's see our candidates, then. Short and prematurely bald, no. Tall, slender, that's promising…but missing part of right foot? Any chance of that?"

Lin shook his head.

"Picky," Bullfinch grinned. "Perhaps this one: average height, no distinguishing marks. Age twenty-five…you would pass for that. A merchant's son, both parents deceased, family name of 'Xing.'"

"Really?" Lin said with interest. "I could work with that."

"So could many others," Bullfinch said, hesitant for a moment, wondering how much he could get from another candidate for that profile. He wasn't greedy, but he needed money to support his practice and pay his erstwhile secretary. There was also a risk—if Lin proved to be insincere, deviant or untrustworthy—then the documents and Jacob's efforts would be wasted, and someone else more deserving of the opportunity would be denied a better life.

"I understand your concerns, Mister Bullfinch, I really do," Lin said quietly. "You have other commitments and obligations, same as me, and I can see in you the same respect for loyalty and fairness that I value. I have little to give you right now, apart from money, but I never forget a kindness or a debt, and you will not regret assisting me."

Bullfinch appreciated Lin's effort to be empathetic, despite the man's obvious desperation. "You're very well-spoken for a farmer, even for one living around English folk."

"I always make an effort to learn the language of the people with whom I must interact," he said. "It helps to minimize conflict and avoid misunderstandings."

"Right," Bullfinch said, intrigued by the young Chinese man's eloquence and polish. He was definitely more than he appeared to be, at first blush, but Bullfinch decided to go with his gut on this one. "Alright, Mister

Lin. Let's start your paperwork." He passed the papers to his new client to review. "Welcome to America, Mister 'Xing'."

1906

Bullfinch had just finished collecting his papers into a neat pile when he heard a knock on his door. His building was one of the few still standing intact amid the devastation and rubble that was the aftermath of the recent earthquake. He had enough space to let some of the excess square footage to displaced business and neighbors. It had only been a few days, so most people were still focused on salvaging their lives and homes, before they could even start to focus on restoring their livelihoods.

Even so, Bullfinch had heard of a banker who had set up a makeshift office on a street corner somewhere in town, to start accepting loan requests from local businesses hoping to rebuild. Whenever the noise and clutter of the cramped quarters started to get on his nerves, Bullfinch thought of all of his fellow San Franciscans who had lost everything in the quake and counted his blessings.

In fact, Annie Hart had asked for the day off, to volunteer at the hospital triage sites tending to the injured, and Bullfinch had given his whole-hearted support; business was slow, and likely to remain that way for a while. He cautioned her to be careful in the streets, as there were reports of looting and riots breaking out, and the situation was bad enough that soldiers had been dispatched from nearby Angel Island to help keep order.

"Mister Bullfinch," Lin Xing greeted from the door. "Is this a good time?"

"Good afternoon, Mister Xing. Sure, there isn't much call for estate and financial planning when people are just trying to survive day to day."

Lin entered with his hat in hand, as usual. In the years since their first meeting, Lin Xing had worked in a variety of businesses and steadily built a small fortune, which he invested in local ventures, rather than sending it back to his homeland, as many of his fellow immigrants did to support their distant relatives. Instead, he and his beautiful young wife, Selina, lived frugally but comfortably, and were known for their generosity, especially to members of the varied diaspora who—like them—were trying to make a home for themselves in a new land.

"It must be a challenging time," Lin nodded. "I've had a few business owners approach me over the past couple of days, asking if I could back their reconstruction efforts. I don't have the full command of the nuances of legal language, so I was hoping that I could engage your services to draw up the contracts."

Bullfinch waved him to his guest chair. "You're doing better than others, then. I'm relieved; I was worried about you and Selina when I heard about the damage around Chinatown. That's going to take years to rebuild, if investors are even willing."

"We owe our good fortune to you, in part, for helping us keep our assets and holdings insulated from excessive legal scrutiny, and to your friend Mercer, for encouraging us to diversify. We have some losses in Chinatown, to be sure, but no more than elsewhere in San Francisco." He took a seat but kept his eyes on Bullfinch. "So, are you available to draft some paperwork for me?"

"I'm just your lawyer and not as financially savvy as Mercer, so I may be unqualified to give business advice, but as a friend…I'd caution you about reinvesting here, given the current instability. By some

198

estimates, at least eighty percent of the city has been turned to rubble."

"And yet, you're still here," Lin said, gesturing to Bullfinch's tidy office. "You could move your practice elsewhere."

"I still have clients who need me, especially the ones who have nowhere else to go," Bullfinch said. "But if you have someplace else, it would be safer for you and Selina. People become stupid and weak-minded when they grow desperate, and right now, there's a great deal of hostility against your people, even more than in the past." He had heard rumblings about local anti-immigrant groups hoping to use the recent disaster to force Chinese and other minority groups away from the high-value real estate within the city borders, relocating them to the outskirts, or other towns, altogether. "The Chinese Exclusion Act is still in effect, you know. It's actually been made permanent, for almost four years now."

Lin nodded sagely. "And it probably won't be repealed for many decades to come—certainly not now."

"So, why do you want to stay?"

"Because people are inherently good, and we will all survive this, if we persevere," Lin smiled. "Some cities and civilizations have fallen into ruin, despite never experiencing a natural disaster like this, while other cities thrive, despite one catastrophe after another. The land doesn't matter as much as the tenacity and heart of its people, when it comes to estimating resilience. It may be a gamble, but it's a risk worth taking."

"And what does your wife say?" Bullfinch had only met Selina Xing on a handful of occasions, but she seemed a sensible sort. She was smarter and more observant than her soft-spoken voice and delicate beauty suggested, and she and Annie had become fast friends.

"She's actually the one who encouraged me to pursue this avenue of investment. She's more compassionate and far-seeing than I am," Lin said. "She's been helping down by the ferry with Miss Hart these past few days, and she's seen the suffering and losses first-hand."

"How much of a risk are you willing to take here? I mean, how much money are you fronting for this endeavor?"

"By my estimate, I can set aside a hundred thousand initially, without compromising my own liquidity. If this goes well, I may increase the fund."

"A hundred thousand dollars?" Bullfinch said, his mouth agape. "That's a significant wager." That was the sum rumored to be pledged by the likes of Andrew Carnegie and the Standard Oil company to help with the reconstruction efforts.

"Not all for one business, of course," Lin clarified. "But Selina estimates that it may be enough to help a good number of people, at least until the fires have stopped, and the bank vaults have cooled down enough to re-open."

"Sounds reasonable, and fair."

"And, I'd appreciate your discretion, please. The last thing some of these desperate sorts want to hear is that some immigrant Chinese is faring better than they are," he said. "I'll return later with the names of the proprietors and businesses for the contracts, as long as you're available. These would be cash transactions, so a paper trail will be important to maintain."

Bullfinch knew that Lin had his own fire-proof vault somewhere in his home, so he didn't bother asking how Lin had ready access to a hundred thousand dollars in cash. "How many contracts are we talking about?"

Lin smiled enigmatically. "Depends on who else approaches me before I return later with the list. You can charge me whatever you wish, once you have a better idea of the effort," he grinned, reminding Bullfinch of their first transaction, all those years ago. "If you need an advance, to cover rent, or assist some of your other clients, or to pay Miss Hart's salary, I hope you won't hesitate to ask."

Lin glanced at the neat stacks of papers and files on Bullfinch's desk, as he rose to his feet. "I imagine, once the dust and ash settle, requests for 'paper son' documents will start flooding into your office, now that so much of the archival records have been destroyed in the quake and fire."

Bullfinch hadn't thought that far ahead, yet, but Lin was right. More Chinese could claim native-born status, if there were no documents to show otherwise, and the government officials had more pressing concerns than policing immigration, when their constituents were homeless, dying or starving. Whatever efforts and legislation were still enforced, were still mostly targeted against Chinese immigrants, with little attention paid towards groups from other regions and countries. Bullfinch found the discrimination grossly unfair, but he would do what he could within the system, until the laws changed.

"In that case, you could've waited a few years for your own papers and saved yourself thousands of dollars and months of anxious waiting," Bullfinch joked, rising from his seat, as well.

"Perhaps that's true, Bullfinch," Lin said, extending his hand for a handshake. "But if I had waited, I wouldn't be in this position now, to do some good."

Bullfinch took Lin's hand easily. "You've done a lot in ten years, Mister Xing. I would hate to see you lose what you've built, and you're taking a bigger risk than your experience here would inform."

"That may be so," Lin nodded, "but my wife is hopeful that this common hardship will repair the poor relations between the disparate groups. We don't expect change to happen quickly, but we don't mind biding our time. Waiting is a virtue that my wife and I have come to master."

Chapter 12

Present Day

Jonah had cased the Nob Hill residence of his target, Thomas Ashford Morrigan II, supposed Baron of Devonshire, for less than fifteen minutes before he found a gap in the weathered wooden privacy fence surrounding the property. It was one of the few remaining single-residence buildings in the area with a yard accessible from the street, and at one time, it must have grand and opulent, but years of neglect had left it looking outdated and careworn, except for the yard, which boasted a manicured English-style garden and well-fed lawn.

He had seen the arrival of a black SUV in front of the house, and was dismayed to see a woman who resembled Selina Xing being escorted out of the car and into the building by the same types who had been surveilling them during their lunch meeting. Just to be sure, Jonah had called Selina's number and heard his suspicions confirmed when Adam answered her phone. Jonah had kept the conversation brief, as much as he wanted to hear Mina's voice directly, and not just amid the background clatter of pots and pans. There would be time to speak with Mina once everything was over, and Selina was safe. *And Yumi, too. Great.*

Selina Xing's arrival was fortuitous, in a way, as the security focus was lessened around the perimeter and diverted to guarding the Baron's new visitor. As Jonah approached the house itself, he noticed a dog-door set into one of the rear entrances, and he estimated the dimensions of the flap with trepidation: could he easily and quickly get through an opening that was less than two feet tall, and about a foot and a half wide...and what was waiting on the other side that used a door that big?

Then Jonah seized on something that Bullfinch had said to him back in New York, about the possibility that he could still shift his form, if he wanted to. Jonah looked down at his new suit and wondered about the clothing situation in his canine form, but decided to give shifting a try, half-expecting to end up looking like one of those unfortunate pets forced to wear people clothes at their owners' whims.

The shifting itself was almost effortless, like tapping into his instincts before going into a brawl, just requiring a little more concentration to start the process. He felt his muscles and bones change and distort, as his senses returned to that heightened, exquisite sharpness that he had enjoyed when he had been a dog.

Mister Gideon, this is your suit, made to accommodate every possible situation, Metzger had explained patiently to Jonah during his fitting, and Jonah finally realized the extent to which his suit was tailored to his needs. Every stitch of fabric that touched him, and even his shoes and items in his pockets like his phone and wallet, seemed to evaporate and vanish into his new fur.

Whoa, that's pretty cool, Jonah acknowledged, shaking his coat and feeling nothing to hinder his movements, and hoping his clothes would return when he tried to shift back later. *Here goes nothing.*

His nose picked up on the drool and dander, and his ears caught the low growls and jingle of collars, before he saw the matched trio of brindle-coated mastiffs with gazes fixed on him. They got up together, towering over his rangy, lean husky form, and Jonah was reminded of the three-headed Cerberus guarding the underworld from would-be trespassers.

Too late to back out through the flap, Jonah came all the way inside and saw that the guard dogs were collared, but not leashed, and they approached warily, with teeth bared. Jonah dug his claws into the hardwood planks and arched his spine, bracing himself. *Fuck. Me.*

Yumi Taira stirred to find herself in an uncomfortable, rickety wooden chair, unable to sit upright because her wrists and ankles were hog-tied together. Her raw left pinky still stung like a motherfucker from the nail being torn, but at least it had stopped dripping blood. She glimpsed her guards through her long hair that draped over her face, but she smelled them with greater clarity; two of the men wore cloying deodorants, while the other two wore none at all and needed to, badly. They stood in a circle with their backs to her, unaware that she had awoken, so they chatted animatedly. They were white, and English-speaking, as in: "Queen's English."

Well, shit, I guess this is the Baron's doing, after all. She had heard stories from her benefactors, mostly Selina, about their years in China and their encounters with the Baron of Devonshire who had taken over their lands, so she understood their reasons for wanting to keep their children safe, but Yumi hadn't expected to be kidnapped, herself. Attacked or shot, in the service of the Xing family, sure, but not darted and held for ransom like an actual, valued member of the family.

Yumi realized with alarm that her jade fox pendant was gone from around her neck, as she no longer felt its weight or the warmth of the gold chain against her skin. That, combined with the nail that her captors had torn from her finger before knocking her out… *Fuck, I've been used as bait!*

She heard the muffled slamming of a door, through the ceiling above her head, and for the first time, she saw the planks of old hardwood flooring, held together with crossbeams and screws. She strained to hear the various voices, including Selina's familiar, modulated alto voice.

"Well, lads, look who's woken up," jeered one of the guards, tugging at one of Yumi's loose black locks. "Just in time to say 'hello' to her boss-lady. Look over there, darlin', and smile," he ordered, grabbing her hair to force her to face a camera atop a tripod several yards away.

Yumi refused to raise her eyes to the camera and instead, followed the wires and cords that dangled from it, to see which one was the power cord, and which one carried the signal elsewhere, presumably upstairs to where Selina was. When she spotted a hand moving in the shadows to tug the cords from the wall, Yumi looked up sharply and automatically ducked as the camera and its tripod hurtled over her head, striking down two of her guards.

Too busy laughing at her helplessness, the guards had missed the stealthy arrival of the silver and black husky and his three brindle mastiff friends, until it was too late. Even she hadn't caught the shift of the blue-eyed husky into the nimble, shadowy human figure, as she was trying to avoid getting struck by flying video equipment, but she froze as the massive guard dogs leapt past her to maul and tackle the remaining guards, until the only figure standing was the man who had brought the dogs.

"Heel," he said tersely, and the mastiffs backed away from the fallen guards, their mouths slack and panting from their brief exertion. The men were groaning in agony, clutching their torn hands and legs and unable to use their guns, but the dogs had left them alive.

"Guard," he said, and the mastiffs stood at alert attention, watching the wounded men with serious, unblinking stares. "Good girls."

As the man crouched in front of Yumi to unravel her ties, she recognized his black and silver hair, and his bespoke charcoal suit from Fournier's. *Jonah Gideon.* "You're here for Selina?" she asked quietly.

"Among other reasons," he said in kind, pulling the loosened ropes free. "Did they hurt you badly?" he asked, glancing at the guards, then noticed her mangled left pinky fingertip. "Fuck, which of these shitheads did that to you!"

"I'm fine." Getting to her feet, Yumi felt the soreness in her wrists and ankles, as well as the nagging stinging in her finger, and mused that her pains were nothing compared to what she planned for her captors, in retaliation for their plot against her mentor and surrogate mother. "But they won't be," she snarled, fixing her eyes on the wounded guards.

"Save it. Let's get to Selina first," Jonah said, spotting Yumi's purse on the floor against the floor and passing it to her.

"Have you seen her?" Yumi asked, hearing a tiny pinging from her phone. "Is she alright?"

"She looked fine when she arrived, but that was a few minutes ago," Jonah said. "There was a crowd of armed guards escorting her inside, so I thought it'd be helpful to have some backup before charging to her rescue."

Yumi looked at the three massive dogs, each heavier than she was. "It looks like you found some."

"Who, the girls? They were just bored and wanted out of the kitchen," Jonah said, taking one of the guns that one of the men had dropped and that had fallen out of their reach. "Now, what do we do with you chuckleheads?"

Yumi gestured to a tiny door. "Utility closet. It locks from the outside, it's where they kept me until they got the ropes and camera ready."

"Hurry, if you want to stay alive," Jonah rushed the men. "Or, a bullet to your head will keep you just as quiet and out of the way."

"We won't all fit!" complained one of the men, looking at his burly cohorts cramming into the tight cubby.

"Suck in your gut, and pretend you're on the subway," Jonah snapped, shoving the last man in and closing and locking the door behind him. It was long enough for Yumi to pull her phone out and see what messages had come through. "You're checking your phone, *now*?" he berated.

Shit, shit, shit. Yumi's mind raced as she saw the missed call and voicemail from Mina, plus a string of unanswered text messages from Lin Xing, growing in urgency: *Check in? Where are you? Status please.* Then the last one, sent ten minutes ago: *Checked house security feed and turning on your tracker. Leaving now.*

"What's that sound?" Jonah asked, hearing the quiet pinging from Yumi's phone, like a sonar sound.

"That's my phone's tracking signal," Yumi said, muting the volume. The signal was still transmitting, though, as only Selina or Lin could actually shut off the tracker. "The fact that it's audible now means that Mister Xing is almost here."

Before they could discuss a strategy, a mature Englishman's voice came over an intercom, taunting in a sing-song tone: "I see you! What a mess you've made down here. Why don't you both come up and join us?" Heavy footsteps plodded down the steps, and several black-garbed men pointed their guns at them. "I'm afraid I must insist."

✧✧✧

208

Selina took a seat on the antique clawfoot settee, aware of the eyes and weapons trained on her from around the room. On the low coffee table in front of her was a clean, folded tissue, with Yumi's pendant and chain, and her blood-caked fingernail, on top of it. She glanced at the guards to see if there was any objection, before she wrapped the macabre trophies in the tissue and tucked the whole bundle in her jeans pocket.

As she waited in the sitting room for the Baron, Selina watched the various monitors that surveilled areas in the house: one was focused on Yumi in what looked like a basement, while others showed the garden and other rooms. In most, she saw shadows from quick figures that passed beyond the range of the cameras, but then she did finally spot Jonah briefly, before he darted out of sight. *Damn it.* She had planned to have a quick exchange with the Baron and secure Yumi's release with minimal violence, but Jonah's appearance was a complication she hadn't anticipated.

Once the Baron joined her, he watched the screens with her—or rather, he watched her reaction to what the monitors displayed—until the camera on Yumi went dark. He began fidgeting with a pocket watch chain that dangled from his waistcoat pocket, until he caught himself and stopped, but the camera malfunction was apparently unexpected. In response, he dispatched several of his hired men to the basement, but then he saw the feed from one of the other basement cameras, and there was a glimmer of recognition.

The Baron turned on the intercom and addressed Jonah and Yumi in that jeering, condescending tone of his, as Selina remained silent, taking a moment to study her adversary up close. After all the intervening years since she had last seen him, he looked the same, with cropped, curling reddish-blond hair, sharp green eyes and pink, porcine skin. After more than a century and a half, he looked *exactly* the same...

"That's not the man I was expecting," the Baron remarked to Selina, as he turned off the intercom, "but I am intrigued by how he's managed to come this far without getting caught. He looks like the young man that my boys reported seeing with you at lunch today. Who is he?"

"You'll have to ask him yourself," she said shortly.

He leered at her. "It is so good to see you again, Jin Mudan, and to hear your voice. I was bereft when I heard that you and your *lin* had given up and fled your land, but when I heard that you had settled in the States, I knew it was just a matter of time before I would find you again."

Selina elected not to engage him in conversation. She had nothing to say to the Baron, even when they were newly acquainted, so she certainly had nothing to say to him now, as an old foe. She let him speak, though, as he seemed to need an audience for his self-aggrandization, and he hadn't yet made his intention clear about whether he planned to kill her, or just keep her imprisoned.

"The years have made you soft and weak, or perhaps, it's your burden of a family," the Baron said. "I cut my daughter and the rest of my family loose decades ago," he boasted. "They would never understand what I've done, what I've sacrificed, for our legacy."

The Baron was rambling now, and Selina was grateful and relieved for Yumi and Jonah's arrival, as she could at least see for herself that they were unharmed. They arrived in the sitting room unaccompanied, however, with their faces and hands slightly blood-smeared, so Selina knew they had already dealt with the security detail dispatched to meet them downstairs. The Baron's remaining guards immediately had their guns aimed at the newcomers, halting their advance.

"Let them in," the Baron said easily. "They were invited to join us, after all."

He looked at Selina. "I can tell that they mean something to you, Jin Mudan, even though they're not even family. You certainly wouldn't have surrendered myself, if you didn't care. Your feelings are your vulnerability, while I refuse to let anyone use emotions as leverage against me. Never affection for an underling, certainly," the Baron said, as he motioned to have one of his guards shoot Yumi. Luckily, Yumi had noticed the gesture and pivoted in time to catch the bullet in her arm instead of her stomach, but she still yelped from the pain.

"Leave her alone!" Jonah barked, wrapping his arm around Yumi and drawing her back protectively. He looked evenly at the Baron. "You are Thomas Ashford Morrigan II, Baron of Devonshire?" he asked, almost derisively.

"You have me at a disadvantage, young man," the Baron said, seemingly taken aback by Jonah's knowledge of his name. Again, he reached unconsciously for his pocket watch and chain, then caught himself and forced his hand away. "You wouldn't happen to go by 'William Grant,' would you?"

Jonah shook his head. "You have the wrong man."

"Sit," the Baron ordered, directing the new arrivals to matching armchairs across from Selina's settee, and his guards to stand watch behind them. "What is your name, then?" he asked Jonah.

"It doesn't matter," Jonah sighed.

"Indulge me," the Baron said, with a similarly light tone. "Your wallet, please, or Miss Taira takes another bullet," he threatened, as one of the guards moved closer to Yumi's seat.

Jonah pulled out his wallet and let the Baron take it without a fight. "You don't have to hurt anyone. You can ask me anything you want. It's just that the answers won't matter," he said indifferently, passing Yumi his pocket square to help staunch her bleeding.

211

"I'll be the judge of that," the Baron muttered, opening Jonah's wallet. "A Massachusetts driver license; you're a long way from home, Mister… 'Jonah M. Gideon.'" At Jonah's casual shrug, he continued. "That's a biblical-sounding name, and peculiar, given your current, ungodly associations. What does the 'M' represent?"

"Ask your mom, she knows," Jonah mocked snidely. "It stands for 'motherfu—'"

One of the guards pistol-whipped Jonah before he could get the whole expletive out, but the Baron's face reddened anyway. Selina met Jonah's defiant blue eyes and gave him a mildly chastising frown, and he grinned cheekily, as he rubbed the back of his head where he had been struck.

Jonah's toying with him, Selina realized, wondering why Jonah seemed so confident about his chances with the Baron. *He called the Baron by his name…*

"If you must know, my middle name is 'Michael,'" Jonah said.

"Ah," the Baron said with satisfaction. "*Quis ut Deus?* It means: 'Who is like God?'"

"I suppose so, if you want to be literal with the translation," Jonah said staidly. "I just think of Michael as being the angel who guards and protects those in need."

"He is also the leader of God's army of angels," the Baron said, closing the wallet and returning it to Jonah. "Are you a God-fearing man, Mister Gideon? Be truthful; I'll know if you're lying."

"I have no reason to lie. I'll admit that I haven't been to church since this morning," Jonah said, "and I believe that devils and angels like to meddle in human affairs. Is that what you mean?"

"Then you must appreciate the work I'm doing, to try to rid the world of unnatural elements and creatures like *this*," he said, pointing scornfully at Selina. "Their wicked, foul existence taints this world and challenges the sovereignty of the Lord."

Selina admired Jonah's unflappable inscrutability, in the face of the Baron's deliberately provocative comments. She had heard all of it, and worse, throughout her years of living alongside human beings, but the rhetoric of zealous intolerance still chafed, especially when she noticed the discomfort it caused younger spirits like Yumi, sitting across from her with a petulant, distasteful scowl.

"Divine forces may choose human agents to do their bidding," Jonah replied, "but humans are fallible and don't always act as we should, especially when we forget what makes us special, like the expiration date on our lives."

Jonah's soothing, cajoling voice belied the warning in his words, which Selina understood clearly, knowing the context. *He's here as a reaper, for the Baron's soul.*

"Yours expired long ago, Baron," Jonah said. "So, born in 1810…how many lives have you stolen, so that you can stay as you are?"

"If you know so much about me, then you know that my work is too important to stop and worth any sacrifice!" the Baron cried. "These monstrous aberrations still overrun the world, corrupting humans with their magic and false faiths. They must be contained!" He glowered at Selina: "I had promised you that I would see you inside a cage again."

"Had you?" Selina asked mildly. "I've never given much thought to your incessant blathering."

Before the Baron could spew a rebuttal, the building shook with a quake-like shudder, and Selina and Yumi exchanged a look. It didn't feel like a typical San Francisco tremor, like the ones they had grown used to over the decades. None of the men around them seemed local, as they were caught off-guard by the sudden, unnerving mini-quake.

"*Zhè shì zěnme?*" Selina snapped in Chinese, noticing Yumi's guilt-ridden expression, in her own shorthand for: *What's going on?* or *What is this?*

"*Tā láile,*" Yumi replied, then mouthed to Jonah: *He's here.*

Selina was displeased that Lin had come, as it meant that he had been alerted to what had happened, and all chances of a peaceful outcome had evaporated. "You didn't tell—"

"We didn't," Jonah said. "He was already on his way."

The brief exchange went largely unnoticed by the Baron and his men, as their eyes were on the monitors that suddenly went black, and they clutched their guns more securely, but the Baron caught the tail-end of the chatter.

"'He'?" then Baron interjected with a wide-eye gleam, whether from excitement or panic, or perhaps equal measures of both.

"None of this involves you," Jonah addressed the guards. "You should leave while you can, and maybe take your friends in the basement with you." There was a shriek outside, followed by the staccato rapid-fire of an automatic weapon amid more screaming. "Last chance, boys."

As the guards rushed from the room, the Baron screeched with indignation at their abandonment. "No! I will have my victory, one way or another!" He aimed his gun directly at Selina's head. "If I die, Jin Mudan, you're coming with me."

He's actually crazy, like Ahab-level insane, Selina thought, *and he sees me as his stupid white whale.* She kept her composure to avoid provoking the Baron into acting rashly and tried to meet his gaze, but he avoided her eye contact, as if seeing her as a human instead of a beast would compromise his resolve.

With the Baron's attention focused on Selina, he missed Yumi's transformation back into her *kitsune* form, as she leapt onto his back and dug her sharp vulpine claws and teeth into his scalp and neck. It was enough of a diversion to let Selina dart out of the Baron's line of fire, as he flailed his arms and convulsed to try to dislodge Yumi—still entangled in her pink sweater— from his head and back.

A low snarl sounded next to Selina where Jonah had stood, followed by a blur of black and silver that swept past her and crashed down, tackling the Baron to the floor, as Yumi jumped away. The Baron howled in agony, as Jonah the wolf-dog clamped his jaws on the Baron's hand and tore the gun free. Yumi batted her paws to flick the gun across the floor, out of the Baron's reach, and leapt nimbly to Selina's side to guard her.

As the Baron stopped struggling, realizing that he was beaten, he stared wide-eyed at Jonah's powerful form looming over him, and at Yumi's diminutive but ferocious vulpine figure. "You're monsters, all of you!" He looked up at Jonah, almost sadly. "Even you, Mister Gideon?"

Jonah growled, as he started shifting back into his human form, his suit reforming against his skin, and it seemed as effortless for him as taking a deep breath. "You have no idea."

Selina's attention was sidetracked by her husband's appearance in the sitting room doorway, and she breathed a sigh of relief that he wasn't soaked in blood. She only took her eyes off Jonah and the Baron for a second, as she ran to greet Lin, but then she heard a yelp of alarm from Yumi.

Selina bit back a cry, seeing the Baron and Jonah locked against each other, with the Baron's fist around the hilt of a dagger whose blade seemed buried deep in Jonah's belly. Jonah frowned down at the dagger, then at the Baron, who looked stricken that Jonah was still standing after the crippling blow and not bleeding at all.

"This was meant for them," the Baron said, perplexed. "Why—"

Without comment, Jonah head-butted the Baron, and the older man reeled from the blinding pain, releasing his hold on the dagger before dropping to the floor woozily and falling unconscious.

"What a dick," Jonah muttered, rubbing his reddened forehead, then looked over at Selina and Lin. "It's good to see you again, Mister Xing. It's been a while."

Lin nodded, gesturing to the dagger hilt protruding from Jonah's belly. "Do you need a hand?"

"No, I got this," Jonah said, drawing a breath through his clenched teeth. "It's just… it was a serrated blade, so it'll hurt as much coming out as it did going in."

Selina returned to Jonah to look at where the dagger hilt jutted from his abdomen. The numinous Fournier suit had absorbed the injury and would look fine once the blade was removed, but Jonah was right: the puncture looked deep and painful. "You seem insistent on endangering yourself to impress us, Jonah," she said, disguising her concern with dry humor.

"It does seem that way, Missus Xing," Jonah said with an effort.

"You can call me 'Selina,'" she offered with a gracious nod.

"Really?" he smiled, momentarily forgetting his pain.

"Yes." She seized his moment of distraction to grab the dagger handle and yanked it out, and she still felt Jonah's flesh catch on the sawed edge of the knife, but he limited his pain response to a wince, despite the tears flooding his eyes. "You've earned it," she said, glancing at the thin, compact blade, gleaming as though never used. "Do you want to hold onto this?" she asked, holding out the dagger, as she looked down at the Baron.

Jonah shook his head, passing his hand over his shirt and belly to make sure that everything was intact. "Not right now, thanks. It's not my style."

Selina tossed the dagger on one of the armchairs and looked around for Yumi, who came forward, still in her *kitsune* form. "Yumi, dear, we should leave soon, if you want me to reattach your fingernail," she said.

Yumi responded with a yip, pawing at her fallen clothes. *It would be easier if I'm in my human form.*

"We'll wait for you in the hall," Lin offered kindly, turning to go. "Are you coming with us, Jonah?"

Selina shook her head "no" to Lin, as Jonah replied: "Thank you for the offer, but I need to finish my work here." He pulled a blank-looking notecard from his jacket pocket and glanced at the Baron. "I'll wait until he's awake, and allow him his final words."

"Let me know when you're done, or if you need anything," Selina said, following Lin from the room. She looked down the hallway to the ends of the house and listened, but the building was eerily quiet and empty now. There was blood everywhere, but no bodies. "Is everyone gone?"

"It seems so," Lin said nonchalantly. "There were some stragglers that I chased off when I arrived, but Jonah did most of the work, or perhaps his new friends…" He stopped and grinned solicitously. "Do you remember when we talked about getting a pet, since the house feels so empty when the children are away?"

"No, I don't recall that at all," Selina said warily, letting Lin lead her by the hand towards a side room that resembled the kitchen. "What is this about?"

"How would you feel about a dog?" he asked, as she caught the odor of canine dander mixed with ample drool, as well as the sound of thick nails scratching against hardwood. She froze in the doorway and stared

217

down at the trio of brindle mastiffs, even the smallest eclipsing her in heft. "Or, three?"

The dogs sat on their haunches and looked at them attentively, their wide jaws slack and dripping with thick saliva.

"Absolutely not," she muttered, thinking of the cleaning effort, not to mention the feeding, bathing, picking up during walks…

"Didn't you offer once, to let me bring home a second wife if I wanted?" he reminded teasingly.

"One wife, not three massive dogs," she returned, "and that was a century ago!"

He looked at her with wide, pleading eyes. "They're sisters and need to stay together. If they're left here, animal control will come in, and someone will see the copious human blood and torn clothing throughout the house and assume they're vicious… If they're not euthanized, they'll be separated and caged for the rest of their lives."

"Alright, fine!" she cried. Between her husband's dark, fretful gaze and the dogs' entreating stares and whimpers, Selina never stood a chance, and she resigned herself to a house full of dog hair and slobber, broken and mangled treasures, scratched-up parquet floors, stains on the antique rugs…

She sighed, as Lin crouched down to carouse with the trio of giants, who had already bonded with him and reveled in his attention. Whatever mess they brought with them, was outweighed by the childlike joy on her husband's face. For a glimpse of that infectious, carefree smile, she would be willing to tolerate a messy house and tumbleweeds of dog hair.

Chapter 13

Jonah averted his eyes, as Yumi shed her lustrous golden-red fur and shifted back into a human figure and gathered her clothes from the floor. She tugged on the garments she had shed when she reverted back into *kitsune* form, and needed to readjust the sweater and bra that had stayed on during her changes.

"You can look now," Yumi said, and he glanced over, but she had lied. She was still adjusting the cups on her push-up bra, with the hem of her sweater tucked under her chin. She laughed at his reticence. "Like you haven't been around a half-naked female before!"

"I don't ogle," he said, keeping his eyes fixed on her pretty face.

"I'd watch *you* dress, if I had the chance," she smiled, finally pulling down her sweater. "Jonah...may I call you Jonah?" She waited for his "go-ahead" wave with a coquettish smile. "Jonah, you're not this uptight and prudish with Mina, are you?"

He was immediately reminded of his intimacies with Mina and shook his head. "I'm not uptight, I just prefer to exercise my self-control. I don't believe in satisfying every urge I feel, just because I can."

"That's such an oddly human sentiment," Yumi said, finding her shoes and bag.

"Maybe because I'm oddly human?" he hazarded, glancing at the Baron to make sure he was still unconscious on the floor.

"You still are, aren't you? You haven't lost that part of yourself, despite your experiences," she said. "I mean, you can clearly take care of yourself in a fight, and then some, but you're not as hard or jaded as some of the other reapers I've met."

"I'm still new at the job, so let's see how I end up," he shrugged.

"I hope you stay this way," she said, stepping closer to him. "You're very sweet, and I can see why Mina likes you." She gave him a chaste kiss on the cheek, then held out his pocket square: neatly folded and pristinely white, just as it had been before she used it to staunch her bleeding bullet wound.

"I was ready to replace it for you, but Fournier accessories are as indestructible as the suits." Selina's bright voice called from the hallway, and Yumi returned: *"Hai, Xing-sama!* I'll be right there!" She brushed the lapel of Jonah's jacket flirtatiously, as she tucked the pocket square back into his breast pocket. "Will we see you later?"

"Depends on how long this will take," he said, seeing the Baron starting to stir. "Go, get your pinky and arm patched up."

Jonah took a seat in an armchair to wait for the Baron to recover consciousness, studying the serrated dagger, then studied the décor of the room. On the side table was a faceted crystal decanter filled with a caramel-amber liquid, with matching glasses. More crystal and cut glass decorated the room, as figurines and lighting fixtures, enlivening the outdated, dusty space with prismatic light and shine.

Jonah returned his attention to the Baron, as he awoke. The older man seemed momentarily confused, then angry, then a little alarmed when he realized that Jonah was still there, observing him silently with the dagger in hand.

"You're still here," the Baron said, sitting up on the floor. He hesitated in moving to the settee until Jonah gave him an assenting nod. "Thank you." He waited for Jonah to speak, expecting some impertinent snark or speech, perhaps, and noticed the stillness in the house.

"Everyone else is gone? Even my dogs?" he asked, and Jonah nodded. "Why are *you* here, then?"

"Your assigned reaper, William Grant, had another engagement," he said, running his thumb along the knife's saw-toothed edge, "so here I am, in his place."

The Baron stiffened, as his eyes darted around for a weapon of his own. "So you're here to kill me."

"No, that's not what I do," Jonah said, shaking his head. "Maybe that was Grant's specialty, but I don't like to kill anyone, unless they try to kill me first." He looked at the blade a last time before setting it next to himself on his seat cushion. "Did you stab me with a steak knife?"

The Baron looked offended. "That dagger is a sacred king-slayer blade, a relic from 13th century Italy, consecrated by Pope Gregory himself."

"Ah," Jonah nodded. "Which Gregory: IX or X?" He was silently gratified that he was finally able to use what he remembered from his high school medieval European history class.

"What?" the Baron asked.

"Which 13th century pope? Because Gregory IX, between his anti-Semitic decrees and the Papal Inquisition—"

"Gregory X," the Baron answered, his green eyes suspiciously narrowed. He was caught off-guard by Jonah's verbal engagement, given his earlier aloofness. "Why are you speaking with me?"

"You tried to kill me. I deserve to know why."

"You weren't my intended target, but you got in my way," he said. "It's not your fault. Clearly, you've been bewitched and seduced by them, as they like to take beautiful shapes to prey on men." He stopped and glared

221

at Jonah, remembering. "You were a wolf when you attacked me—you're a cursed beast, also."

"I was a dog," Jonah corrected tiredly. "Speaking of which, you didn't treat your pets very well," he added, recalling the mastiffs who had greeted him. "They told me they were taught from the time you bought them as puppies, to fear and distrust any human who showed them kindness, and to attack anyone who would try."

The Baron seemed unmoved, even proud of the viciousness he had instilled in his dogs. "What did you do with them? Did you have to put them down?"

"No, we got along just fine, since I wasn't human when I met them," Jonah smiled. "I asked them to greet Mister Xing nicely when he arrived, and judging by the quiet, they behaved themselves, so they're probably on their way to a safer, more loving home."

"You've denied me my quarry, routed my guards and taken my dogs," the Baron said. "What's next, Mister Gideon?"

"That's up to you," Jonah said, pouring two fingers worth of the amber-colored liquor from the crystal decanter, into a highball glass, which he held out to the Baron. "Any last words, or last thoughts? Any regrets or confessions?"

The Baron took the glass and sat back with a dubious scoff. "To share with *you*?"

Jonah remained expressionless. "If you don't want me here, I'll go, but you'll still die. Your soul can either haunt this place forever, consumed by whatever you're feeling now, or you can move on from this world and stand for judgment. If you believe in your piousness, then you should have no qualms about meeting your judges."

"I don't have to explain or justify myself to you," he muttered, gulping down the liquid.

As Jonah refilled the Baron's glass, he felt the familiar shimmer of air and energy of whenever a spirit was in the vicinity, and sure enough, a couple of ghostly figures wavered into his periphery. They looked like Chinese men from an earlier era, based on their outdated hair and clothes, with the younger one dressed in typical Victorian fashion, while the older one wore a simpler farmer's tunic and trousers. They glanced at him curiously but saved their more critical gaze for the Baron. They exchanged a few words, in a terse, guttural dialect that Jonah didn't understand but had heard spoken by Mina and her family.

Jonah wondered about the men's link to the Baron, who were unaware of their appearance, then pieced together what he recalled of Selina and Lin's complicated, prolonged history. "You knew Jin Mudan?" he asked, referencing the name that the Baron had used for Selina.

The younger man looked over in surprise. *Jin Mudan, the* huli jing*? She's alive?*

"She is," Jonah said, relieved that the spirit understood English. "And she's safe," he added, and the man nodded with relief.

"Who are you talking to?" the Baron asked, looking around the seemingly empty chamber.

Our family name was Bo, the older man said, his diction more accented but still proper and clear English. *We were the Baron's game wardens in Fujian, when he used to hold our lands there.*

"There are spirits here to see you off," Jonah said to the Baron. "Anything you wish to say to Mister Bo and his son?"

The Baron shook his head vehemently. "You're lying, playing a trick on me! They've been dead for more than a century!"

You stole their lives. You ruined us all. A woman's ghost wavered into Jonah's view, and she circled behind the Baron's seat on the settee. She was dressed in a full-skirted gown adorned with frills and lace, as befitting a

223

fashionable, wealthy woman of the late 19th century, and while the colors of her features were muted, Jonah imagined that her shining curls would have been bright red like the Baron's, and her pale eyes perhaps equally green.

She leaned over and whispered against the Baron's ear: *You knew I loved him, Father, and you kept us apart.* The Baron shuddered in response to her close presence and looked around but saw nothing.

Catherine. The younger man's spirit left his father's side and stepped closer to the woman.

The woman sighed heavily. *Isaac. I thought you would be spared, if I left. I'm so sorry, I didn't know...* She turned sharply and looked down at Jonah. *Don't let him take it!*

Jonah reached down and grasped the dagger hilt instinctively, as he saw the Baron edge closer towards it. "Why? What's special about it?"

The Baron was tight-lipped and glowering defiantly, but his daughter, Catherine, was more forthcoming. *Push down and twist the pommel*, she directed. *These king-slayer blades had hidden compartments in the grips, that assassins would use to hide their orders.*

Jonah did as Catherine advised and felt the pommel release from the hilt, revealing a tight scroll of parchment hidden within. With an effort, and with the Baron watching closely, Jonah unfolded and uncurled the yellowed, brittle paper, lettered with faded brownish ink in some form of Latin. "It looks like a contract."

"You have no right! That belongs to me!" the Baron demanded shrilly, but Jonah wordlessly brandished the dagger to remind the Baron that he was no longer in charge.

It was my father's contract, allowing him to kill with impunity and steal years of life from others, Catherine said. *My father showed it to me, once, and swore to me that he wouldn't take from Mister Bo's family, if I returned to England, but they were all lost in a generation.*

"You killed Bo's entire family?" Jonah asked.

"I did not!" the Baron replied hotly. "Life was wasted on peasants like them, so I borrowed a few years from each of them. They deserved it for their treachery and lies, for trying to protect the creatures that infested my land."

"*Their* land," Jonah corrected. "They lived there long before the Europeans started carving it up after the Treaty of Nanjing and the other forced concessions." He noticed the surprised stares at him from the spirits. "What? I know some history." As Jonah looked over the contract, the letters reshaped themselves on the paper into English to make themselves understandable to him, similar to how written text in a dream could distort itself to become more or less legible.

"History books won't tell you what savages the people were," the Baron defended. "We brought them civilization—"

Catherine shook her head sadly. *You haven't changed, Father, even after all these years.*

"You said you 'borrowed' their years," Jonah interjected, and he finishing reading through the contract. "But you never planned to provide restitution for any of them, did you?" From the look on the Baron's face, it was clear that the idea had never crossed his mind. "You'd read the fine print, I presume, so you knew that if the contract were destroyed, your life would be restored."

"Why would I destroy the contract? It gave me time, to fulfill my life's purpose," the Baron said.

Because you entered into a devil's bargain. Jonah was fairly certain that no angel would have negotiated with the Baron to allow him to steal life from others, in exchange for his soul, or have the contract written in blood, as this one was. Just as an angel was unlikely to

225

include a clause to void the contract if the Baron ever acted against "any divine entity, present and past, or agent thereof."

"There is no one left to give you more time," Jonah said, holding out the contract. "I suggest you make peace with that."

Refusing to accept his fate, the Baron began to recite an incantation under his breath, and Jonah felt a cool tingle against his skin.

Those are the words he used against us, Isaac recognized. *He's trying to steal your lifeforce, as he did from us.*

"You're wasting your time," Jonah warned. "It won't work!"

But the Baron only raised his voice, drowning out Jonah's advice, so Jonah tossed the frayed, discolored scrap of paper on the coffee table between them, threw up his hands in disgust and sat back, to let the Baron reach his own conclusion.

After a minute, the Baron realized that his words were ineffectual, and Jonah was unchanged. "How are you unaffected?"

"Your contract has a condition that forbids you from harming certain parties," Jonah reminded, pointing to the yellowed parchment scrap. "Your stabbing of me was accidental, but what you just tried was a deliberate violation of the terms," he explained carefully, "so your contract is void."

"No, you tricked me!" the Baron raged, snatching the contract off the table to read it for himself. "There is nothing divine or holy about you!"

"That's true, I'm more like a subcontractor," Jonah said blandly, watching the Baron mentally unravel before his eyes, as he tore the fragile parchment into bits in a desperate attempt to destroy his contract.

Father, you cannot escape your fate, Catherine said.

226

"The contract is gone, so I'm freed from it!" the Baron cried. "My life is restored," he said, breathing more easily.

"That's not how it works," Jonah said solemnly. "Your life is now restored to what it would have been, if you had never made your bargain—your true, natural lifespan, which was supposed to end over a century and a half ago."

As the spirits stood watch, Jonah waited for the ravages of age to consume the Baron, and the doomed Englishman was helpless to escape his fate. Within minutes, the Baron's hair and skin faded and thinned, his vibrant green eyes had clouded and dulled, and his stout, robust frame had shrunken and wasted to a husk of how he once was, but the process continued.

The Baron's rheumy eyes bulged in shock and recognition, as his gaze passed over Jonah, to the stoic ghosts who came to witness his end.

He can see us now, Catherine said, realizing that her father's time was nearly over.

Isaac moved closer to her and touched her hand, tentatively, and was amazed that he could actually feel her ghostly skin against his own.

The Baron could only watch his daughter reunite with her love, and he leaned back against the cushions when he could no longer hold himself upright. It was a quicker, less agonizing and more merciful demise than the Baron perhaps deserved, given the cruelty he had shown to others, but Jonah was only there to oversee the passage of the soul, not its judgment or final fate.

Unlike Millicent Krantz and William Grant, who had left their mortal bodies with a kind of transcendent peacefulness, the Baron's spirit seemed stuck, almost entangled and embedded within his rapidly decaying body. Only when the Baron's remains had reduced to little more than a withered skeleton, did the spirit finally release its hold.

I'm not ready to go, he lamented, still looking longingly at his physical body.

Your victims were not ready to go, either, Catherine scolded her father. *This is a just end for you.*

Catherine, he called, reaching for her. *I wanted to keep you safe from his ungodly influence. I had to send you home.*

She shook her head with a forlorn sadness, avoiding his hand. *You lied to me, Father! You told me that Isaac had wed another, so that I would agree to marry Crain. By the time I learned the truth, my children were born, and Isaac was already dead. I betrayed him because of you!*

Isaac tugged at her hands and kissed them. *You didn't betray me—you were tricked. If we had to be apart, then it was good that you shared your life with another, so you could raise a family like you always wanted.*

Like we wanted, she said. *To my last day, I never stopped thinking and dreaming of you.*

I dreamed about you, also, he smiled, *so perhaps we have always been together*.

Finally accepting his mortality and powerlessness, the Baron's spirit began to fade, and his eyes stared off in an empty, unfocused gaze. *I will receive my just reward during judgment?*

"I don't know where you will go, but there's nothing left for you in this world." Jonah said. Whether the Baron's fate would be fair or just was not for Jonah to know or decide.

Bowing his head a final time, the spirit of Thomas Ashford Morrigan II, the one-time lord of Devonshire, faded like a fine mist, as Catherine and Isaac Bo bore witness. When his presence was gone, the spirits of the lovers joined their hands and combined their glows into a blinding incandescence that passed through the ceiling and out of the chamber, leaving the room felt noticeably dimmer and cooler.

Still, there was one spirit that lingered.

"Did you need something, Mister Bo?" Jonah asked, watching the ghost of the Baron's elderly game warden pace the room.

No, reaper. My son has reunited with his love, and with Ashford gone, my family can now be at peace. I think I am here to help you find something.

Jonah tracked the spirit, as Bo went to examine the skeletal remains of the Baron. "I don't understand. What am I missing?"

Bo noticed the long, straight red-golden hairs on the rug and chair where Yumi had been in her spirit form. *These are fox hairs. Did they come from the* huli jing?

"They didn't come from Selina…Jin Mudan, but yes, there was another one here with her," Jonah said. "Is that important?"

The Baron hunted the golden fox, but he also hunted her companion, a mighty, noble lin *who protected her fiercely. Ashford never caught either of them, but he did wound the* lin *on a couple of occasions over his decades of pursuit.* Bo peered at the Baron's pockets for some tell-tale clue. *The Baron had us deliver to him any evidence of the* lin*'s injuries: blood-stained bullets or torn fur, especially.*

"As trophies?" Jonah scowled.

Bo straightened and took a step back. *No, to use for a talisman. The Baron has a pocket watch in his waistcoat pocket. Left side.*

Jonah spotted the chain and pulled out the anachronistic timepiece. "It's not even working," he said, noticing the unmoving hands, and the lightness of the watch, as though it were hollow. He found the catch that held the mechanism closed and carefully cracked the watch open. Instead of metal gears and fittings, the watch held bits of hair, fur, nail trimmings and flecks of blood,

229

bound together by clear wax into a disgusting-looking cake, like something fished out of a clogged drain.

"This is all from the *lin*?" Jonah asked, then the significance of the name of Mina's father finally struck him. "His name is 'Lin.'"

Lin *was the kind of creature he was,* Bo said, *but throughout the centuries, he's been called by many names: Baphomet, Xing'tian or just Xing...*

Lin Xing. "Oh, shit," Jonah blurted, snapping the watch shut. "The Baron created this as a talisman against him? Did it work?"

I cannot say, but the Baron was never wounded in any of the pursuits after Jin Mudan or her lin.

Jonah had dismissed Lin Xing's lack of aggression towards the Baron—even though the man had threatened his wife and family—as a matter of self-restraint, but perhaps there had been something else at work. Jonah pocketed the watch. "I don't know yet what I should do with it, but it can't stay here for someone else to find."

Better with you than with others, Bo nodded in agreement. *The dagger should remain with you, as well. It is still a consecrated weapon and too dangerous to leave for anyone to misuse.*

Jonah found the sheath for the dagger on the floor, near where he and the Baron had struggled earlier. As he rose from the floor, Jonah heard sirens in the distance. "I should probably go. There's too much here that I can't talk my way out of."

Jonah bowed his head to the spirit. "*Xie xie nin,* Mister Bo."

No need for that, Bo smiled and shook his head. *You said the* huli jing *Jin Mudan is still alive?*

"Yes, and married to the *lin* you described, unless I'm mistaken," Jonah said, trying to envision Lin Xing as anything other than Mina's intimidating father.

It is good that they have survived this long. As a boy, my son swore to always protect her and keep her

230

free, Bo said, accompanying Jonah from the sitting room, towards the kitchen. *The front door is the other way.*

"I know," Jonah said, securing the pocket watch and sheathed dagger, and pointed to the pet door. "But I'll draw less attention as a stray dog than as a strange man lurking on the property."

Bo chuckled, as Jonah shifted back into his canine form. *That is an impressive trick, reaper! Lady Crain had a fascination with the arcane and would have enjoyed seeing that.*

Lady Crain, Jonah echoed, rattling the name around in his head. *Catherine Crain.*

Bo nodded. *As she and my son grew closer, she spoke against her father often. After she was widowed, she moved from England and settled in New York, to get herself and her red-headed sons as far away from the Baron as she could.*

Jonah ducked through the pet door and waited for Bo's spirit to join him outside. *Red-headed sons?*

Two of them, Bo said, strolling alongside Jonah across the thick, emerald lawn. *She named the elder one after her husband, Alexander, and the younger after her grandfather, Morrigan. Their descendants are still somewhere in New York, I would guess.*

Perhaps, Jonah said, thinking of Xani and Morgan Crain, with their red hair and green eyes. He looked at Bo and noticed: *You're fading now.*

The spirit looked down at his near-transparent form, as they neared the fence line. *I must be done, then. Good-bye, reaper.*

Good-bye, sir.

Jonah trotted towards the broken fence where he had gain entry earlier. He paused and looked over his haunch towards the garden, but the elderly ghost had already gone. Where the spirit had stood was a new addition to the garden: a cracked granite boulder, with a gnarled, knotted rock pine firmly rooted in the fissures, and the pine's long, silver-green needles waving and basking in the golden afternoon sun.

Mina and Adam rushed to the front door at the sound of their parents' voices, and they breathed a shared sigh of relief to see that their mother and father were both unharmed and in good spirits, and that Yumi had accompanied them.

Their parents dropped their shoes by the door, and Yumi tried to follow their example, but she winced as she reached down towards her feet, and Mina noticed the blood on Yumi's left pinky and right forearm, not to mention her cut lip and bruises on her face.

"Oh, fuck the shoes!" Mina cried, as she came forward to help Yumi. "If she tracks any dirt in, *I'll* mop, if you want," she offered, as her mother opened her mouth to comment, then stopped dead when she saw what was still waiting outside the front door. "Mom?" she called over her shoulder.

"The mop and bucket are in the hall closet, Min-Min," her mother said breezily, as she led Yumi to the kitchen. "According to their tags, they're Goneril, Regan and Cordelia, but you know your father won't let that stand."

Three oversized, jowly, drooling brindle dogs sat on the landing, watching Mina expectantly, their muscular tails slapping the ground like batons. Adam joined Mina at the door shortly and was just as startled to see the gargantuan dogs.

As they heard their father's sharp calling whistle from inside, Adam tugged Mina aside, and the dark-coated trio barreled into the house, towards the sound of their father's voice in the office. As Adam shut the door, he and Mina exchanged a *WTF?* look that conveyed their mutual confusion.

232

"You help Mom with Yumi—"Adam started, heading for the office.

"—and you ask Dad about the dogs," Mina finished, pointed towards the kitchen.

As he approached their father's den, Adam called into the crowded room: "So, Dad, did you ride home on those things, or something?"

The kitchen was quieter and less cramped, as Selina was preparing a concoction in another saucepan from her innumerable cookware collection. Yumi took a seat at the counter, with her blood-stained sleeve pulled up over her elbow, and a small slug on a napkin next to her. On a crumpled-up tissue lay a delicate nail, pearlescent pink and smudged with dried blood.

"Ouch," Mina grimaced. "How can I help?"

"You didn't use up my ginseng, did you?" her mother asked, as she sifted through her spice pantry.

"I used the last of the American for Adam, but there should still be a tin of Korean red, next to the organic mugwort," Mina said, taking the seat next to Yumi. "Do you want some tea?"

"Water it down," her mother cautioned. "Caffeine will raise her blood pressure."

"Just some water, thanks, and a wet paper towel, please," Yumi said.

"Coming right up," Mina said, getting a water glass and tearing a paper towel to take to the sink. "You know you could've said something, earlier, when you walked me home. You could've come inside, and we would've figured out together how to deal with the Baron's goons."

Yumi lowered her eyes, and Selina answered: "That would've gone against my wishes. Yumi's role is to deflect risk from you and your brother, and to defend you, if avoidance is not an option. Yumi did exactly as I had requested of her; under no circumstances, were you to get anywhere near the Baron."

233

"*Arigato gozaimasu, Xing-sama,*" Yumi replied with a bow of her head. She took the glass of water and dampened paper towel from Mina with a grateful nod. "Thanks."

Mina frowned at her mother. "And whose job would it be to keep Yumi safe?"

"Mine, of course, if the situation calls for it," her mother said with infuriating calm.

"Yours!" Mina exclaimed. "You were marched into the Baron's house by armed gunmen…"

"Who told you that?" Selina asked mildly, then glanced over at her phone, next to her purse on the counter, at the sound of an incoming text chime. "Jonah, of course," she said, distractedly.

"Yes, it was Jonah!" Mina replied hotly, then noticed that her mother was reading the new text. "Mom?"

"Sorry." Selina turned her phone face-down and smiled at Mina and Yumi. "Jonah's done with securing the Baron's soul."

"Wait, why is Jonah texting *you*?" Mina asked, suppressing the urge to check her own phone.

"I asked him to keep me apprised," Selina said simply, returning her attention to her simmering saucepan.

"Is he coming here?" Yumi asked, gently cleaning her scratches and lip, as she held her arm out for Mina to check her bullet wound.

"I didn't ask," Selina shrugged, "and he didn't say."

"Then probably not," Mina said quietly, trying not to pout. "Jonah's not the type to assume that he can just stop by without an invitation." *Shit, at this point, it looks like everyone's either seen or spoken to Jonah, except me*, she thought glumly.

"*Kawaii, desu ne?*" Yumi whispered slyly. *He's cute, isn't he?*

234

"*Hai, totemo kawaii*," Mina smiled, despite herself. *Yes, very cute.*

"He probably just wants to clean himself up before he sees you again," Yumi suggested. "He's very bold and not afraid to get dirty in a fight. Is he that way about everything else, too?"

Selina was pretending not to hear their hushed exchange, but the edge of her lip twitched with amusement. "Min-Min, can you please get me the bandages from the guest bathroom, while the poultice cools off?"

"Sure, be right back." Buoyed by the thought of seeing Jonah soon, Mina skipped into the hallway and stopped when she saw her father by the front door, slipping his shoes back on. "*Ba-ba*, you're not going back to the office, are you? It's almost five."

"I have a meeting that I need to take," he said, scratching the jowls and chins of his three new pets who had accompanied him to the door. "This should be quick, and I'll be back for dinner, but I'll let your mother know not to wait on me."

"But, Dad—"

Her father shut the door firmly behind himself, as Adam emerged from the office.

"Where is Dad going?" Mina asked, continuing to the powder room for the supplies her mother requested.

"Not entirely sure," Adam said. "He got a text from Bullfinch while we were talking in the office."

Mina flattened herself against the wall to avoid the pack of mastiffs that raced past her, in pursuit of their Tibetan spirit dog, Dawa, who floated past in a cloud-like blur of snowy white and led the stampede back into the office. Mina flinched at the sound of something ceramic crashing onto the office floor.

"What was that?" called Selina warily from the kitchen.

"I'll take care of it," Adam replied, turning on his heel to return to the office.

"Wait, Bullfinch isn't in town, is he?" Mina shouted, chasing after her brother.

"Nope, he was calling from New York," Adam said, shaking his head at the blue and white antique vase that had chipped in its fall from their father's bookcase. He gave the dogs—the three mastiffs and the white *ruishi*—a reprimanding frown, which curtailed their collective exuberance at once.

"Wow, that's impressive," Mina remarked at Adam's easy command of the dogs. "Do you know who set up the meeting through Bullfinch, then? If it's work-related, wouldn't it be scheduled through the office?"

"If they coordinated through Bullfinch, I'm pretty sure it's not business," Adam said, gingerly picking up the shards of the vase, of which there were thankfully few. "Maybe check with Mom. Dad said that he would text her on his way to the meeting."

Mina rushed back to the kitchen, with a sneaking suspicion that her father was on his way to meet Jonah. Before she could ask her mother, however, Selina put Lin on speakerphone to keep her hands free to treat Yumi's bruises and scrapes with the fragrant herbal poultice. Mina passed the bandages to her mother and listened without interrupting, as her parents discussed how long her father's meeting would take.

"It was his request to meet," Lin said.

"Yes, but you set the time and place," Selina returned. "You could've scheduled something for the morning instead, when he's had a chance to think about what he wants to discuss."

"Even more reason to meet sooner," Lin said. "He could've waited until morning to contact Bullfinch, too, so perhaps he has his own reason for urgency."

Selina noticed Mina's intense focus on the conversation and mouthed, *Your father's meeting Jonah.*

236

As Mina started to interject, she felt her own phone buzz against her hip, and she saw Cindy's name on the screen. *Fuck this timing!*

Storming from the kitchen, Mina put the phone to her ear, taking a breath before she answered, "Hello?"

There was a pause on the other end before Cindy replied tentatively, "Did I catch you at a bad time?"

"No, sorry." Mina sagged onto the cold marble steps, hearing the guardedness in her friend's voice. "What's wrong, Cin? What happened?"

"I'm..." Cindy started, then paused. "It's not a big deal. Morgan and I split up, that's all," she said in a rush, so quickly that it took a few seconds for the words to register.

"What? How is that not a big deal?" Mina snapped. "What did Morgan do?"

Cindy laughed tiredly through a sniffle. "Why do you assume that it was something he did?"

"Because I know you," Mina said, petting Dawa's head as the *ruishi* tucked his head under her free hand to solicit her attention. "You don't repeat your mistakes, and you'd sooner pluck out your eye than do anything that might hurt Xani."

"I know, she's so *sensitive*, right?" Cindy joked melodramatically. "That's true—I love Xani to death, but... I could make an eye patch work, if I had to, couldn't I?"

Mina could tell that Cindy was fishing for an ego boost, despite her jocular tone. "Cindy, you could rock a *Phantom of the Opera* face mask without even trying, even with the goofy cape."

It was good to hear Cindy's laughter. "Thanks, honey. How's everything over there? How's Jonah?"

"I haven't the slightest idea," Mina said, sobering. "He's been in town since last night, and I haven't even gotten a text from him. I was hoping he would come by the house—"

237

"No, sweetheart, you do *not* want that!" Cindy cut in with a laugh.

"Why the fuck not?"

"Because it's one thing for your parents to know that you're a grown-ass woman, but they don't need to watch you undressing your man with your eyes," Cindy reminded. "And if, somehow, Jonah gets invited to stay the night, your whole family would hear the two of you going at it like rabbits."

"They would not!" Mina said, her face reddening. "I mean, we wouldn't be…" Her voice trailed, as Adam passed her on his way to the kitchen. "Shut up, Cindy," she muttered.

Cindy broke into all-out laughter on her end of the call. "I'm glad I called you, honey," she said. "You always know how to make me feel better."

"I'm glad I could help," Mina said. "You still haven't told me what Morgan did."

"It doesn't matter," Cindy sighed. "I'll get over it."

"Yeah, you will," Mina reassured. "If you're still in a funk by the time I get back, I'll bake a batch of triple-chocolate cupcakes for you."

"Could you bake some for me, anyway?"

"Whatever you want," Mina smiled. "Love you, Cin."

"Love you more, Min," Cindy returned. "Give your fiancé a big hug and kiss from me, when you see him next. Whatever you want to do to him after that, is up to you, but I hope you make it worth all your waiting. At least *one* of us should be having some fun."

Chapter 14

Jonah looked up at the sound of the elevator doors opening, and noticed how most of Lin Xing's employees watched for their boss's arrival. Jonah had been silently observing and listening as the business day drew to a close, and he had found the common comradery and good humor of the colleagues heartening. The employees of the Xing Corporation appeared to enjoy each other's company, and their goodwill extended up the chain of command, as well, judging by the smiles and nods that Lin received as he strolled through the lobby.

Jonah stood to greet Lin and took a moment to take a closer look at him. Prior to the brief exchange they had shared at the Baron's house, Jonah had last seen him years ago, shortly after Mina and Malcolm's wedding, and the man was still as imposing and handsome as Jonah recalled. With his hair still jet-black, and his eyes dark and piercing in his sculpted face, he resembled a slighter older version of Adam.

"Jonah," he greeted with his hand extended. "You didn't have any trouble getting in, I hope."

"Mister Xing," Jonah answered, taking his hand with a deep nod, almost a bow. "Not at all, sir. Your security guard downstairs had everything ready. Thank you for seeing me on such short notice."

Mina and Adam's father had a thin but handsomely-shaped mouth, that had the natural appearance of a smile, even when the rest of his face was definitely not broadcasting joviality or warmth. "We can talk in my office," he said leading the way to the corner office, with its view of the bay. "I asked for some tea to be brought in, while I was on my way over, but I can request some water?"

"Tea is fine, sir," Jonah said, spotting a tray with a stout cast iron teapot and two ceramic cups and a small towel, at one corner of Lin's desk.

As Lin closed his office door, Jonah felt his critical, careful gaze as he repeated the ritual that he had seen Mina perform whenever she served tea at home: wipe the inside of the cups dry, swirl a teaspoon of steaming hot tea in each cup to warm and rinse them, pour out the tea into the towel, dry the cups again, then finally fill the cleaned cups with fresh tea. He presented one of the cups to Lin, holding the cup with both hands.

Lin nodded, as he took the cup and gestured Jonah to sit. "Your cousin never served me tea."

"Malcolm wasn't a tea drinker," Jonah said, taking the guest chair across from Lin's seat.

"I know, but neither were you, as I recall," Lin said, taking a small sip of the steaming brew. "It shows respect, to know how to serve what one doesn't usually drink."

Jonah took his cup of tea and lifted it to Lin before he took a tiny, scalding sip. *Shit, that's hot.* He had a short list of items that he needed to discuss with Mina's father and wasn't sure about the priority, so he opted to start with what was foremost in his mind, as he met his dark, unreadable eyes: "You scare the hell out of me, sir."

"Really?" The edge of Lin's lips curved in a wry smile, as he sipped his tea. "After all that you've experienced, *I* am what scares you? Perhaps you'll feel better, once we've cleared up some things."

Jonah blew softly on his tea to cool it. *Good things? Bad things?*

240

"Let's start from the top: you proposed to my daughter," Lin said.

"Yes, sir," Jonah said, trying not to grimace or smile.

"And she hadn't given you her answer before you parted ways."

"That's true." Jonah didn't want to overshare with Mina's father about their complicated exchanges but knew he was expected to clarify. "She hadn't rejected me out of hand, but I didn't want to force her for a definitive answer."

"That was a wise move on your part," Lin said. "My daughter doesn't respond well to being pushed." He paused. "Or struck," he said, more quietly.

He knew what Malcolm did to her. Even though the guilt wasn't his, Jonah felt his face heat with shame over his late cousin's conduct.

"You've won over my children and my wife, so my blessing is just a formality, isn't it?" Lin said. "Mina still wears your ring. I assume that it's a piece with sentimental value, as it's not very big or showy, and you don't strike me as the type to skimp on romantic gestures."

"No, sir, but I'm more inclined to show my feelings through actions than words."

"Like jumping into a pit of certain doom, or in front of a madman's dagger?" Lin took a sip of his tea, seemingly unbothered by the scalding heat. "I hate to see my daughter in pain, so be certain that you've explored all your options before you risk yourself again. Is that clear?"

"Yes, sir." Only Lin Xing could make Jonah feel guilty for hurting Mina through his self-sacrifice. At his core, Jonah hadn't expected Mina to mourn him as she had—he had given himself because he loved her, but not with any expectation that she loved him as deeply in return.

241

"You look intact, so I presume that everything went smoothly with the Baron, after we left you?"

"I had some help," Jonah said, setting down his cup. "The Baron's daughter, and the spirits of Bo and his son."

Lin looked thoughtful. "A curious ensemble. How were they able to help you?"

"Catherine guided me to the Baron's contract," Jonah recalled. "Once the contract was destroyed, he seemed to fall apart, mentally and physically. Bo's son, Isaac, was there to reconcile with Catherine."

"And Bo, himself?"

Jonah replayed Bo's description of Jin Mudan's *lin* companion: *Throughout the centuries, he's been called by many names: Baphomet, Xing'tian or just Xing…*

"Jonah?" Lin prompted.

Jonah met Lin's dark, assessing gaze, then pulled out the Baron's sheathed king-slayer dagger, setting it on Lin's desk. His heart was pounding, as he was taking a huge risk handing over a consecrated weapon to a powerful entity like Lin—if his hunch was right—but Jonah had no use for such a weapon.

"Are you really Baphomet, or am I mistaken?" Jonah asked.

"I've been called many things over my lifetime," Lin said. "I've been called that, as well one of the Four Horsemen of the Apocalypse, and even *the* Devil. Would you believe me, if I told you that my existence actually predates most of my names?"

"I don't know enough to be certain of anything," Jonah admitted. "But I have no reason to wish you any harm, so there's no reason for me to keep that," he gestured to the dagger.

"Thank you," Lin said, but made no move to take it. "Did Bo tell you anything else about me?"

Jonah felt the hard, smooth metal of the Baron's watch and chain in his inner pocket, against his chest.

"He said the Baron had been hunting you and your wife for a very long time."

"The Baron chased us for well over a century," Lin said, finishing his tea. "I promised Selina that I wouldn't try to kill him, although I did try to hurt him, but he always escaped unscathed."

Lin set down his cup and picked up the dagger, examining it briefly before setting it back on the desk, in front of Jonah. "Hold onto that, just in case."

"Just in case of what?" Jonah frowned.

"I haven't survived this long by trusting humanity," Lin said quietly. "I know the Baron took measures against me, such as holy weapons like *that*, and even protective wards and charms to prevent me from harming him. My wife takes similar precautions to guard our home and our family, also—but I've learned to embrace and welcome my vulnerabilities. They remind me to cherish what I have, to not become complacent and assume my good fortune."

Jonah shook his head, not entirely understanding. "If the dagger is a threat, why give it to me?"

"Who better to keep an instrument of death, than a reaper?" Lin smiled grimly. "The knife by itself has no special powers against me—I'm not a demon or foul, fell beast, despite what the Baron believed. But the dagger wielded by the keeper of the Baron's talisman...now, that would sting a bit."

"His talisman?" Jonah asked, even as the metal casing of the watch rested against his breast.

"It protected the Baron from me, but also made me susceptible to his attacks," Lin said, refilling Jonah's cup of tea, and smiling when Jonah instinctively rapped the desk in a show of politeness. "I know you have it with you; you would've been a fool to leave it behind and unsecured, just as with the dagger." He nudged the knife an inch closer to Jonah. "Take it. I insist."

"How did you know that I kept them with me?" Jonah asked incredulously.

"You had just left the Baron's house a few minutes before you called Bullfinch, so of course, you still had them with you," Lin said. "I couldn't invite you to our home for that reason. If somehow you managed to get through our front door with those artifacts in your pockets, you would have gone into cardiac arrest. Or gotten turned into stone, depending on what my wife finally decided to cast."

"Selina's protective wards," Jonah realized. "Mina has similar ones around her apartment."

"You know the perils of being part of this family, then," Lin said. "You still want to marry my daughter?"

"Yes, sir, more than anything," Jonah said.

Lin smiled at Jonah's ready answer. "In some ways, I feel sorry for the Baron. In isolating himself from his family, he deprived himself of a truly full and happy life and left no one behind to mourn his passing. I imagine he left a will, but he left no descendants to miss and celebrate him."

Jonah reserved comment, not knowing enough about the Crain family to be absolutely certain about whether Xani and Morgan were part of it. That could be awkward, if it was revealed that Xani and Morgan's ancestor tried to kill Adam and Mina's parents…

"Something on your mind?" Lin asked.

"Nothing that's for me to share," Jonah deflected quietly.

"You've had a long couple of days, Jonah," Lin said, implying that Jonah looked as tired as he felt. "You could probably use a long nap and a hot shower," he said, rising to his feet. "I won't keep you, unless there's anything else you wanted to discuss with me?"

Jonah checked his mental list, and got to his feet, as well, following Lin's cue. "Why did you go to the

Baron's house for Selina, knowing that you wouldn't be able to take action against him?"

"Because she is my wife," Lin answered readily. "And we do complement each other: I may not have been able to do anything against the Baron, but Selina has no such limitations. I just needed to make sure that no one else got in her way. As it turned out, you did most of the hard work for us, so thank you."

"No thanks necessary." Jonah was curious about whether his next assignment had come in, so he pulled out his dog-eared card and was relieved to still find it blank. "It looks like my handlers have given me the night off."

"Good, you deserve a break. Don't forget to take that with you," Lin said, gesturing to the dagger, as he opened his office door.

Jonah tucked the dagger into his pocket, with lingering reluctance. "You're entrusting me with tools that have the power to seriously weaken you."

"Oh, more than that," Lin said lightly. "You have the power to destroy me, if you really wanted to."

Jonah stopped at the door and faced Lin. "What?"

"I'm entrusting you with my children, Jonah," Lin said solemnly. "I'm putting my full faith in you, to keep them safe and sound; Mina and Adam are more precious to me, and have more power over me, than a couple of dusty old trinkets ever could."

As Jonah let the gravity of Lin's words sink in, he reached absently for the other man's outstretched hand. "I won't betray your confidence, sir."

"I know you won't," Lin said, patting Jonah's shoulder as he squeezed his hand. "You're welcome to join us for breakfast in the morning, if your schedule allows."

"That would be nice, thank you." Jonah felt the weight of the pocket watch and the dagger weighing down his jacket. "That will give me some time to figure out what to do with the Baron's sh—" He stopped himself, noticing Lin's raised eyebrow. "His things."

Lin nodded, leaning against his office doorjamb. "I could recommend a few shielded and consecrated vaults that would accommodate you, but it would be safer if I didn't know. Good night, Jonah, and good luck."

Jonah felt trapped in his body, unable to fight against what was happening to him. He knew he was in a dream, as nothing he saw or felt was a true memory, but the sensation of his bones reforming and his flesh reaffixing to his skeleton was visceral and maddening.

He recalled his conversation with Lucifer and Gabriel before his resurrection, when he was told that he was being remade, in a very literal sense. It was one of the few cogent thoughts he had, as his ability to think clearly was compromised by the hysterical, tortured screams of others around him, feeling their own bodies in various stages of disintegration or reconstruction.

Jonah forced himself awake and lay for a moment in bed, staring at the plain white ceiling of his hotel room, appreciating the pain-free wholeness of his body and the stillness of the room. Well, mostly pain-free; he had a bruise on his side and a slight soreness in his shoulder where William Grant's bullets had almost pierced him, plus a deep, purplish contusion over his belly where the Baron's dagger had torn into him, but Jonah would take a little discomfort over actual holes.

Jonah sat up and realized that he was starving. Apart from his dim sum meeting with Selina at noon, he hadn't eaten anything substantial since leaving New York. He had intended to get something to eat while he was waiting for Aciré to return his text, but she had replied promptly, and Jonah had gotten distracted with following the protocols that she had recommended to secure the Baron's artifacts. After he was done, Jonah had returned to his room, shed his suit and stretched out on the bed, expecting to take a quick nap before showering...

Apparently, that had been several hours ago, according to Jonah's phone display. He confirmed it with a quick glance out his window at the soupy, cloud-thick fog suspended below the star-specked night sky. Despite the late hour, Jonah didn't want to skip dinner again, but nor did he relish the idea of getting dressed just to go searching for a place to eat.

Fuck it. After the day—the week, even—he had had, he deserved to take a break and treat himself. Deciding to splurge, he called room service and ordered an aged strip steak, cooked rare, with a baked sweet potato, and two glasses of ice water, since he was feeling parched.

While he waited for his food, Jonah jumped in the shower to wash off and wake up a little more. After his nightmare, he wasn't eager to go back to bed just yet, and he needed some quiet time to think about what he would say to Mina when he saw her in the morning. He hadn't felt so skittish and juvenile about talking to a girl since he was a teenager.

Among his concerns was the reason for the silence on her part. Mina undoubtedly knew by now about his role in dispatching the Baron who had hunted her parents, and maybe she even knew what he had discussed with Selina and Lin, but his phone was still quiet. Not even a text to say "hello."

Jonah toweled off just in time to hear the knock on his door announcing the arrival of room service. Unable to locate the bathrobe he had used in the morning, he answered the door with a towel securely tucked around his hips. Jonah was conscious of the surreptitious glances that the young room service waiter was sneaking, as Jonah checked the order, added a generous tip and signed the receipts.

247

The waiter set the food tray on the desk near the bed without comment. "Anything else we can get you, sir?" the waiter finally asked, returning to the door.

"An extra glass of ice water, please," Jonah said, gesturing to the single goblet on the tray. "I had asked for two. It's not a rush, but I'd appreciate it."

"Oh, please accept my apologies," the waiter said, chagrinned. "I'll bring it right back."

"It's okay, whenever you can get to it," Jonah said dismissively, and shut the door.

Smelling the rich, savory steam from the steak and sweet potato from across the hotel room, Jonah was tempted to skip the utensils and just eat with his hands; he could always just jump back into the shower if the meal got messy. Standing over the neatly-arrayed tray on his desk, though, complete with cloth napkin and even a fresh purple-and-white dendrobium orchid spray in a bud vase, Jonah opted to eat like a civilized human being, but he stayed in his towel. He also ignored the complimentary, shrink-wrapped mini-bottles of ketchup and steak sauce served alongside his food.

He had just finished his second bite of perfectly seared steak and sampled the creamy sweet potato when a knock sounded at the door again, with the waiter announcing himself as room service. Jonah chuckled at the alacrity of the hotel staff, but when he answered the door, he was stunned into silence.

The waiter stood sheepishly on one side of the doorway, with the second goblet of ice water held out, and next to him, stood Mina, with an inscrutable smile on her face.

"My apologies, sir," the waiter fumbled, "I didn't realize she was right behind me."

Jonah was thankful that the waiter had spoken first, as he had a few extra seconds to recover from the shock of seeing Mina in person. "It's alright," he said, finally,

taking the goblet from the waiter. "I was expecting her."
Not really, but, whatever.

"Oh!" the waiter said with relief, suspecting that she was the reason that Jonah had ordered two glasses of water.

"Do you need me to sign something?" Jonah asked, gesturing to Mina to come inside while trying to shoo the waiter off without being rude.

"No, sir," the waiter said, backing away from the door. "Can we bring you anything else?"

"No, thank you," Jonah said absently. "Good night."

"Okay. Great, thank you. Have a good night, sir."

By the time Jonah had shut and locked the door, Mina had already made herself at home, taking off her hoodie—*his* hoodie—and shoes and dropping her bag on the desk chair. She wore a snug black t-shirt and faded jeans, and in that moment, she was the most gorgeous woman he had ever seen. And she was helping herself to his dinner. "Hello?" he said with mock indignation.

"Hi. Do you always answer the door in a towel?" Mina grinned, taking a sip of the ice water from the goblet on the tray. "That's a really good steak. I'm surprised you didn't finish it," she teased.

"I haven't had a chance," Jonah said, returning to the desk to reclaim his late-night meal. He didn't mind sharing with Mina, but he was ravenous, too. "How did you know where to find me?" he asked, taking a sip from the second goblet before setting it down. "I know Bullfinch told your parents the hotel name, but the room…"

"Aciré made your reservation, so she gave me your room number," Mina said, cutting and feeding him a morsel of steak. "I got tired of waiting for you to call or visit me."

"What?" he asked between chews. "I was trying to give you space and keep you out of danger."

Mina laughed, scooping a forkful of sweet potato. "Are you serious? There's no avoiding danger here. Compared to New York, this city is a minefield. There's a reason I haven't been back in years."

"Right, so you already have your hands full," he said, letting Mina feed him.

"Not yet," she whispered, setting the fork down and tugging him closer by his towel. "I've missed you."

"I've missed you, too, baby." The touch of her fingers against his belly blotted out any consideration of food or sleep, and he edged her against the desk, bracing his arms on either side of her. He looked down when he felt the prong setting of her ruby ring scratching lightly against his bare skin.

"So, does this mean we're official now?" he asked, stealing a kiss, then another. "The word is that you're my fiancée, but you never actually gave me your answer."

"I would've, if you'd stayed around a little longer," Mina joked. "Do you still want *me*?"

"Now that I've had a chance to think about it, I'm not sure," he teased, but his body's response to her proximity was more certain and harder to ignore.

"Uh, huh." With a laugh, she unraveled his towel and flung it aside. "Let's be sure, then."

Selina took a last walk through the quiet house as her usual nightly ritual, to make sure that all the lights were out, the kitchen burners and any candles were all extinguished, the leftovers were put away, and the front door was securely locked for the night. Tonight, she kept her phone close by, in case Mina texted that she was coming home, but Selina doubted that she would.

Ever since Lin returned home from his meeting with Jonah, and throughout dinner, Mina had seemed preoccupied, and Selina was well aware of where Mina's thoughts were focused. After they had cleared the table and checked Yumi's finger and arm dressings together, Selina had suggested to Mina that she pay a visit to Jonah.

At first, Mina had been hesitant, both of barging in on Jonah uninvited, and going out during what was most likely one of her last evenings at home before returning to New York, but Selina had encouraged her to follow her heart…and take a quick shower and pack an overnight bag.

As Adam had already retired to bed, and Yumi had left to visit a Shinto shrine before heading home, Selina was curious about who was in the office with Lin, having a quiet, cordial phone conversation at such a late hour. Their three new dogs were snoring quietly on the Persian rug around Lin's desk, oblivious to the chatter.

Selina paused in the doorway and narrowed her eyes, as she recognized the calm, dulcet cadence of Lucifer's voice. She didn't trust any of the devils with whom her husband was well-acquainted, but Lucifer was especially annoying, since he interfered in Mina's life, also.

"I should go," Lin said, answering her glare with a smile. "I need to give some attention to my wife."

"Until next time, then, Mister Xing," Lucifer's voice floated over the speaker.

Lin waited until the line disconnected before he broke into a guffaw at Selina's look of distaste. "At least he didn't visit in person."

Selina crossed her arms. "I'd like to see him try. His skin would erupt into boils, as soon as he crosses the threshold."

"Now, my love, you know he would never act openly against us," Lin soothed, holding his hand out to her as he came from behind his desk to stand amid the minefield of slumbering dogs. "Luci's much too fond of the children, especially Mina."

The smallest of the dogs picked up her head to sniff at Selina's leg and settled back down, and Selina gave her a little scratch behind her ears. She had to admit: they were messy and clumsy, but they were guileless and endearing, like giant toddlers.

"You're far too trusting of Lucifer's attention towards Mina," she warned, letting Lin gather her into his arms. "I know you've been acquaintances for millennia now, but his nature is suspect and as immutable as yours."

"I'm aware," Lin said, nuzzling her cheek. "And we have a new tool in our arsenal, should the need arise."

Selina looked at him askance. "Jonah's not a tool."

"I don't mean Jonah," Lin said, "although another reaper is always a helpful ally to have. No, I meant what Jonah salvaged from the Baron's house: his dagger and his talisman."

Selina stiffened. "You didn't mention that before!"

"It's not exactly a dinner conversation topic," Lin said lightly, holding Selina by her waist to keep her from squirming away. "Jonah's holding onto both items, and I trust him not to try to use them against me."

"How would the talisman help us?" Selina asked. "The Baron had it created to use against you, specifically."

"I'm letting Jonah safeguard the watch, to keep me in check," Lin said soberly. "He's a fair and just reaper, like Bullfinch, and if my time comes soon, I will request that Jonah send me off. If that comes to pass, and if he needs to defend himself against me, then he should have a way to do it." He looked evenly at Selina. "The dagger, however, is a holy weapon that can pierce almost anything—as you recall from when you pulled it from Jonah's stomach."

Selina looked at him with suspicion. "Are you sure that your opinion of Jonah isn't clouded by the fact that he was carrying the talisman when you met with him?

252

You have a great deal of faith in him, given how briefly you've spoken with him."

Lin cupped her face in his hands and kissed her softly. "I'm not the one who sent our daughter off to spend the night with him," he reminded teasingly.

"Mina would've been moping until morning, if she didn't go to him. She's already committed herself to him, more than she may realize," Selina smiled, feeling her contentious mood lightening. Lin's loving touch always ameliorated her temper, regardless of her sourness, and over the years, he had mastered and expanded his techniques for winning her over. "If they're to be married, they should spend time together."

"Oh, really," he said, brushing his lips against her ear. "How many years were we married before you even let me kiss you?"

"Hmm," she mused, as he turned her around and leaned her back to rest against his hips. "We were married in 1885, and I joined you in California in 1896, so eleven years, give or take a few months?"

"Mm-hmm," he said, brushing his lips along the slope of her neck and shoulder. "And how long did you wait before you finally came to my bed?"

"Too long." Feeling his welcome, intense warmth spread throughout her body through his contact, she recalled her reasons for resisting him, which she now realized were unfounded and inane. She had feared his sheer power and the overwhelming size of his natural form, witnessing enough of his ferocity to know that she would be helpless against him, if he ever wanted to dominate her, or if he lost control of his impulses.

Eventually, her trust and desire had overcome her fear, and she put herself in his hands, literally and figuratively, and was rewarded by her husband's generous and unflagging passion. His touch still stirred her, after all their years together, and she couldn't imagine ever giving herself to anyone else as completely as she had to him.

Selina wished that kind of unconditional devotion and love for their children, and with Jonah, she could see it within reach for their daughter. "Mina deserves to find happiness, after everything she's experienced. Now that Adam is better, he may be on his way to finding his, too."

"Even if he wants to be with Alexandra Crain?" Lin murmured.

"If that's his path," Selina said. "The Baron was *our* enemy, and the conflict should end with us. The Crain children have no knowledge of Ashford's cruelty, and it's not our place to tell them." When Mina was younger and had named Xani and Morgan Crain among her friends, Selina had been guarded about their fortuitous acquaintance, but the twins had since shown themselves to be genuine friends, to both Mina and Adam.

"You are as wise as you are beautiful," Lin whispered, wrapping his arms around her waist.

Selina recognized his amorous growl and pushed half-heartedly at his strong hands. "We still have one child in the house, and three dogs snoring at our feet. I'd like some more privacy than this."

"If we needed privacy for lovemaking, Adam would be an only child," Lin pouted.

"You've waited for me before," Selina laughed and extracted herself from his embrace. "Once the children are on their way back to New York, you can have your way with me. Until then, to help you control your urges…" She pivoted on her heel and shifted back into her *huli jing* form, shimmying out of her clothes with practiced efficiency. She flicked her lustrous gold tail and bounced out of the office and towards the stairs.

As he trailed after her, picking up her discarded clothes, his teasing voice floated after her. "Bestiality is still a 'no,' then?"

She circled around mid-way up the stairs. *If you're in the mood for sharp teeth and claws, maybe one of your new girls will accommodate you.*

He ascended the stairs slowly after her. "No, thanks, I'll wait. I've waited longer for you." At the upstairs landing, he stopped at the buzzing from Selina's phone in her shirt pocket, and pulled it out. "Mina texted you a thumbs-up emoji. What does that mean?"

Selina's laugh came out as a shrill yip. *It means she's doing fine.*

Lin frowned, as he opened their bedroom door and let Selina slip inside past him. "You mean Mina's having better luck than me tonight. Should I ask her for details?" he joked, picking Selina's phone back up to answer the text.

Put my phone down, right now! Selina reared and planted her front paws on her husband's legs, which looked as thick as trunks from her shorter vantage.

He looked down at her with a mischievous glint in his eyes. "What's in it for me?"

She reshaped herself back into her human form and snatched her phone from his hand, while Lin was admiring her unclothed form. "Shut the door," she said, with a deep kiss, "and if you're quiet, I'll let you get lucky, too."

Jonah finally found his bathrobe hanging behind the bathroom door when he went to wash his face and take a quick shower. As Mina continued to doze in his bed, he pulled on the robe to take the room service tray out. As he nudged the tray away from the doorway and stood back upright, he jumped at the figure watching him from across the hall, who wasn't standing there a second ago.

Son of a bitch, Jonah glared at Lucifer. "What are you doing here?"

Lucifer stayed leaning against the wall. "I didn't think you or Miss Xing would appreciate my appearing inside your room, although my view is about the same."

Jonah reached around his door to swing the buckle clasp around, to keep the door from closing shut and locking him out of his own room, so he could focus on his conversation with his uninvited visitor. "You were watching us?"

"Briefly. Long enough to check that everything is in working order, Mister Gideon," Lucifer said with a measuring glance, passing his sharp blue eyes over Jonah's figure. "You've had a busy couple of days, and yet you still mustered enough energy to please your fiancée. Well done."

Jonah gritted his teeth at Lucifer's mention of Mina, even without speaking her name.

"No comment?" Lucifer asked. "Not even a word of thanks, for giving you a break to enjoy your reunion with your love?"

The door opened quietly, and Mina appeared behind Jonah, wearing one of his t-shirts. "Well, this is a surprise. Are you here for him, or me?" she asked Lucifer, her gaze and voice still seductively indolent.

Mina closed her eyes sleepily, but Jonah caught Lucifer's flash of jealous desire before the devil answered, "It depends on what's being offered."

Jonah noticed a subtle twitch of Mina's brow, but her tone remained giddy. "You're still not allowed to touch me, so you'd just have to watch."

"I don't mind watching, as long as you're enjoying yourself," Lucifer returned easily. "You're better than most pornography."

"Just 'most'?" Mina pouted in mock insult. "You'll have to excuse us, then, as we practice some more," she said, tugging Jonah's hand. "Whatever you need from us, I'm sure it can wait until Gabriel's available to join the conversation."

256

Jonah suppressed the urge to snicker at Lucifer's confounded scowl, as Mina led him back inside and released the buckle clasp lock from the door. "Has he always been like that with you?" he asked. "He gives off a 'creepy stalker' vibe sometimes, and 'inappropriate uncle' at other times."

Mina laughed and wrapped her hands around his hips, drawing him back towards the bed. "Not too far off the mark, I guess. He's a little like a fairy godfather, if you replace 'fairy' with 'devil,' and 'godfather' with... 'devil-father'?" She burst into giggles at her own haplessness.

"You can be so goofy when you're tired," he remarked, shaking his head. "So, what are you saying: that he's your demonic guardian, or something?"

"No," she said, soberly. "Devils and demons are very different, following different rules. My father is an entirely separate type of entity, but he and Lucifer have a history and a mutual respect. I don't recall all the details of their arrangement," Mina yawned, lying back on the bed, "but Lucifer has to be nice to me."

Mina closed her eyes, and Jonah started to ease her back onto a pillow, but she hadn't fallen back asleep yet. "He's not allowed to fuck me," she said drowsily, "so he wants to watch you do it."

"What?" Jonah stopped and looked at her. Had she heard the start of his conversation with Lucifer in the hallway?

"He can see us through your eyes," Mina said matter-of-factly, sitting up. "Gabriel could, too, but he doesn't care about any of our messy human habits. Lucifer, though... he's more voyeuristic."

"How long have you known that he's been doing that?" Jonah asked, feeling a little queasy that his reunion with Mina had been surreptitiously observed, and that Mina had been aware of it.

"When I saw you tonight, something about you seemed different," she said. "Then I remembered that you had been remade, with some of you coming from Miranda. Those bits of you bind you to Lucifer, so I knew there was a chance that he could use you as a conduit. When he made that crack about watching me like porn," she said with a roll of her eyes, "that confirmed it."

"If you suspected that he was using me, why did you stay?" Jonah asked.

"Because I wasn't sure yet," she said, "and it doesn't matter to me, anyway." She knelt in front of him on the bed and draped her hands around his neck. "You're still the same man I fell in love with," she said. "All he can do is observe—he can't control your actions or act through you."

"You sound more certain about it than I feel," he said, feeling her melt against him.

"I am," she said and kissed him. "Lucifer didn't force you to jump in front of the Baron's dagger, and he couldn't stop you from contacting Aciré to keep the Baron's artifacts locked away."

Jonah looked at her. He hadn't mentioned anything about that to Mina, so how did…

"Aciré told me you coordinated with her to secure some items in one of local, ward-protected vaults, and given the timing, I assume you had picked up something from the Baron's house," Mina said. "She didn't say much more than that, so the 'what' is still a secret to me, and I don't need to know."

"But Lucifer knows, because he can see everything that I see," Jonah said, trying to keep his eyes riveted on Mina's face, instead of her scantily-dressed figure. "He can see everything we do."

"So what, if he sneaks an occasional peek?" With a laugh, Mina toppled Jonah and pinned him to the bed. "Besides, he's not obsessive—he has other mortals to torment, the whole world over," she said, peeling off the t-shirt she had borrowed from him. "Plus, the blue in your eyes is a little different when he's watching through you," she whispered. "It gets a little darker, closer to the color of his eyes."

"You know the color of Lucifer's eyes?" Jonah asked. "What else have you noticed—"

She fused her mouth against his to quiet him and reached down to untie the sash of his bathrobe. "Just shut up, and trust me, okay?"

"Okay." He blanked on anything wittier to say, and could barely get the single word out, as he watched Mina's silky hair sweep down his chest, and felt her warm breath against his belly.

"If it helps," she said, brushing her fingertips across his sensitive skin, "you can shut your eyes, and he won't be able to see through you."

As she lowered her head, he shut his eyes automatically, drowning in the intense pleasure of her mouth and tongue against him. He didn't need to see her—he smelled her perfume, as her hair slipped through his fingers, heard her soft moans as she savored the taste of him, and felt the sensual, rhythmic rise and fall of her body against his.

Even with his eyes tightly closed, he could easily envision Mina's beautiful shape, and his hands flowed over her curves easily. He refused to be Lucifer's window to peep at her whenever the devil felt the itch. Mina was not for sharing, not even a glimpse, if Jonah could help it. *She's mine, motherfucker.*

And Mina made clear that she considered Jonah hers, too, in the way she touched and used him with abandon, in her furious rush towards release. She had barely recovered her panting breath, when she caught him between her long, lean legs and let him sink into her, slow and deep.

Without sight, his other senses were flooded by his awareness of her: her heat, her cries and her scent, and the sweetness of her lips when they kissed. He felt her shudders and stillness, then the slower, sweeter rhythm as she began again, to bring him to his resolution.

Time was hazy and unimportant; maybe it was fifteen minutes, but it could have just as easily been two hours. Sated and spent, Jonah and Mina sank into each other and the tangle of bed linens, and Jonah felt like a piece of seafoam on a wave. He felt removed from his own body, not quite aware of where his extremities landed on the bed.

He was very conscious of Mina's cool, smooth form molded against him, though, with her head tucked against his shoulder and under his chin, as she drifted back to sleep. As she fell into deeper slumber, Jonah felt her slipping free of his arm, almost shrinking away, and he opened his eyes partially to see where Mina was.

Lying next to Jonah on the bed was a small sleeping fox, with a lustrous scarlet-auburn coat, a snowy-white breast and delicate black paws. Her chest and breath continued to follow the slow, peaceful rise and fall of Mina's patterns, and her closed eyes twitched the way Mina's often did when she slept. In her unconsciousness, as she had fallen asleep feeling safe and secure, Mina's *huli jing* nature had decided to manifest itself for a little while.

She's still beautiful. Jonah reached over and stroked the silky fur on Mina's black-tipped ears and muzzle. During her shift, the ruby ring had slipped off her finger—*toe, claw?*—and Jonah picked it up to avoid losing it in the bedsheets. As he turned briefly to put the ring down on the nightstand, he heard the quiet scratch of a nail against the bed, and looked back to find Mina nestled against him, her thick red pelt and tail warming his bare chest. She continued to snore quietly, still deeply asleep.

"So, I guess this is a thing now," he murmured, scratching Mina's head between her velvety ears. He shrugged and closed his eyes, tucking his hand around Mina's shoulder to pull her closer.

Jonah took a quick inventory of his life: he was a resurrected, shapeshifting reaper of souls, with few worldly possessions left to his name, engaged to a witch born to a fox spirit and a powerful, primeval inhuman entity. Jonah's life had certainly taken a turn for the strange, in a matter of weeks, and becoming stranger by the day, it seemed.

I can deal with strange. With Mina in his life, he felt like he could deal with just about anything. Snuggling with Mina in her fox form, feeling her soft fur and whiskers against his bristly chin, felt nice and serene, normal and natural. For Jonah's screwy new life, it felt just about perfect.

Chapter 15

Thursday morning, Adam went towards the front door as soon as he heard the latch open, but he was beaten to it by the new family pets, as the trio barreled past him down the stairs like a waterfall of black and brindle, to greet the arrivals.

The mastiff girls were happy to see Mina, but they seemed more excited to see and sniff Jonah again, and he rewarded their enthusiasm by briefly shapeshifting into the black and silver husky form that Adam remembered so well, to play wrestle with the dogs. Just as effortlessly, he shifted back into his human form, with all his clothes intact.

"Hey, you can go full-dog, now!" Adam remarked, coming down the steps. "With that beard, I can't tell which version of you is fuzzier."

Jonah beamed at Adam and opened his arms for a hug. "Come here, shish-ke-brain."

Adam hadn't realized how much he had missed Jonah's company and humor until he locked his arms around his friend. It was true that Adam had known that Jonah was back, and they had even spoken briefly on the phone, but being able to see Jonah's grin and sparkling ice-blue eyes again was sublime.

Mina's glowing smile, also, was something that Adam had missed, and she seemed unable to keep from grinning whenever she glanced in Jonah's direction.

"You're dressing like our dad, now?" Adam chuckled, glancing at Jonah's tailored slacks and fitted broadcloth shirt. "You're in, already—you can stop kissing ass, now."

"The uniform's part of the new job," Jonah said. "Stays on during shifting, too, which is a plus." Jonah looked him over, top to bottom. "Looking good, Adam."

Adam nodded at the cue. "Feeling good, Jonah," he returned readily. "Between all the blood cake soup and earthworm tea, and catching up on sleep, my head's finally intact again. Oh, yeah, speaking of blood cake and earthworms," he grinned, turning to the kitchen, "I hope you're hungry."

The dogs trotted alongside Mina and Jonah as they joined their parents in the kitchen, where Lin was setting the table for breakfast, while Selina was preparing the platters on the counter. It was a heartwarming scene of domestic bliss, even with his parents stealing moments to grope and fondle one another whenever they were close enough.

As Jonah humbly offered a box of pastries to Selina, Mina drew Adam aside for a private word.

"Did you get a chance to call Global Pacific yesterday about their offer?" she asked. "They wanted your counter by mid-week, as I recall."

"I did." Adam smiled at recalling the brief conversation he had had with Sobol about the job that Lin had negotiated. "I told Stanislav that I'd work for them, but not as an employee," he said. "I would be a freelancer, contracted to them through Xing's corporate services division." He had decided to call his old company's bluff—if they wanted him, they would have to accept his conditions, as he refused to return to their yoke.

"Back to the corporate world, just working for Dad instead of Global," Mina said. "What did Sobol say?"

"They'll consider it and get back to me. I should know by tomorrow, before the weekend."

"Freelance research?" Mina asked dubiously. "Is that even a real thing?"

"It can be, if they're serious about their offer," he said. "I'd still be working for them, but I'd spend more time here, keeping tabs on Mom and Dad." He noticed Mina's twitch of trepidation. "It's time I stopped hiding, isn't it?"

"What do you remember?" Mina asked quietly.

"I remember everything," Adam said. Once all the pieces of his restoration gelled, he recovered memories and pieces of himself that had been lost for years, some since he was a boy. "Mom and Dad suppressed and hid so much from us to protect us from the Baron, but now that's over."

"Are you coming back to New York, or are you staying here?" Mina asked, nodding at Selina's searching glance to call them to the table.

"I haven't decided yet," Adam said, holding Mina's chair for her, as she took her seat between him and Jonah, across from their parents. Jonah intuitively picked up and kissed Mina's hand, and Adam felt a kind of peace, knowing that his baby sister was no longer alone, and with Jonah around, he could worry about her a little less.

Selina, as always, was meticulous about the positioning of platters, to ensure that her guests had easy access to the dishes they favored: the porridge and tea in front of Lin, bacon and smoked salmon next to Jonah, the fresh pastries in the middle between Adam and herself, and a tray of individual savory egg custards in front of Mina.

Mina was positively giddy, as she took one of the warm glass yogurt cups and cradled it between her palms. "Crab and corn?" she asked hopefully, breathing in the aromatic, slightly sweet and briny steam wafting from the jiggling egg concoction.

"Yes, Min-Min," Selina smiled, enjoying Mina's girlish excitement over something as simple as a favorite food from childhood.

Mina sighed at the first spoonful of the savory custard. "Oh, my God, I have to teach the elves at the Lotus how to make this." She beamed at Adam. "Xani loves soft-cooked eggs! She would totally do—"

Mina stopped herself, remembering their audience, and Jonah chuckled at her furious blush, while their parents pretended not to hear. Adam, in the meantime, was reminded that he and Xani needed to have a conversation about his decision, and its impact on their relationship.

Lin poured some tea for Adam. "Are you going to call her today?"

"After breakfast," Adam said. "Xani was taking Cindy out last night, to get her mind off Morgan."

"Do you need to get back to New York, then?" Selina asked, looking directly at Mina.

"Cindy and I texted this morning," Mina replied. "She's feeling better and told me not to rush back, until everyone's business is finished," she said, sneaking a glance at Jonah.

Lin sipped his tea. "Perhaps you should take advantage of this lull, Jonah, before you're given another West Coast assignment," he said. "And before I can accidentally sabotage it," he added in a semi-apologetic murmur.

Jonah raised his tea cup to Lin. "I'm grateful for any support you wish to provide, sir."

Lin looked at the three seated across from him. "The word is that the Baron's house will be put up for auction soon. It's not old or historical enough for preservation. Any interest in a bid?"

"A bit macabre for a souvenir," Mina commented. "Didn't he have any heirs to inherit it?"

Adam caught the subtle glance between his parents before Lin answered, "They might want it, but they're already settled comfortably in New York, so they may not want to bother with San Francisco."

"Are we sure about that connection?" Jonah asked.

"What connection?" Mina asked.

"Morrigan," Adam said, pulling names from a distant memory. "The Baron's name was 'Morrigan,' and he had one child, a daughter named 'Catherine,'" he said, looking pointedly at Mina, "who married someone named 'Alexander Crain.'"

"Shit," Mina blurted, then winced at their parents' glowers. "Sorry."

"You remember all that?" Lin remarked.

"You had a file open on your office chair, and I saw the names," Adam said. "I must've been around seven because I tried to read everything in front of me, whether I was supposed to or not." He looked around Mina at Jonah. "*You* knew?"

"I had a hunch, but it's not my place to say," Jonah said. "Xani and Morgan have nothing to do with any of this, if they're even aware about who the Baron was."

Adam felt the buzz of an incoming text on his phone, which he pulled from his pocket to read. As if she had read his mind, Xani had texted: *Call me when you have a sec. Just heard from Mom: I need to fly to San Fran for a distant relative's estate.*

"Everything okay?" Mina asked, breaking an almond croissant in half to share with Jonah.

Shit. Adam slid the phone to Mina to read the message. "If the twins didn't know about the Baron before, they're going to find out soon."

Xani heard her name and spun around, peering into the crowds around her at the arrival gate, when she spotted Mina and Jonah coming towards her, with Mina sprinting ahead to reach her first. Xani was glad to get an enthusiastic reception in San Francisco, after a long, uneventful flight from Newark; the traffic to the airport from Manhattan on a Saturday afternoon had only prolonged the already-excruciating journey.

"Guys, what are you doing here?" Xani asked, returning Mina's hug. "Don't you need tickets to get past security?"

Jonah adjusted the strap of his messenger bag over his hoodie. "Our flight leaves later tonight, but we didn't want to miss you on your way out, so we came a little early."

"God, I'm so glad to see you!" Xani laughed, giving Mina another hug. "These past couple of days have been nuts. Well, I don't have to tell you that."

Ever since receiving the first cryptic text from Catherine Crain on Thursday morning, letting her know that there had been a death in the family, Xani was caught in a whirlwind of activity and preparation to get ready for her trip to California. Between going over the work appointment schedule with Morgan, covering shifts with Cindy at the Red Lotus, and getting some details from their mother on what she could expect regarding their estranged "cousin or other, I believe," Xani had barely enough time to think about how to pack for the weather and pull her overnight bag together before she had to catch her flight.

"Adam's waiting for you by the bag dump," Mina said wryly. "Our parents booked you a suite at the hotel where Jonah was staying, and it's walking distance to our house."

Xani bristled at the thought of the bill. She didn't know what to expect from the estate, but she was traveling on a budget. "That really wasn't necessary…"

"My mom insisted," Mina said. "She wanted to avoid the potential awkwardness of having you stay with them, but she also wanted you to be comfortable, so they're paying for it."

Xani's jaw dropped. "No, wait, they paid for my plane ticket, already. I can't…"

Jonah set his hand on her shoulder gently. "Just accept it, Xani. They're trying to be nice."

"No, I get that, but…" Xani sighed, realizing the futility of the argument. It wasn't like Mina and Adam's parents were trying to buy her loyalty, or patronizing her with their overbearing generosity. Mina's tone and smile would've been much more cynical, if that were the case. "Okay."

Mina hooked her arm with Xani's, as they walked her towards the exit. "If my folks invite you over to eat, bring a light dessert, something with fruit, or a potted herb."

"What about flowers?" Xani tried.

"Not so much. Food nourishes, but cut flowers die," Mina said. "My mom also collects aloe vera plants, for some reason, so she'll appreciate those."

"Biscuits," Jonah suggested.

"Yes!" Mina said. "Bring some dog treats, too." She grinned. "Be sure to wear something that's resistant to drool."

They parted ways near the last exit, with Mina's parting offer for Xani to text her if she had any questions and Adam seemed clueless, and also to relax and enjoy San Francisco.

Xani's visit was unexpected, for everyone, so no one was adhering to the structured formality of a first-time meeting between Xani and Adam's parents, and there were no real expectations or protocol for how she should act or say. Jonah was different; he was already known to the family, albeit in another context, and he had experiences and insight into the family that Xani didn't.

Xani passed through the baggage claim area quickly, just to reach the exit, as all she had brought was a rolling duffle that had fit in the overhead bin. She hadn't known whether to pack for two nights or a week, so she kept her bag light, with some extra room in case she needed to buy something for a longer stay.

"Miss Crain."

Xani almost didn't recognize Adam with his short, clean-cut hair and slightly tanner complexion, but he still filled out his t-shirt and jeans nicely. "Hi," she said breathlessly, meeting him halfway.

He swept her up in his arms and greeted her with a swoon-worthy kiss. "Hey, Red," he smiled, setting her back down, then took her duffle from her and draped his hand around her waist. "How was the flight?"

"Good," she said, still recovering her breath, leaning her head on his muscled shoulder. *Wow, he's solid.*

"Are you okay?" he asked laughingly, noticing her stare. "It's been less than a week since we saw each other."

"Yeah, I know, it's just…"

Adam seemed different. Not in a bad way, but like someone who had just snapped out of a daze or a trance. He seemed more alert, more confident, and it dawned on Xani that this was his natural state of being, and that his pensive, methodical manner when he had left New York earlier in the week had been a side-effect of his impairment. *That* was different—this was Adam, the way she remembered him from years ago, the way he was when she fell in love with him.

"You seem better," she said finally. "I guess the time away from New York helped."

"It did, and I think Mina and I needed to reconnect with our folks," Adam said, guiding Xani to the sliding door exit. "They're learning to see us as adults, and I think we've gained some perspective on what they've given and done for us."

Xani smiled wistfully. "I think my mom and I need one of those interventions. She doesn't share much with Morgan or me. The last thing she told us about our family was that our dad believed that destiny brought the two of them together because she had the same name as his grandmother."

"Your great-grandmother was also Catherine Crain?" Adam said easily, walking her to their waiting black town car and holding the door for her.

"Yeah, weird, right?" Xani laughed. She waited for Adam to put her luggage into the trunk and join her in the back of the sedan. "Our dad named us after his ancestors, but it was always unclear which ones. I thought Mom would want to come for this, but she said she had another engagement, so here I am."

Adam smiled, taking her hands. "I'm glad you came. Holding your mom's hands would be a totally different experience."

"This, too, I bet," Xani laughed and gave him a quick kiss, but once she felt the warmth of his cheek and lips against hers, she lingered and rested her head on his shoulder. She wrapped her hand across his midriff and settled against him, feeling a tranquility that had been missing since he left. "I see tinted glass, but I don't suppose there's any soundproofing in here," she whispered, glancing towards the driver through the privacy glass.

Adam chuckled. "Not enough. Besides, it's less than half an hour to the hotel," Adam said, cupping his hand over hers. "We could just talk. How are Cindy and Morgan doing?"

"They're both fine," Xani said, looking at him. He had greeted her with an amazing kiss, but now he seemed distant. "Did I do something wrong?"

"No, it's nothing you did," Adam said.

"So, there *is* something going on, just not with me," she interpreted.

Adam hesitated. "I countered Global Pacific's offer, and they accepted, and I think you should know the details."

"Okay," she said warily. "What did you decide?"

She listened closely to the particulars, and mostly what she heard was that he would be traveling between coasts, and occasionally overseas. It was similar to his life before he had settled back in New York, and before they started their relationship, and it sounded like what he genuinely wanted.

"That sounds great," she said hollowly.

"No, it's shit," he said bluntly, "but it's the only way I can think of, to spend time in New York with you and Mina, while still staying close to my parents."

"It sounds like you've accepted it, already," Xani said. "What do you want me to say?"

"You don't have to say anything right now," Adam said, looking down at their joined hands. "In fact, it's probably best if you think about it for a couple of days. You're going to learn a lot about your family, and it may change how you feel about us."

Xani shook her head, confused. "How do you know that?" She considered the coincidence of her relative dying in San Francisco the same week that Adam, Mina and Jonah were there. "What do you know about my family and about what happened?"

"Everything I know is second-hand," he said, "so it's probably better if you get the facts, first, from someone more objective than me."

She straightened. "But you do know something."

"I'd be lying, if I said I didn't, and I know how you feel about liars," he said. "Look, I don't want to say anything that would cause you to—"

"To what?" she cut in. "Hate you, or hate some part of my family that I don't even know? No one's ever truly

271

objective; everyone has an agenda, so nothing that anyone tells me is going to sway me to feel one way or the other. Not when it comes to you, because I love you." She stopped when she blurted that last bit.

"I love you, too," he said quietly.

"So, this won't change us," she said. "Whoever this relative is, he's never been part of our lives. I don't wake up every morning missing him or thinking about him, the way I've missed you this week." Xani still wasn't keen on the idea of spending additional time apart, but she would rather be with him partly than not at all, as long as they were committed to each other.

She felt his fingers cupping her cheek and raising her chin, so that he could look at her. "I'm yours, as long as you want me. Or, if you don't think this arrangement will work, you can be honest about it. Whatever happens with us, I want it to be your choice. It's only fair, since I went ahead and made my deal with Global Pacific alone."

Xani considered the visit earlier in the week from Gabriel, when he had advised her to have faith in her time of uncertainty. She didn't know what awaited her for the next few days, but she trusted Adam to keep her grounded. Whatever doubts she had about anything else, she believed in what they had together.

"Whatever happens, I want you with me." She leaned over and kissed him. "I choose you."

Mina fell asleep in the cab ride home, after sleeping for most of the plane ride, too. She stirred when she heard Jonah giving some directions to the cabbie on where to stop, as they approached the building. It was odd to see that it was early morning, when she still felt exhausted and bleary-eyed. The sky had darkened to night by the time their plane finally took off from San Francisco, and they had touched down at Newark Airport

272

before the sun had risen, so she should've caught up on sleep, but it sure didn't feel that way.

Galen was near the front door when they came inside, and it appeared from his broom and trash bin that he had been cleaning the hallway. "Welcome back," he said, looking at their bags. "You weren't gone very long."

"Long enough," Mina said. "Why are you out here, at this hour, with *that*?"

Galen played with the broom handle in his hand. "If we're not paying you rent, we should at least make ourselves useful. We're early risers, anyway." He stood back against the wall as the two younger fae children, Fern and Fallon, swept past him on propeller-like wings, with dust rags in hand.

At seeing Mina and Jonah, the children detoured from their trajectory towards the stairs and charged into them, instead. Their voices were as excited and unintelligible as squirrel chatter, as they talked over each other to update Mina and Jonah on the latest news.

"You can talk to them later," Galen spoke over them. "They just returned home."

The children fell silent, and Fern gazed up with her wide, dark eyes. "Did you bring us anything?"

Jonah laughed. "Let us unpack, and we'll see what we find."

"That's more than fair," Galen said, before the children could question further. "Go, the railings won't clean themselves!"

Clutching the dust rags, the children shot skyward, spiraling around each other and giggling in a race to the top, to start cleaning on the top floor. Still feeling the fatigue in her legs, Mina dreaded the thought of climbing all three flights, just to get back to her apartment.

"You look exhausted," Galen said. "Couldn't sleep on the plane?"

Jonah grinned at Mina. "She snored and drooled for most of the trip back."

Galen laughed. "Your pantry is probably sparse, and we still have some of your pans, so if you want Gia to bring you back anything from the Lotus, just let us know."

With a grateful nod and murmured "thank you," Mina started up the stairs and stopped on the second floor landing when she heard the door to the Krantzes' apartment open. To her surprise, Morgan emerged from the apartment, and he hastily tucked his shirt and checked his jeans zipper.

"Hey, you're back!" he said, a flush coloring his cheeks.

"Hey," Jonah said. "Surprised to see you here."

"Yeah, I was just…" He stopped and met Mina's stony gaze, as the sound of a young woman's voice singing along to Britney Spears came from inside the apartment. Mina was making an effort to not show any expression, but that seemed to make Morgan more nervous. "Never mind. I'm just gonna go."

"Yep," Mina said, continuing up the stairs without watching Morgan go. Fundamentally, she knew that Cindy and Morgan were both adults, capable of making their own decisions and working out their own issues, but that didn't mean she didn't feel the urge to shove Morgan down the stairs for his cheating on Cindy. Just a little.

"I'm guessing there was more to Cindy and Morgan's split than just a normal drifting apart," Jonah said, following Mina up the stairs.

Mina shook her head. "I'll get the full story from her when she's ready to talk about it. I'll ply her with some chocolate cupcakes first." She leaned heavily against the doorframe and let Jonah open the door with her key. "You did leave me some eggs and butter in the fridge, right?"

Jonah gave her a sheepish grin, and a noncommittal murmur and shrug, as he held the door open for her.

Mina kicked off her shoes and sank onto her couch, taking a deep breath of the familiar air of her apartment. It had the funky mix of spices, dried herbs, candle wax and orange oil wood polish, and even stale, it was the smell of home. She closed her eyes and sighed, as Jonah kissed her forehead on his way to the fridge. "Yes, two sticks of butter and four eggs left," he reported. "There's some iced tea and juice, if you want, unless you want to crack open a bottle of wine."

"It's barely seven in the morning," Mina laughed. "If anything, I'd have green tea or coffee." Maybe it was her euphoria of being home, with Jonah, but the idea of a full-bodied red or a shot of Japanese whisky didn't have the same appeal as it had earlier in the week, regardless of the hour. All she wanted to do, now that she was back, was sleep for days. Once she had some energy back, perhaps, she would entertain the idea of christening her chaste bed with a hot, steamy session with Jonah, but for right now, she just wanted to lay her head down.

"Do you want me to sleep on the couch tonight, or the bed?" Jonah asked, slipping onto the couch next to her, and she curled snugly against him.

"It's nice waking up next to you," she said groggily. "Unless you think my bed is too small."

"It's cozy," he said diplomatically, and she laughed tiredly. "If you're sleepy, why don't you go back to bed for a while?"

She opened her eyes to look at him. "Will you still be here when I wake up?"

"Baby, I'm not going anywhere, if I can help it," he said, wrapping his hand around her shoulder. "If an assignment comes in, it can wait until you get up."

"I don't know," she murmured. "I might be sleeping for a while. Why am I so tired?" she whined.

"Maybe because you insisted on visiting my hotel room every night, instead of sleeping in your own bed at home?" he smirked. "I was waiting for your folks to offer me their guest room after Thursday night."

"Nope, we're still traditional like that," Mina said with a yawn. "Besides, we were leaving Saturday, so there didn't seem to be a point of asking you to stay for just one night."

"It doesn't sound like you wanted me to stay over, either," he said.

"My dad's hearing is exceptional," Mina said, her eyes closing on their own. "If you'd stayed with us, and I'd snuck into your room, he would've heard every minute, and his eyes would've eviscerated you over breakfast."

"Knowing your dad, you're probably being literal," Jonah muttered. "Of course, we could've just abstained for one night, too."

"Actually, I just really liked the king-size bed in your suite," she simpered, "and wanted to use it as long as we could."

"That, I would believe," he chuckled. "Come on, sleepy-head, let's get you tucked in." When she balked and pouted, he offered, "Okay, I'll carry you to bed."

Mina wrapped her arms around his neck and frowned at his little grunts of effort, as he carried her down the hall to her bedroom. "You're mean."

"You're grouchy," he shot back, setting her down on the bed gently. "And probably dehydrated. I'll bring you some water." He kissed her cheek and went to the door.

Mina wanted to tell him not to bother, as she actually felt bloated and discombobulated, even before they boarded the plane. She wriggled her toes and felt their stiffness, as the circulation returned to her feet, now that her shoes were off. *Wait a second.*

276

She counted back the days to when she had her last period and realized she was overdue by several days. Combined with her discomforts and overall mood and muddle-mindedness…

She lay back on the pillow, wide awake. "Oh, fuck."

Jonah returned with her water. "What is it?"

Mina propped herself up on her elbows and looked at him in panic. "I think I'm pregnant."

Thanks for reading!

*If you've enjoyed this story, and the series so far, please
connect with me or leave me a review!
It's always great to hear from fans and readers!*

Ande Li

About the Author

Ande has lived in Hong Kong, China, and the various boroughs of NYC, and has settled in the NJ suburbs with her husband and occasional collaborator Maurice X. Alvarez, their children, their free-range budgie and incredibly forgiving and patient shelter dog.

Discover other titles by Ande Li

The Xonen Archives
Book One: The Healer's Girl
Book Two: The Children of Xon
Book Three: The Second Life of Cyrus Ex
Book Four: The Trickster's Game
Book Five: The Souls of Stars (coming soon)

The Gideon Files
Book One: Red Lotus
Book Two: White Jade
Book Four: Black Rose (coming soon)

Team Spirits *(as Anne deLys)*
Art Appreciation
My Husband's Best Friend
Ever Faithful

co-written with Maurice X. Alvarez
The Trouble with Thieves
Book One: Return to Averia
Book Two: Trials of Halgarin
Book Three: Elmar of Tranquility

Connect with Me!
On Twitter: *twitter.com/andeliauthor*
On Amazon: search "**Ande Li**"
On Facebook: *facebook.com/Room808Press*
On the Web: *room808press.alvarezli.com/*